COLLABORATIVE CAPERS

Some writers feel that collaboration requires twice the work for half the reward. Barry N. Malzberg is not one of them.

You hold the proof in your hands. In *Collaborative Capers*, you'll find more than two dozen extraordinary short stories written in collaboration with an assortment of wild talents during the past five decades. That includes writers like Mike Resnick, Kris Neville, Jack Dann, Paul Di Filippo, Batya Swift Yasgur, Robert Friedman, and many more.

In these remarkable duets, Barry N. Malzberg's powerful, compelling voice blends with those of his collaborators to create unique harmonies that linger.

Are two heads really better than one? Read *Collaborative Capers* and find out for yourself.

AF113236

Collaborative Capers

by Barry N. Malzberg

Edited by Robert Friedman

STARK HOUSE

Stark House Press • Eureka California

COLLABORATIVE CAPERS

Published by Stark House Press
1315 H Street
Eureka, CA 95501, USA
griffinskye3@sbcglobal.net
www.starkhousepress.com

ISBN: 979-8-88601-046-6

Cover and text design by Mark Shepard, shepgraphics.com
Cover art by Susann Mielke

First Stark House Press Edition: September 2023

CONTENTS

ACKNOWLEDGMENTS

Introduction

What better way to introduce a collection of collaborative short stories than to collaborate on the introduction? Here Barry N. Malzberg and his occasional partner in crime, Robert Friedman, discuss Mr. Malzberg's long history of collaborating with other fiction writers.

RF: The stories in this book span five decades so obviously you started collaborating with other writers almost from the start of your career. Why?

BNM: I started on essentially a whim in 1971; I had a trunk story which had been merrily bounced from *Ellery Queen's Mystery Magazine*, *Alfred Hitchcock's Mystery Magazine*, and *Mike Shayne's Mystery Magazine* and asked Bill Pronzini, already a close friend, if he could perhaps attempt some corrective surgery. He did so, the two better paying magazines still bounced it but *Mike Shayne's Mystery Magazine* did not and it became easy to slide into a redraft of a few of my mystery rejects just as he puttered with a couple of SF stories I had had bounced.

Gradually—more for recreation than money—this became a habit and two years later we were into an attempt at a major suspense novel which became the Putnam novel, RUNNING OF BEASTS. Collaborating successfully with him led me to an open interest in trying the same with others and over the decades although he was my primary collaborator I must have shared bylines with a couple of dozen writers.

Somewhere I had written, "I can simulate the style of any writer living or hopefully dead" and that rather disreputable skill made an expansion of range and opportunity ever more possible.

RF: I can think of a few writers you've simulated in this collection, including John Cheever in CALLING COLLECT (you even name check him) and perhaps Shalom Aleichem in THINGS PRIMORDIAL. Certainly in your favorite novel, UNDERLAY, you borrowed playfully from Damon Runyon and Vladimir Nabokov (quite an unlikely pair), while in other stories you've paid homage to writers like Stanley Elkin, Robert Silverberg, Alfred Bester, Harlan Ellison, and C.M. Kornbluth.

As for collaboration, I can add from my own limited experience that it's a whole lot of fun. The ideas go back and forth and you can sometimes feel the other writer prompting you to head in certain directions. Has the process of collaboration been different for you with every writer and story?

BNM: That's like asking, "What is sex? Has it been different with every partner (or no partner)?" The answer is Russell Galen's, "Yes and no". Different among writers and stories, similar in molding two voices (or narrative predilections) into one.

RF: That sounds like a challenge but it must come with its own rewards.

BNM: The challenges—molding two styles into one—are obvious, the "rewards" on the downside is that it can be twice the work for half the money which I add for the provinces is a feeble attempt at humor. Another reward is that the collaborators in some cases are able to write a story beyond their individual means.

This was particularly true in the case of the 20-25 stories written with Kathleen Koja who pushed me beyond what I had thought were inflexible limits and with whom I wrote some stories which transcended my individual work. LITERARY LIVES (ALTERNATE OUTLAWS) is one such, another is THE TIMBREL SOUND OF DARKNESS, both buried alas in anthologies long out of print and forgotten. Then there is THE HIGH PURPOSE (*The Magazine of Fantasy & Science Fiction*, 11/85) with Carter Scholz which I felt at the time was my best short story. That was a little florid, my wife insisted, but I still put it in the top ten. (Hammett and Chandler fleeing their two famous detectives who are chasing them cross-country for nefarious purposes.)

RF: Speaking of mystery writers, you've written both stories and novels with Bill Pronzini. Did you approach them in the same way? For example, with the novels, did you need to outline them first?

BNM: We outlined our novels painstakingly; the short stories were more a matter of writing alternate sections a cappella with Pronzini on the final draft.

RF: That's similar to how we've written our own epistolary short stories with me doing the final draft. The epistolary approach is one you've used to great effect in earlier stories such as AGONY COLUMN, which was published in *Ellery Queen's Mystery Magazine* back in 1971. What prompted the use of it in our much more recent story, LET THE GAMES BEGIN?

BNM: This was your story; your format. You sent me the opening section and I climbed aboard. See comment above.

RF: That's right as far as it goes. However, as I recall, you actually prompted the story in an email by suggesting we collaborate. Since we've been carrying on our voluminous email correspondence for some years now, that was the most natural format for me to use. The result was successful enough for *Asimov's* to publish it.

While on the subject of success, how can you tell if a collaboration has been successful? Is it when a new style emerges that's different from your respective solo styles?

BNM: In a word, yes. Bill Pronzini said, "We created a third voice" and that more or less sums.

RF: I think we have two distinct voices in our stories but neither is quite the voice we normally write in. It's more like two musicians riffing off each other, which takes you places you wouldn't go by yourself.

Your stories written with Batya Swift Yasgur and Mike Resnick explore religious themes from a different perspective than you do in your solo work. It seems to me that a benefit of collaboration is the opportunity to expand your subject matter and point of view. I'm guessing it's Jack Dann's experience of working in a cable company sales pit that's described in BLUES AND THE ABSTRACT TRUTH. And certainly the descriptions of my own experience as a communications consultant in LET THE GAMES BEGIN add something to the story that's not part of your own background. Of course, you could have researched those professions and written about them convincingly but collaboration saved you the time and effort.

I'm wondering whether you feel the same sense of accomplishment when completing a collaborative story as when you complete a solo one? It felt different to me. Maybe it's just that a team effort is less isolating than wrestling with a story on your own.

BNM: Solo work (as a finished product) was more satisfying overall but there were always exceptions; Ms. Koja and I were capable of work so far beyond my own scramblings that something like TIMBREL SOUND makes me gasp.

RF: I guess sometimes two heads really are better than one. Any plans for future collaborations?

BNM: Why not?

—June 2023

Collaborative Capers

by Barry N. Malzberg

PATER FAMILIAS

by Kris Neville and Barry N. Malzberg

People keep saying the past is dead. You hear it on practically every street corner. I think my father had something to do with it. But then I may be wrong. I may still tend to overvalue him on some level of my being to compensate for my real feelings.

The last time I saw him alive, there was something profoundly moving to me about his condition, considering all the times he had humiliated me, and considering that for all intents and purposes he had been dead for five years and five months.

When my father straightened, finally, from the Fox Temporal Couch, I passed him the remains of my drink.

"Ah, you bastard," he said, sipping. "You caught me in the middle of a TV program that time. I was lying straight out on the chair and hassock, watching the draft riots. I told you last time, I never wanted you to do this to me again."

"It isn't easy on me, you being dead these five years and five months," I said. "I was sitting here drinking and looking at the Transporter, just sitting around, and I said, 'Hell, I feel like having a chat with my old man again.'"

"Stop telling me when I'm going to die," he said. "There's absolutely no need for that." Still half-locked in the Couch, he managed to make it to his knees, clutching the glass, bringing it to his mouth two-handed as if it were a baby's bottle, which, of course, in at least one sense, it was. All of this was bringing back memories. I half-hoped, but did not expect, that he would begin one of his circuitous analyses of the world, as in times past, as though trying to teach me something that I again, as in times past, and in the last analysis, would not be able to completely figure out. Such was his way and mine, I guess. I think it may be the way of all parents, but I suppose some are more direct and maybe better organized and really teach you something, but I doubt it. Then, of course, it is a mistake to generalize like this.

Not the least of the Transporter's appeal, the brochure said, was its poignancy, the nostalgia of it all. It infused the present with the past, brought you back to your origins from which you were now so distant as not to be touched. And, also, as the brochure said, "You don't have always to be a child with your parents, now," although that may be wrong.

"Let's talk about the old days," I said. "Remember that time in 1982 when we were playing softball and I broke your finger with a pitch? And you gave me a shot and broke my nose? That's what I really want to talk about—the basics that we both understand. The cut-off is only five minutes from now, and we really ought to do some talking before I have to send you on your way."

"Five minutes, eh?" he said. "Well, what if I just don't go back? What if I sit right here in your basement and refuse to let you put me back in that circle?"

As if, any longer, he had the strength to resist my determination. And, besides, they wouldn't let him, anyway. They turned everything upside down when people tried to do that, finding them. Some people said it was so you'd have to keep renting the equipment.

"It won't make a shade of difference," I said. "The past is immutable. That's the point of the construct ..."

But, of course, what *was* the point? How could one really know the past was immutable: perhaps it was fluid or semirigid like gold gelatin, or something else entirely.

To pursue our ignorance on this point: how might one account for why the Transmitter could bring back only parents and no one else—except once in a great while, grandparents? Was there some psyche force between generations grown up from an early dependency? And yet, there were occasions when the father who came back was a stranger to the child, and so ... Was there some transcendent genetic continuity, some scientological myth, that the Transporter responded to? Or was it the circle that was necessary like the pentagram of old, and was this black magic entirely, as the world fragmented itself on the New One Thousand, having broken an obscure equivalent of the sound barrier? It's academic now, I guess, but no one admitted to understanding it, even Fox, any more than anyone admits to understanding time itself, or, for that matter, reality, either. Now, of course, Fox is working on a machine to let us visit the future. He seems to be having unexpected problems that perhaps my father also contributed to. I like to think something will go wrong with his research, but maybe this is merely because I have come in other areas to distrust the uses technicians make of science.

But then, I could not admit any ignorance to my father, could I? Was he ever less than certain with me about things of which he knew nothing?

"Come on, Dad," I continued, mindful of the time, "loosen up, relax. Let's tell a few old yarns. Yours is the first generation in recorded history that has been given the advantage of time travel to your descendants—the privilege of seeing your works in their fullest flower—

when you're dead and gone."

"Know what I'm going to do?" my father said, managing to make it fully to the top of his warmed legs and stand at last. "I'm going to kill myself, that's what. Right here in your basement. That way, the way I figure it, none of this ever happened, then."

I wondered what he thought he was trying to teach me this time.

He reached into his inner coat pocket. "Get this!" And he waved the knife at me. "Been holding it for the time those draft rioters get too close to the old man and start to mess with him! Been my protection, this little sweetheart: clean and sharp, really does the job! Good luck, son. I can't take it anymore; I can't spend the rest of my life wondering when you're going to get the urge to pull the old man all to pieces...."

He held the knife two-handed against his heart and then brought it all the way through his shirt.

He stiffened in the midst of a good deal of blood and kicked right out on the floor. Despite the fact that he didn't look good at all, there was a smile on the small fragment of face that hadn't gone completely white. I was sure then, and now, that nothing like this had occurred in temporal transport before, and I waited for something awful to happen.

I was scared. I admit it. If my father had really died here in my basement in 1988 rather than 1933, then my whole life would be unalterably changed, to say nothing of the consequences of his being found suddenly missing sixteen years ago. I would never have had the fight with him that sent me away from home, but that eventually got me into the job where I had made enough money to buy the Transporter in the first place. But, if so ...

The only thing I could think to do was to get him back. This may have been a bad decision, and, if so, then I'll just have to take the blame for it.

I picked him up—it was the most disgusting event of my life—and staggered into the circle with him and tossed the corpse in, and, putting the Transporter on manual so as not to take any chances, set it for a quick return. Then I pressed the lever and closed my eyes.

I said "Thank God" when he vanished, although who can possibly believe in God anymore, although, of course, I guess there are some who still say He's not really dead; He's just senile.

Well, it meant at the worst the old man would be found dead in 1988 instead of 1993, which would be very bad, but not as bad as the other way, or so I supposed. Perhaps the shock of his death like that would have sent me away from home. Best of all, it could be that the effect was self-negating.

I sat in the basement in front of the Fox Temporal Couch with all the doors locked, waiting for myself to vanish or something, but some time later, when nothing had happened and my memories hadn't changed, as far as I could tell, and it was fairly obvious, I thought, that nothing was going to happen, I let out a long breath and decided that I had beaten it. The Transporter had beaten it. Time, indeed, was immutable, as the brochure claimed, and my father's action had, for all intents and purposes, never happened.

I brought my father back twice after that. The second time, decomposition had progressively advanced. On January 4, 1999, I decided that I wanted no more part of it, so I gave up using the Transporter. When the Government call-in was announced, I was more than happy to turn it in. It was a pleasant novelty there for a while, but who in hell wanted to see corpses, lots of corpses, coming back, and have to think about all those moms like that, too?

And I still hope Fox keeps having problems, for there could come a day when some parent may wish to continue his instructions into the far future, thereby succeeding in killing it, too.

HUMAN ERROR

by Kris Neville and Barry N. Malzberg

ONE

The investigation involved a thousand and took five years. Even then, no one was satisfied. The mars colony had, of course, been completely destroyed as if by a massive explosion. Government officials and investigators went through the wreckage, piece by piece for months, looking for evidence. Bizarre theories were compounded, some even raising the possibility of long-hidden Martians coming to implode the barrier. No one had ever *seen* a Martian but the disaster had no rational explanation.

Among minor discoveries was a short in the output unit which would have caused massive overheating. The operator upon seeing this naturally would have switched over at once to one of the standbys. Bradley had been a thoroughly trained man; since it was his first night on the monitor, the possibility of his dozing off could be completely discounted. They would have to look elsewhere for explanations. In the meantime, the wiring on the next generating unit was revised to prevent any recurrence of the short. So they never did, really, find out what had happened although the Second Colony lasted for eight hundred years.

TWO

The Barrier, which protected the colony from the nearly airless environment, drew virtually unlimited power. Fortunately Mars, almost alone in the solar system, was able to provide it.

Bradley, trained as a geologist, was asked by Garfinkle who was going on leave, to take the shift. "The unit," Garfinkle said, "is really handling power, and that's the only difference from the ones you've played with. I've watched it for the last year and nothing went wrong except once when I had to cut in auxiliary for a molecule leak."

Bradley was impressed. He admired Garfinkle and the Barrier. The Barrier was one of the great inventions of the 21st century. No malfunction was conceivable. It had been built to last a small eternity and had been fifty years in the construction.

Nonetheless, Garfinkle conceded, there were various unlikely conspiracies which might influence the quality of the field allowing its air to leak into the Martian atmosphere. They were indicated by complicated light patterns and Bradley had been trained on Earth for over six months to handle developing emergencies. Garfinkle himself did the training and pronounced Bradley qualified. There were no problems. Garfinkle went home. Bradley went on duty. The colony continued its tasks as Mars slowly fell before them.

On watch, Bradley felt the pride of responsibility; beyond that he gloated in the quality of the equipment itself. The Barrier was impermeable; the computer was performing complicated quantum calculations that no human would ever understand. A low hum filled the area; Bradley added to it.

He sat at the console and watched the calculations move from the output unit. Light patterns continued on the board before him and he wondered idly what might happen if a bulb failed at a crucial time as well as the warning buzzer. But even as the question arose, the answer from training reassured him, the thing had so many fail-safe units that the need for a human monitor was purely administrative. The bureaucrats would never concede that the machinery was perfect even though, at least in this case, it was.

Bradley thought about sleep. All of the monitors did it on duty; the buzzer was loud enough to wake up the most profound sleeper and if that didn't, there was the gong. The gong would awaken anyone.

A little green light flicked on and the output unit in front of Bradley activated and typed: LOADED 260? He checked the printer and depressed *yes*. Operations continued. The bell of the output unit chattered away, making intricate mathematical tracks across the unrolling paper.

Bradley smiled: he knew that this was the normal response to a solar flare. The calculator might continue at this pace for over an hour. He put his hand over the moving ball, wondering idly what it would do if he stopped its progress (bite him?) and was surprised at the heat the machine was giving off. The cabinet was really uncomfortably warmed. He had no idea that the equipment operated this hot; Garfinkle had never mentioned it in his training program.

The ball continued as Bradley touched the case again. It seemed even hotter.

A little concerned, he looked at the lights on the panel, but they were making ordinary patterns. Everything was normal. He decided that during sunspot activity, with the machine in continual output, heat was not unexpected and he speculated on the contingencies the designers had accommodated. Doubtless the insulation was one of the new ladder polymers, capable of withstanding temperatures over 400° C or even higher and quite possibly, heat resistance had been designed into the circuit all the way through. As a matter of fact, he would not be surprised if as a safety factor, many of the components were not made of one of the newer alloys with virtually infinite melt temperatures. Technology was absolute; they had not missed an option in design.

The console was now too hot to touch and as Bradley, dreaming, ran his fingertips lightly over the board the field failed, killing 500 scientists and technicians and setting back the Mars colonization program by half a century.

GETTING BACK

by Jeffrey W. Carpenter and Barry N. Malzberg

"Ken," Bev Gallgher said, "he's due here any minute. What did you say his name was?"

Ken Gallgher was watching Speedo on the set. He said nothing.

"Ken!"

"Huh?"

"What did you say his *name* was?"

"Spo," Ken said. "Something like that."

"Spo?"

"Yeah. I know that sounds strange but that's the name they gave him. They all have funny names."

"He hasn't bothered changing it back, then."

"Not yet," Ken said.

"It's weird how they sometimes don't."

"Don't do what, Bev?"

"Don't change their names. Keep their space names, I mean. Why are we always stuck with breaking in the new ones?"

"Beats me."

"Turn off that set, will you?"

Ken turned up the volume.

"I *hate* Speedo," Bev said.

Spo, meanwhile, sat apprehensively in the rear of the taxi as it inched its way through midtown congestion toward the Gallgher's. He was hot and tired and still thinking of the brotherhood of space. They had been much kinder to one another in the orbiting station, but then circumstances had been different there. Home was different. The rhythms were different. A car cut in front of the cab, and Spo pitched into the seatback as the driver slammed on the brakes.

The driver swore. "Ain't got no *right*," he said. He wrenched the taxi left, swerved into the next lane and pulled alongside the other car, thrusting his middle finger at the old woman driving.

Spo was awed. The driver's rage had genuine authority. He held up his own middle finger and inspected it; a cyclist to the right pulling alongside, returned the gesture, shouting. Spo looked at the cyclist, then again at the finger, then sat on it.

I've got to get reacclimated, he thought.

"Ken?" Bev Gallgher said, "what was it like in the space station?" The Speedo game was on lag; visuals splashed noiselessly.

"Nice," Ken said. "It was nice."

"How was it nice?"

Ken shrugged. "Don't know," he said. "They were nice to each other, that's all." He paused. "Maybe *too* nice, you know what I mean? A year in orbit up there, locked away."

"He'd better not give us any trouble," Bev said.

The Speedo came back to volume. "Why should there be any trouble?" Ken said. He was puzzled.

"A pardon," Spo said to the driver, "how long will it be before we arrive?"

"I'm going as fast as I can."

"But how *long* will it be? That is all I asked."

"You want trouble, clown?" the driver said with sudden viciousness, "I'll give you trouble."

Another car slid ahead, cutting them off. The driver screamed. Spo closed his eyes, shuddering, and thought of the brotherhood of the mindless night, five thousand miles distant. Well, that was all over now.

"Ken," Bev said, turning from the window. "I think he's here."

Ken looked up, shook his head. The Hammers were too far behind anyway. He cut down the volume and went to the window. A plump, scared little man came out of the cab. Funny, Ken thought, he didn't look like a spacer. But then they weren't supposed to, were they? The little man staggered on the pavement. The driver came out of the cab.

Ken had picked up lipreading from watching Speedo; he could see what they were saying. "That's fifteen dollars, friend," the cab driver had said. "Don't give me any of that away-too-long stuff; you know what's going on."

The small man reached into a pocket of an ill-fitting jacket, took out a white envelope. "He must be paying the driver off now," Ken said.

"Why don't you help him?"

"Handle it *himself*," Ken said savagely. "Those were the orders."

They watched the driver snatch away the envelope, take out all the contents and then walk back into the cab, smiling. The little man stood patiently. The cab went away. Overpaid, obviously, Ken thought. They were all the same. Unless they were reacclimated quickly, this kind of thing would just go on and on. Do the *job*, he thought. Got to do the job.

"He's really new, isn't he?" Bev said. "To this, I mean."

"He's been away for three years, Bev."

"He looks scared," Bev said. She giggled.

Ken giggled too. They watched while Spo stood before the house, indecisive.

"That's cute," Bev said. "He's even afraid to come in. We ought to go out and help him." She took Ken's arm almost jauntily and led him toward the door. Funny how close we are at this moment, Ken thought. The two of them against the man from the space station. That was ridiculous, of course. They weren't against anything.

And Spo was no threat. In the station it was like one big happy family. They all took care of one another and so on. To Ken it sounded awful.

"Hello, Spo," he said on the porch.

Spo trembled. He looked terrified.

"Come on," Ken said gently. "We'll watch Speedo." He motioned toward the door with his hand. Start gentle, that was the way you did it. Later on, after you had their trust, that was the time to get rough. "Don't be afraid," he said.

Spo looked at them with luminous eyes. "It's okay, Spo," Bev said. "Isn't he cute? Come here. Here, Spo."

"He's not a dog," Ken said. Bev glared at him. "Well," he said mildly, "I mean he *isn't*. Is he?"

"Spo," Bev said, "don't be nervous. You're welcome here."

This is going to be really hard, Ken thought. Worse than most of them. If it takes this much to get him now into the *house*—

Spo took a few hesitant steps toward them. Ken smiled at him warmly. "Come in," he said. He took Spo's cold hand and, holding on, dragged him into the house. "How was it up there in orbit?" he said heartily. Spo did not reply.

It would be bad all right. Usually they had changed their names anyway on return. Spo didn't even want to give up his space handle.

Spo looked around the room, fascinated by myriad knobs, dials, switches and cord. There is real order here too, he thought. Just like above. Everything has a place which is tied into everything else.

"Boxing to four," the announcer was saying. "Klein is down and bleeding profusely. He's moving oddly on the boards; it looks like a spinal injury up here. That will set them back a little."

"He is cute," he heard the woman say.

"Shut up, Bev. They're not supposed to be cute any more. You're making it even harder."

"Klein is in real pain," the announcer said.

"Sit down, Spo," the man said.

"I don't want to be in real pain," he said.

Ken said, "Just relax. You're back home now and we'll make you comfortable. Have a seat on the couch and we'll get you some coffee. You still drink coffee, don't you?"

"I don't want real pain!"

Oh, my, Ken thought. He knew what to do, anyway. He took Spo firmly by the collar and pushed him onto the couch. Spo sat in a terrified lump, heaving. Bev stared at him admiringly.

"Spo," Ken said, "you're home now. You've got to readapt to our ways. You have no alternative; those gamma rays or whatever would kill you if you stayed up there. You can't live in space any more, you have to come back here." He paused, looking for a reaction. But Spo said nothing.

"Bev and I are your friends," Ken said reasonably. "We're here to help you."

"We'll help in any way we can," Bev said. "That's what we're here for. To help you get back. Why don't you just watch the nice Speedo, now?"

Spo stared at the set, shriveling into a corner of the couch. "Don't want to get back," he said weakly.

Bev said with a wink, "Ken, why don't we just forget about Spo. He won't even try."

"Not the right approach," he said.

"Don't tell *me* what the approach is."

"I'll tell you anything I want." Ken felt the anger beginning, anger at Spo, at Bev. It was always the same. They got back, but the price you had to pay was too much. "It's *my* office who sent him and I'll handle him as I see fit."

"Yes," Bev said, "but it all falls on me. Who does the cleaning up after they've left? Who has to look at their frightened, meek little faces?"

"*I* do."

"You're a stubborn, selfish man. You have to be to keep on taking them in time and again. Aren't you sick of them?"

Ken seized his wife's wrists. "Listen," he said, trying to be calm. "You're not helping this. Shut up! After he's reacclimated then we can deal with this."

Bev tore free of his grip and slapped him hard in the face. "Damn you!" she cried. "Damn you!" She ran out the front door and slammed it.

Spo stared at him, interested.

Ken rubbed his cheek. "Would you like a drink?" he said. "You can drink, can't you?"

Spo said nothing. "Ignore her," Ken said pointlessly. "The marriage was a mistake. But we just have to go on."

Spo's luminous eyes were curiously empty. "Isn't that what it's all about down here?" Ken said bitterly. "Going on. Maybe you think with your experiences in orbit that you're different, but you sure as hell aren't. That's all over, friend, and you've got to live right here like the rest of us. And the hell with you." He walked to the liquor cabinet, took out a tall glass and, his wrist trembling, poured it full of vodka, downed it in three burning swallows. Bev, he thought. That damned woman. The reacclimatization job, and now this. A man had a right to more than this.

Spo watched the host stagger away from the drinking place and into the adjoining room. There was the sound of retching. I don't want to be reacclimated, he thought, but it lacked urgency to him. They took it out of you. The man came back from the kitchen and squatted tensely before Spo, holding his empty glass. "Look," the man said, "it is important that you listen to me. I'm trying. We're all trying. You can't go back. You have to accept the way things are, just like I do. You have no choice."

"I don't want to live here!" Spo cried. "I don't want no other way of life!" He leapt from his seat and turned toward the door.

The man grabbed his arm. "This is the only way!" he screamed. "For all of us. You have to accept—"

Spo whirled frantically and struck the man in the jaw. The man fell backward into the speaking thing. His head struck its corner with awful force and then he lay quietly.

Spo looked again at the knobs, dials, switches and cords. Only then did he smile as he sat in the chair, alone with the speaking thing and with the terrible sounds that filled the room.

His name had been Jim, Spo thought. Jim. All right, he would be Jim again.

Jim sat in the room and thought about what he would do to the woman when she returned. And then he would be *fully* reacclimated.

CALLING COLLECT
by Arthur L. Samuels and Barry N. Malzberg

I

"I'll do it," Irma Green said after a long pause. She pushed a strand of hair distractedly back over her ear. "I mean," she said, "I have no choice."

Her visitor shrugged and said, "That is your decision."

"I mean I *do* have a choice," she said, "but then—"

"Vanity of vanities," her visitor said calmly. "All is vanity." His eyes glowed.

"Ain't *that* the truth," Irma said reluctantly.

II

Martin Green staggered from the rear patio toward the shrilling phone, looking remarkably like an angry Doberman. Even there, he could not escape the sound of the telephone which sounded peculiarly, malevolently fixated on him. That was ridiculous, of course; the call, as always, would be for Irma. No peace, he thought. No peace. "Hello?" he said.

"This is Jack Jacobs," an unctuous voice said. "Jack Jacobs, you know? We met you at the pool last week—my wife and I, we met you and your wife at the swim club." The voice paused, wavered. "This *is* Martin Green, isn't it?"

"She's not home," Martin said. "She's out. She's at a *club* meeting."

"Oh," Jack Jacobs said. He paused again. "When will she be back?"

"Later. Listen, Jacobs, what do you want? Why are you calling my wife?"

"We—my wife and I, that is—wanted to invite you over some evening. Generally I do the calling." Jack Jacobs coughed into Martin's ear and said, "I know that isn't conventional—in the suburbs it's usually the *wife* who does the social things like that, I know, but we have kind of a liberated marriage, share and share alike, so I thought I'd put through the invitation—"

"Jacobs," Martin said flatly, "I don't think I want to see you. I don't even remember you and I don't want to renew acquaintances. You understand?"

There was a long silence at the other end and Jack Jacobs said, "Oh yes, I understand."

"Don't call my wife anymore, Jacobs," Martin said and put the phone down so abruptly that it bounced off the pedestal. He caught it on the fly. "*Don't do it*," he screamed and slammed it down again and went back to the patio. But his mood was ruined. He could not do bicycle repair. Strange men were calling his wife now on what was already an instrument of destruction. I can't take it anymore, he thought, but he knew that this was only a pose. Of course he could continue to take it.

What was the alternative?

Irma Green was obsessed with the telephone. Martin could sit and read for hours, work on household equipment; Irma *talked*. When she didn't talk, she went out. In between times, when feasible, she prepared dinner, slept, engaged in sex. When she was home she was on the telephone.

The calls came in and went out. Irma scurried off on her activities, wooed new acquaintances from her own bed until after midnight. I don't have a wife, I have a switchboard, Martin thought. Once he had even said it to her. She did not take to it kindly. Fifteen years of marriage counted for something, she said. Like autonomy and trust. Trust was vital to any marriage. Beaten, Martin had dropped the issue. But now she was getting calls from a man. Who was Jack Jacobs? What did he want? What was going on?

Martin pondered the issue into the evening, long after Irma had come home, dropped her coat and car keys, returned five telephone calls. She had laughed when told about Jacobs. He had almost *drowned* in the pool trying to show off last week, she had said. Didn't Martin remember? No, he did not remember. Well, it did not matter; certainly she was far too busy to want to deal socially with people like him or his fat liberated wife. "You look angry, Martin," she said at eleven, the phone mercifully still. "Are you jealous? Do you think I'm having an *affair?*"

"You're never off that phone," Martin said pointlessly. "You're always calling someone or they're calling you. There's no peace."

"It keeps me young," Irma said.

This was probably true, Martin thought. At forty-five she looked thirty; throughout their marriage she had softened and deepened, while he had merely wrinkled and spread. "It's not keeping me young," he said. "If I haven't got Jacobs for a correspondent, I have the telephone."

"Don't be ridiculous," Irma said. "I sleep eight hours a night, I maintain a full schedule, and we have an active sex life."

"All between. Between phone calls. We haven't had twenty minutes together awake in years—"

"Really?" she said. "How about last Monday?"

Martin tried hard to think of last Monday. It was hard to isolate the day in memory; time kind of flowed. Of course, that was a characteristic of mid-life. He had read that in books.

The phone rang.

Irma picked it up. "Oh," she said, "hello. *Hello.*"

"Good-bye," Martin mumbled. He stood, left the bedroom, stalked into the living room. Behind him he could hear Irma with appalling brightness talking to someone called "Dorothy" about "plans" for a "bruncheon." Martin brooded. The voice from the bedroom rose and fell. The conversation ended; he heard the faint clang of the receiver being replaced. The phone rang again.

Martin closed his eyes, sat at attention in a bright red chair. The new conversation was relatively brief. The receiver clattered. There was a pause. He heard the sound of Irma dialing.

Martin sighed. He stood, shuffled back into the bedroom, looked at his wife as she talked. Her voice was blissful, her eyes lustrous, her skin gleamed with the force and innocence of youth. The telephone did marvelous things for her complexion. As we live so we will die, Martin thought. Irma was immortal. How could you die in the act of returning a phone call?

"You're ridiculous," Irma said nervously when he finally was able to bring up this thought safely after midnight. "You're a strained man, Martin, you're spending too much time hanging around the house. It's never been the same since you free-lanced accounts. Get out into the world, look for a job, *see* your accounts, go to the racetrack. Try golf. I mean, that's really bizarre thinking."

"What? That you think you can cheat death by that damned phone?"

"I want to go to sleep," Irma said. She pushed the phone away and lay with her back toward him.

He reached—but found that she really did.

Maybe she was right, he thought later. Other interests. Get out of the house. Cease to brood. Martin got up in the shadows of another dawn and drove to the local public golf course, waited outside the gates, rented a set of clubs, went out in the mists alone, swinging wildly. He had not played golf in a decade, didn't even watch the sport. Inhaling great drafts of polluted air, looking at factory smokestacks from the south cheerfully pumping out their industrial filth, Martin plodded through nine holes, trying earnestly to break a hundred. By the fourth hole, however, his internal attention had left the course and shifted to the figure of a man.

A man. Who? Where? Martin could not identify him, but it was definitely a man and he had a picture: the man was in bed with Irma. Right now. An affair. Just like in the works of John Cheever. Skulking through the rooms of desire, the shadow lover while the husband, all ignorance and bouncy cheer, is out at sport. What else? What else!

She had sent him out, hadn't she? It had been her idea! And the incessant phone, the whispered arrangements—the man who had called her a couple of days ago. Jim Jacobs? No. Not quite. Jack. Jack Jacobs. That was it. Martin tore out a divot.

He understood everything.

Martin stumbled through a twelve-stroke ninth, tossed his clubs into the cart, plunged through the pro shop cursing. In his head Jacobs and Irma tinkled ice cubes in post-coital cocktails, discussed Martin's sexual inadequacies. The phone, he thought. The phone did this to me. I'll kill him. No, I won't. I'll be civilized. Maybe it wasn't the phone, he thought; maybe it was Jacobs who was keeping her young.

He drove home. No strange car in front of his house. Still, there wouldn't be, would there? He knew how it was; what you did was park the car blocks away, sometimes miles, and speed fleeting through the neighborhood to land panting with desire at the side door. I'm no fool, Martin thought, I know about this stuff too. It isn't all bills of lading and statutory unemployment funds here; there's educational television and the Literary Guild. I read and think. He came up his steps briskly, opened the door soundlessly, took off his shoes and went up the stairs toward the bedroom to the open door. Shameless! I won't kill him, Martin thought, I'll be civil, offer him a drink. *Then* I'll kill him.

He heard Irma's voice.

Inside, she sat on the bed, her legs crossed, smoking a cigarette, the telephone cupped to her ear, talking with intensity. "*Friday*," she said. "Friday is *good*, Emily. Of course have to call Rona and Harriet to make sure—"

Something within Martin Green broke.

He plunged toward his wife, seized the phone, ripped it away and flung it against the wall. "I am not merely an accountant!" he screamed. "I suffer!" She stared at him uncomprehendingly. "I can't stand it anymore!" he said piteously. Her eyes were luminous. He went to the closet, seized an overnight bag, stuffed clothing indiscriminately. "I've got to get out of here!" he said. "I don't even have the dignity of being cuckolded by a man!"

He fled down the stairs swinging the bag, got into his car and drove away.

Later, he found it hard to recall the details.

Twelve hours and five hundred miles later, however, Martin awoke to find himself in a small motel on the outskirts of Erie, Pennsylvania. The air was, if possible, worse here than on the golf course. He belched uncomfortably, the residue of many drinks, a bad dinner, remorse. Shame lifted him toward the cashier, self-pity paid the check, self-loathing carried him from the dining room and to the elevator, the elevator carried him up one flight and shame, doing double duty, took him into his bleak room. He locked the door, tossed aside a tissue box and a Bible, picked up the phone and gave the switchboard his home number.

"And make it collect," he said.

He entered a long tunnel of possibility. The phone purred in his ear. That it was not busy was in itself further inducement to remorse, more fodder for self-loathing. Perhaps he had misunderstood her. Or perhaps she was out with Jack Jacobs.

Irma answered the phone. The switchboard said that it was a collect call. There was a long pause. "I'll take it," Irma said shakily. "Martin—"

"I'm sorry," he said. "I'm sorry."

"Martin—"

"I am," he said, "I am sorry." He said other things.

He talked for a long time. He would not let her say much; he said it all himself. To her credit, Irma had a wonderful telephone manner. She listened. He told her that he had been a fool. Unstable. Recriminatory, immature. Hateful. Suspicious. And selfish. The selfishness had driven her to the telephone for companionship. "It won't happen again," he said. "I'm coming home. I can't stand Erie, Pennsylvania!" he added desperately.

"It's too late, Martin," Irma said.

"There is someone else, then. Is it—"

"No," she said, "it isn't that." There was a sickening pause. "It's too late, Martin," she said, "too late for any of this. I accepted the call."

"You accepted the call? Of *course* you accepted—"

"Postage due," she said sadly. She hung up.

Martin clutched the phone and stared at the Bible. Well then? he asked it. What now?

III

Irma walked from the telephone, her gait hobbling and cautious. Inside she felt the crumbling, the organs caving into dust, but she would not collapse. Nor would she cry. Not then, not ever. It was the pact, that was all. You accept the conditions; you accept the risks.

She went into the bathroom, supporting herself on the door, wobbling on the tile, grasping at the wall for balance as she came before the mirror. Her heart thudded to a thicker, older rhythm. She stared at her face in the mirror.

The crevices and hollows of that ruined face looked back at her, the mouth of the old woman opened and closed.

Irma whimpered.

"Vanity of vanities," her visitor said behind her softly.

"You're here to collect," Irma said weakly.

"*You* accepted the charges," Jacobs said reasonably.

BRINGING IT HOME

by Jack Dann and Barry N. Malzberg

Jay Remsen was coming home from St. John's Law School when he saw the soldier across the street. This was the fourth time Jay had seen him, and he should have gotten used to it by now. But it was still a jolt.

It was a hot day, maybe ninety degrees, more than that in the subways; and it must have been even worse than that for the soldier, who was in full field pack and steel pot, the rifle drawn to port across his chest, the heavy combat boots raising the temperature even higher. Just like the army to dress you that way, dress you as if you were going out on the tundra looking for the invading Siberian hordes when instead it was Brooklyn in August, and it was literally too hot to fight.

But that was the army for you ... irrational, even more irrational than the appearance of the soldier himself. That was what enabled Jay to keep perspective: the foolishness of it, the stupidity—the soldier was less a threat in his hallucinatory aspect than he was another evidence of the sins of bureaucracy and how lucky Jay had been to arrange his medical deferment.

This was the fourth summer of that peculiar, personal war, which Jay had taken to be the gift of his parents' generation to his own. Perhaps he was taking this too personally (it had been an old character failing), but these were the terms in which he saw it. Meanwhile, on the other side of Avenue U, keeping pace with him, was the soldier, his rifle at port arms, his steps a more measured version of Jay's more shambling stride. Together they walked past the myriad shops and bars and delicatessens. They strode past the neighborhood kosher butcher and the synagogue, the Chinese restaurant, which was so convenient and cheap, and the laundromat, where once a week he washed his shirts and underwear and sat on a bench, looking for the kind of women who never came into laundromats on Avenue U. He walked past the children sprinting out of school, past the older couples—there were many older couples in this fading neighborhood, and he looked now and then across the street, casting little glances at the soldier pacing him.

The man wore green khakis, a helmet, flak jacket, and pants were stuffed into his boots. The rifle, Jay guessed, was an M-16. He knew that this model had succeeded the old M-1; he kept up with the stuff like that in the newspapers. When his number in the draft had come up 3 two years ago, and he had thought he was actually going to go, he began to take a pained, doomed interest in many of the aspects of combat. But then his father found him a friendly doctor who had accommodated Jay's history of a spontaneous pneumothorax.

Maybe the National Guard is meeting, Jay thought. Or maybe Jay's guilt at not being in the war was becoming manifest across the street in the form of a hallucination. Or then again maybe it was some nut who donned khakis every now and then again and went out on the streets of Brooklyn in the heat ... but wouldn't the cops have taken a look at the situation? The fact that the soldier was being ignored, that everyone seemed to take the manifestation with entire matter-of-factness, was certainly a strong point for the hallucination argument. But then again, this was New York.

Jay ducked into the luncheonette two blocks south of his apartment. It was time to get out of the heat, and the situation was getting to him. Personal or impersonal, sane or insane, there was something very personal about the soldier ... personal in the way that the war itself had been. He did not want to deal with it. In the cool abscess of the luncheonette, Jay told himself all of this would go away. He would come out and, just like all the other times, the soldier would be gone. Actual or hallucinatory, the soldier's appearance at least did not seem to last long. Jay picked up a *Wall Street Journal* and paid for it before the owner could tell him that the place was not a library. Then he sat down at the counter, ordered a chocolate egg cream, and read the human interest story which was always the center column of the first page. It was an article about a man in Seattle who thought he was the reincarnation of Leonardo da Vinci; the man had invented an ornithopter that experts thought might just work. "Experts" were good. Jay had admired them for most of his life until he had come to the realization that "experts" were one of the main reasons why we were four years into the war now.

He drank his egg cream.

He checked the second section to see how his uranium stock was doing. His father had made him buy it with some money that had been left to him by his uncle. The stock hadn't done anything since yesterday. He really didn't care about the uranium, nor did he care about the stock market, his father, or law school. But he dutifully wore a tie every day, studied late every night with his study group, and saw his girlfriend who lived upstate every other weekend—there was no question of her dropping out of the college from which they both had graduated to join him in Brooklyn, not with a graduate assistantship.

Jay had wanted to be a writer, or at least a journalist of some kind. But his father was a lawyer and was paying for the shot. Jay had thought of freelancing and had actually written and sold a story to a men's magazine, a story about the war in fact (a tough whore in Saigon who seemed to be working for Charlie, but at a crucial moment turned out to be an American sympathizer, giving a virginal Spec 4 his first oral experience, and so on), but he hadn't been able to sell any others. So the best idea seemed to be to go to school and write on the side, but there was little time for anything except his studies. If he had any faith in himself, he would have gone out on his own. Instead, he was filled with self-loathing: he was a draft-dodger, half a law student, and a tenth of a protester (now and then he signed petitions, but he didn't even give contributions any more: protesting the war had begun to seem like undergraduate stuff).

He paid the owner for his egg cream, left the paper on the counter, and walked out of the store.

The soldier was waiting for him in the street. He leveled his rifle at Jay and said, "All right, you." He had a very high voice, but it was authoritative for all of that. He made a slight gesture with the rifle. "Just get moving."

Jay stared at the man, then looked up and down the street. It *must* be a hallucination because no one was looking at them at all; at least he was only getting the routine, sullen stares that older people in this neighborhood would give a young draft dodger on the streets.

"Move!" the soldier said. His voice squeaked a little, but he jammed the rifle into Jay's rib. The impact was shocking. Jay gasped. He felt little alleys open underneath his skin, felt them embossed with his sweat.

"Yes," Jay said, "but where?"

"Just *move*," the soldier said, and Jay obeyed. He put his hands at his sides and walked towards 10th Street; the soldier fell in behind him. Every third step or so he could feel the rifle prod his back. "What is this?" he asked. "What the hell is it?"

"That doesn't matter," the soldier said. "Just keep going. You're doing fine. Faster. Watch out for the wire. Watch out for the mines, Charlie's dug in."

Could a hallucination be crazy? Jay considered this as a metaphysical question and then elected to consider it no more. The traffic light was red. Jay came to a reflexive halt, but the soldier pressed against him, pushing him forward. "What are you *doing?*" Jay asked. "Tell me what's going on."

"We're bringing the war home."

"What?"

"Bringing it home," the soldier said. He prodded Jay with the rifle and said, "Face front. Walk!" Jay crossed the street and the soldier continued, "Each of us, one to one, you know? And you're my assignment." He seemed to giggle.

There had to be a perfectly reasonable explanation for this. It was his own guilt, that had to be a part of it, either that or the heat, the conditions of isolation ... he really was alone in this neighborhood all the time, except when his father came in from Westchester and patronizingly took him to dinner. And the war was getting even worse; even the *Wall Street Journal* could not ignore it; the stories had been terrible, the testimonies from the battlefields ever painful (Jay would not own a television), and this might have been the cause of his isolation. He had at last abandoned his commitment, had given up and gone to law school, had isolated himself from his friends in the anti-war movement. He had even stopped talking to his girlfriend about anything important; she, being more conservative, was happy that Jay had stopped being so "radical." There had even been one summer when he frequently went to demonstrations in Washington and started talking about joining the Weatherman. Still—

"Still," the soldier said, "there's no choice." They were on the corner of 11th Street now, a sudden absence of people all around him. They might no longer have been in Brooklyn, but on the Delta itself, that oozing, swamping plain about which Jay had read, and which he took in his mind to be green, odorous, infested with Asians of homogeneous menace. In this space, it was just he and the soldier then, the man raising the rifle. "It's personal," the soldier said. "Do you understand that? Everything here, all of it. I could have picked anyone, but I picked you."

"Wait a minute," Jay begged, "you don't understand. I did what I could, we all did what we could. I *tried*. I've fought the war over here, three years ago I almost got arrested—"

The soldier's eyes were closed tight; under the steel pot he was crying, his face curiously aged by this rather than rendered infantile, the tears of an old man, but the hands on the rifle were tight and authoritative as they leveled the instrument. "I'm dreaming this," the soldier said, as if he was trying to shake himself out of a dark, sweaty nightmare of epiphany. "It's not real, I'll wake up and be back there, but right now it's happening, it's no dream at all, it's happening. I prayed that I would somehow find someone like you, and I *did*. I know who you are, you sonofabitch. You're a protester with a deferment. That's all I wanted and here you are."

He leveled his rifle.

The first bullet took Jay's breath, slammed him into a one hundred and eighty degree turn, left him staring at the soldier; the first wands of blood erupting from the wound.

"Oh my God," he said, but the soldier could not hear him, the soldier was screaming *Oh God* too, the two of them bellowing and then Jay was falling; he fell a long distance, through all the spaces of street and stone and woke then in the pit to the second morning of his great adventure holding the rifle, listening to the flak, the sounds of ordnance full in his ears. *Bring the war home*. This time he would get himself someone down in the VFW, some old jerk with a pot, yelling about the hippies and protesters. Tear him open. Bringing it all back. He tilted his head back and laughed, letting go, and no one, no one in Brooklyn heard a thing.

BLUES AND THE ABSTRACT TRUTH

by Jack Dann and Barry N. Malzberg

This isn't a spiritual or a prescription. It is, however, a precise diagnosis.

Bear with me. To explain and explain.

So this is how it happens: It's 1963, and you are with a girl named Mollie. John F. Kennedy was killed three weeks ago on the 22nd (you can look that up), and LBJ is telling us that we will continue ... continue with what? "Danke Schön" and "Call Me Irresponsible" are playing day and night on the radio, God help us all. You went out to a college bar in Hempstead, Long Island, where they had a guy who played terrific jazz organ, and you picked up this girl who is a freshman at Hofstra and hails from upstate somewhere, maybe Cohoes. She says she was the only Jewish girl in her high school, and she makes every other word sound like "aou."

You've brought her back to your rented room on the second floor of Mr. Seitman's rooming house in East Meadow. You thought you'd have to sneak her into the house, but dictatorial, half-blind Mr. Seitman has gone out to play bingo, and now you're safely behind closed doors and impressing the hell out of Mollie with your knowledge of jazz. You're studying music at the same college she's attending (she's a theater major), and you are absolutely certain that one day your name will be listed in *Playboy's* Annual Jazz Poll. And you're smart because you're studying musicology; worst comes to worst, you can teach during the day and play in the clubs all night. You have a 1-Y draft status because you have a nervous stomach, and right now you're playing the classic recording of Louis Armstrong's "A Monday Date," where he cuts in with a brilliant vocal rendition right after his trumpet solo.

Mollie has been saying something like she's a virgin and that she believes chastity to be the only valid option for a woman in these times, although she's not opposed to oral sex. Not *bitterly* opposed, anyway. In 1963, before and after JFK's extraordinary run of bad luck, it was very chic in college circles to be a virgin, even if you weren't, so this is not surprising or objectionable.

"Sure," you agree, understandingly. "Sure."

She looks like she has nice breasts under her skin-pink mohair sweater, and you are hopeful of seeing them naked soon, but (and this is the kicker) you are for sure the virgin in this crowd. You don't know how to tell her this or cover your inexperience.

Luckily, she knows that you want her, and senses your awkwardness, and she takes you off the hook easily by making the first move. The important thing is, you are going to come.

Coming is definitely not a routine event in your life—with a woman, that is to say. You have been thinking about it all night. Now the black lights are on, and so is the rotating sparkle globe you've installed on the ceiling, and all your posters are glowing like neon: peace signs and astrological signs and all manner of fantastic beasts and Nereids are suddenly brought to radioactive life while the room seems to twirl with every possible color. You and Mollie are smoking some unbelievably good Panama Red, which a buddy from your band has left with you to stash, and Mollie's clothes are off—almost all of them, anyway—and you are so stoned-out now, the two of you, that you are confusing the music with your thoughts, but you're getting it right, sliding your fingers over her goosebumped skin, pushing and grinding against her, tasting her cigarette-soured mouth, thinking musically of this and that and nothing at all and that poor bastard JFK, fucked over now by a Texan, and then you are

Transformed.

You are taken up and out, Stony-o, you are lifted like the bullets lifted JFK in the Continental, you are *yanked*, and then....

You are bearing with me. I am doing what I can to explain. Over and over this goes, but it is vitally important to get it right; there is no understanding without memory, Mollie, and I can still almost feel your arms tight around me, and your tongue, and then

You are somewhere else.

You are *here*.

You are in this *place*.

It's like being six sheets to the wind and falling down the stairs.

It's like being jolted out of a deep sleep.

But here you are, young man, no transition, yank, bang, and you're in a large office separated into cubicles. The pushpin fabric of the five-foot-high cubicle dividers is powder blue, the commercial-grade carpet a dismal brown. The dividers are on your right, and six people are crammed into the cubicles, one to a spot, phoning, until suddenly they all turn to look at you, staring at you, waiting for an explanation. You must have made *some* kind of squawking noise, and who can blame you, what with Mollie's face taking up the field of vision one minute, and now this....

You look at these six people, and what you really want to say is, "What the fuck is going on here?"—but that would expose your position immediately. It's not for nothing that you have a little sixties smarts, a residue of late-fifties cunning. You still have a buzz on from the grass (maybe that pot was *too* good), and you say, keeping your cool, adjusting yourself to the situation, "Back to work, gang. I just got a shock from the computer."

The word just comes to you. *Computer*. In 1963 that was a tech-word like *astronaut* and *New Frontier*, but you somehow had access to it. Be that as it may, you're still new to all this, and as you look at your hands, you can tell you have aged. You are not twenty, that is for sure. (Would that you were!) The hands are solid and bear the heavy imprints of time, and you know, now you know, that if you raise your hand to your face, you will feel texture, wrinkles, a bristly stiff mustache.

Such is the rush of chronology. It is much more than a physical dislocation. Much has shifted.

But under the circumstances, you are amazingly calm.

You have had all of this latter time to think about that, of course; your calm, your amalgamation, your *synchronicity* with the impossible. Because, of course, you are of two parts: there is the strangling, stunned part of you that has come *here,* and there is that distant and cold part with which you have just merged; it is that distant "you" that knows about computers and the precise function of this office, which is to sell the unneeded to the unloved under the guise of love and need.

You're selling entertainment.

This is a cable-television sales pit.

But the young, dislocated part of you asks how the fuck you got *here*, of all places. This is absolutely nowhere. You were supposed to become a goddamn musician. You should be out playing a gig at the Metropole or maybe The Half Note. At the very least, you should be teaching, maybe not at Juilliard, but a decent university wouldn't have been out of the question. You certainly shouldn't be managing six part-time temporaries working on a Friday night. And your distant, older part—the self you are quickly coming to know, the self that has been ground smooth as a stone by forty-two years of experience and frustration—doesn't have a word to say to you.

Because you know, Stony-o. You *know*.

A young woman of about twenty says, "Yeah, I've had that happen to me, too, when I'm putting stuff into the computer. Shocks the hell right out of you, doesn't it?" she says crudely, smiling. She is swarthy and doe-eyed, and it is obvious that her long shock of white-blonde hair is dyed, the ends burned by countless applications of bleach. The part of you with whom you have merged, the worn-out and cynical "you" who knows computers, understands that her name is Franny. She had been here for six months—a long time in the telemarketing game—and not so long ago you asked her to have lunch with you, but she said, "No married men; I've been through that door once, and that was enough." Another humiliation, even though you are the boss, even though you are supposed to be in control.

So now you know of this and other incidents of this man's life. Although everything is new and terrifying, now you *know* that twenty-odd years have passed and that you have merged with an older self, but whether it is really you or a defeated facsimile, you are not yet sure. There is still a tendril of hope in your heart. After all, this couldn't really have happened to you. But with dislocation comes instant maturity, and you really do know the truth, just as you know that it would be a kind of death to accept it completely.

Slow and tentative, fast and desperate, you have the answers. And yet you have none.

The buzz from the grass has ebbed—the yanking will do that to you—and you are very cold and very clear on a level of functioning that is so precise that it is the most terrifying thing yet. You are out of control, and yet you are in control. JFK, you understand, has been dead for half as long as he was alive, and Phil Spector is gone, gone.

"Come on, now," you say, cheerlessly enough, as you are in a supervisory position, "let's get back to *work*"—just as if you knew what you were doing here, as if you belonged (but you do! you do!)—and you go back to the computer. As one part of you gazed in wonder, the other part is monitoring the telemarketing service reps (you also know they're called TSR's) and at the same time typing names and addresses, answering *Y* or *N* to arcane questions coming up on the screen of the monitor, which reminds you of the fluorescent black-light posters in your room in East Meadow, the very same room where, moments before, you were kissing and tasting Mollie's lips, which were sticky and deliciously red from a recent application of strawberry lipstick gloss.

Well, that is how it began. Or how it ended.

Outside looking in ... inside looking out; my mantra.

One moment I'm twenty and trying to score; the next moment I'm forty-two and supervising cable sales in an upstate district that includes Mollie's hometown of Cohoes. I am married to a woman named Ellen Aimes, my first and only marriage, her second. We have been married for eighteen years and have one daughter, Mollie. (Through the insane coincidence of a malign but stupid fate, Mollie was the name of Ellen's mother.) We have careful sex once a week, always in bed and in a missionary position. Ellen is a mathematics teacher at a junior high school. I make about twenty-five thousand a year; she makes thirty. I drive a 1983 Pontiac Catalina and collect bebop and modern jazz, although I don't play any gigs, nor do we have instruments in the house. I don't need eight hundred pounds of piano to remind me of my failure. In the years since my ... merging, return, amalgamation, whatever you wish to call it, I have had three adulterous involvements for a total of eight fornications, none of them particularly successful, all of them with younger co-workers. Ellen knows nothing of this, nor does she know that I was recently yanked out of my past and spilled into my future, all middle having been taken away from me.

But I know that if I were to tell this to anyone—anyone at all—I would be in severe trouble. Life would tremble. Life would topple. Life would become dangerous and ill-considered. I cannot manage this. I have bills to pay. I have a life—yes, a life—to lead. Mollie needs a father. She is eleven years old and is beginning to hate me in a healthy, bored sort of way.

How, I ask you, can I tell anyone of this? How, outside of this recollection, can I make my fate, my condition, clear?

Only this: Once I was twenty, and the shot that killed JFK somehow seemed to have catapulted me into my life; all the years outside looking in, and now I was going to be on the inside myself, and then, and then—

And then another shot, another catapult—and I am forty; married; a father; an unsuccessful adulterer (although perhaps I should count it a success that I haven't been caught); a panting, heavy, sad case of a man on the lip of middle age; and I now *am* on the inside looking out. Evicted and entrapped without a single moment, a single moment in the middle.

But I do have a facility for amalgamation. I could have just as easily lost it in the first moment of middle age, but instead, I interfaced with the future and saved it.

Interfaced....

And I pick up a work order for a sale to a new subscriber in Cohoes (which precipitates all of this, you understand), and I just stare at it and stare at it.

Is that you, Mollie?

Is that you, I see, first name, middle name, new last name? Is that what I have made of you? A name and address on a sales card?

I'll never call you. It would be a disaster.

I will call you. It will be a disaster.

I'll never call you. It would be a disaster.

You think of calling her, don't you, Stony-o?

If you do—oh, you poor bastard—if you do, *will it take you back*? Will it will it will it?

GETTING UP

by Jack Dann and Barry N. Malzberg

In the middle of the night, the old urge comes over the President of the United States. He slides from the huge, canopied, eighteenth-century bed provided for him, careful not to awaken the First Lady asleep in the adjoining bedroom, and dons the fatigues he has carefully hidden in the back of his suitcase. He is unshaven and stooped-over, slightly slack-jawed, and his shock of fine hair—which is dyed black as the great Valentino's—is uncombed and flattened from the pillow; he could pass easily for any of the old peasants and beggars and drunks and hustlers ghosting and stumbling around the wet, steaming streets of Tegucigalpa, the capital city of the Republica de Honduras. He puts on a wide-brimmed hat and conceals a point thirty-eight under his shirt. (The president has *always* carried a gun.) Then he takes an ancient, musty-smelling secret passageway through the bowels of the fortified palace (the president also always does his homework), and slips out of a little used servant's exit where he joins the crowds on the razor straight boulevard, blending easily into them.

It is all a matter of assimilation.

He has been praised for his common touch, for his ability to amalgamate, to become one with the people. Never has it been better put to use.

Encampments outside the palace. Peasants and intellectuals alike are jammed up against one another in tent shelters and crowded into outdoor cafes, where they drink spirits and smoke pot and take drugs. There, and in a thousand alleys and cellars and seedy cockroach-infested hovels, the revolutionaries make their plans and plot the downfall of law and order.

The president bumps and pushes his way through the crowds. No wonder it is impossible to instill any order into these situations, he thinks. They let the masses come right up to the palace walls. The point thirty-eight is heavy, and he feels its steel coldness under his belt and against his slightly distended stomach. Soon the gun will emerge, a tool of reactionary justice.

What was it he said to his wife at the party earlier tonight? "These people do not understand anything but violence on the one hand and corruption on the other. They don't understand politics. They must be educated into democracy." Something like that. She had nodded approvingly. It was a point of some subtlety, one that he at last was able to share with her. "I guess they must be guided to find their own way," the president had said, suddenly noticing that the First Lady's hair had been sprayed and lacquered into what looked suspiciously like a 1950s-style beehive. Well, if we were going to go back to good, honest, traditional values, why not traditional styles too? As president, he had certainly helped pioneer the former.

The president knows his time is short, surrounded as he is by desperadoes, rustlers, thieves, and revolutionaries, all the clamorous forces of unreason. But he knows what he's doing. He approaches the Casa Regime, which he has information is a haunt of Juan Byhan Branaa, a self-styled *coronel* in the "Army of the Revolution."

And big as life, there sits Branaa sipping a *licor de whiskey com mel* at a street-side table under a dingy red- and-white umbrella. He is thin, as if he were made to be hard to hit. His black mustache is flecked with gray, and he has dozens of tiny brown moles on his neck and jaw. He wears a powder blue short-sleeved shirt, open at the neck, and is talking to a stoutish woman with long, beautiful hair, probably his wife.

Well, these things have to be done, the president reminds himself. He bows his head and pulls his red scarf over his nose and mouth. Then, as if by magic, the gun is now in his hand. He has played it all out perfectly. He is at the best vantage, and he fires at once. He has always had courage, determination, and nerves of steel.

There are people around him, gaping, but he has tunnel vision. There are only he and Branaa, and Branaa falls away, slipping off his wrought-iron chair, banging his head, which has a neat hole between the eyes, on the table. There is a glistening of blood on the white plastic tablecloth.

Dead hit. Dead connection.

The president turns abruptly, playing to the crowd. "*There* is your revolution, lying in the dust. That man was a communist. Do you know what he wanted to do? He wanted to take your country away from you." They stare at him vacantly, as if they cannot believe he is talking to them after killing the *coronel.* It is often impossible to get peasants to grasp the point. "You must *all* fight the revolution," he says in his best oratory style, waving his arm and then adjusting his scarf to allow for a little more breathing room. "If you don't, then others like him will surely take away all the hard-won freedoms that your government has guaranteed you." They don't understand, but he felt impelled to say it anyway.

Then he makes a swift exit, heading back to the palace before he will be missed. The crowds part for him. Here in this part of the globe, there is a long tradition of crowds parting for a man with a gun. He ditches the point thirty-eight at the first opportunity by tossing it into a huge pile of reeking, maggot-infested garbage.

He slides back into the palace undetected.

He looks in on the First Lady, who was as insensible of his absence as she has so often been of his presence. She is snoring quietly.

Then he gets back into his own bed, pulls the covers up to his chin, and falls into the oblivion of the righteous.

When he finally dreams, it is of western range wars raging eternally.

There is, of course, no news of the revolutionary's death in the days to come. The government insists that there is no trouble, no revolution, no dissatisfaction, no abrogation of individual rights, and the news is not considered important enough for a page five squib in any of the Western papers. *Pravda* made one outraged mention and blamed the murder on the ubiquitous CIA, but the president knows nothing of that. He returns to Washington in *Air Force One*, certain of the success and confidentiality of his mission. One less revolutionary, one less desperado in the world.

He imagines the desperado's body growing ripe as an avocado and drawing flies before it is finally dragged away to an anonymous grave. Such is the fleeting daydream of a vigorous president, who has proven to himself once again that he is ageless and in the pink, as he stares out the window at the clouds and landmass below.

Fortunately, the disposition of the remains of revolutionaries is not his problem.

In his most recent and profound engagement with the premier, the president had suddenly found himself inflamed with a desperate generosity. The incident in South America had obviously exhilarated him, and he was responding in terms of that euphoria. But the premier had kept bringing up the defensive screens over and over again; he just could not let go of it, even though the President explained they would become the premier's defensive screens, too. To that the premier replied that he knew all about that American propaganda, as he had called it, and *his* answer was "*Nyet, nyet, nyet!*"

Enough was enough.

The president would not be threatened.

"I cannot compromise on that," he said.

The premier blustered and slapped the table, causing water to spill out of the crystal glasses, thus losing all of the superficial sophistication that had become his trademark.

But the president was imperturbable; he stood his ground as he knew he had to. As the First Lady had reminded him the night before, a bear dressed in a seven- hundred-dollar pin-striped suit is still a bear. If honey doesn't work, bang him on the nose. And it was getting down to banging time.

He had been in a situation just like this in his old movie days. Damned if he could remember the title of the movie, and it had been one of his favorites, but he could remember the plot exactly: He was in love with a long, leggy, clean-cut, ponytailed gal; and her blustering father had threatened the character the president was playing with all kinds of revenge and difficulty if he, the president, didn't give up his grandiose ideas of marrying the gal and inheriting the ranch. But the president's character had stood firm (which meant that the *president* had stood firm, as there was no difference, after all, between what you did and who you were), and in the end the old man, a gruff fellow with mustaches—a veteran character actor whose name the president for the life of him could not recall—had backed off, ceded the gal and gave him his blessing. "It's because you're the kind of man who won't be bluffed, can't be backed off, and won't take his guns off the table when he knows he's right," the gal's father had said, and that had been the end of *that* damned situation.

Same thing here, the president thought. You took a position and you followed through.

"The defensive screens stay!" he said, pounding the table for effect. That was the only kind of behavior the premier understood anyway. He pounded the table again, and the glasses jumped on the table as if coming to attention, water slopping onto the polished table. "Do you hear? Stay!" The last said for good measure and because the president suddenly found he enjoyed finally getting it off his chest. He was sick of being diplomatic, which was nothing but a euphemism for cant and hypocrisy. And it seemed to have worked, for the premier could do nothing for a long moment but stare icily at him. In fact, he looked frozen as a fish stick. Then his face crumpled. He stood up, shook his head in disgust, and without another *nyet* left the room, followed by his interpreters. The president stood blinking at the doorway, oblivious to his own two interpreters standing beside him. It occurred to him at that second that the premier was mad as a hatter and could start a nuclear war over less provocation. But you could not give ground, that was the point. You had to take your position and follow it through to the ultimate end, damn the torpedoes or nuclear warheads or whatever else was at stake. If you didn't, if you allowed them to perceive that instant of weakness, which was only their own uncertainty mirrored in you, circumstances would change utterly and there would be a terrible reckoning, a reckoning beyond all possibility.

He knew then what he should have done: lean over the table, push the interpreter to one side, seize the premier by one cheek, stretch the skin, distend the face and then land that one solid punch that would bring the bear to his knees.

That they would understand.

Of course, there were all kinds of frightened bureaucrats and functionaries who would tell him that this was not diplomacy.

The phone rings just as the president is hunched on the verge of a truly satisfying, climactic, freedom fighter's dream. Scrambling in the silken bedclothes, he reaches for the receiver, tries to simulate alertness, for he knows there have been scurrilous rumors about his age and efficiency and attention span. "Yes," he says groggily nevertheless. "What is it?"

"That business in Honduras," the president hears the colonel say. "That was a nasty business."

"How did you find out about that?"

"Word spreads. Do you think we're ineffectual, without our spies and networks? Now, why did you do that without orders?"

The president feels the flush of shame spreading through him; he is fortunate at least to be alone. "I thought you would be pleased," he said. "I thought you wanted—"

"We didn't want! None of that at all!" The colonel sounds infuriated, deeply outraged; the president has never heard him act like this before. "You are to do nothing political without specific orders!"

"But it was a simple assassination," the president says hopelessly. "It seemed so simple."

"You can't go out shooting rebels in the night at whim! Assassination is a highly sensitive matter, to be decided collectively. That's what it means to be part of a democratic entity. Don't you think that someone on the other side is going to put it all together someday, and then where will we be? Besides," the colonel says, his voice dropping to a confidential murmur, "we know what's best to do, when it's right, when it will *work*. Don't you know that by now?"

"Of course," the president says guiltily, realizing how wrong he has been.

"Have we ever failed you?" the colonel asks, and then, as if the president had indeed answered, went on to say, "But that business in Honduras, that was bad. Well, never mind," he says, perhaps sensing that the president will try to justify his position—after all, he *is* the president. "We have no time to talk of that now. We have another assignment."

"Yes," the president says eagerly. It has been quite a while since he has last had a specific order; perhaps that's what accounted for that unexpected, indefensible business in Honduras. "What is the assignment?"

"In a moment," the colonel says. The president listens to the static on the line and the soft rasp of the colonel's breath, which seems to warm him, caress him in its exhalation. There is something almost palpable about the sound of that purr over the wires. The president has seen the colonel often enough in photographs, has come to know him well enough in these contacts to have judged him as a real American hero. Still, it is difficult to keep up, sometimes, with what the man is thinking. You want to respond. You hope to please. You want only to get along. But sometimes they will utterly evade you. The president used to have the same kind of trouble with directors. The worst were the ones who just assumed that you would follow orders; they didn't care at all for your own thoughts or motivation. But the colonel does not really fall into that category, the president tells himself. He has always shown unusual consideration, far more than most. "All right now," the colonel finally says. "Are you listening?"

"I'm listening."

"It's the premier we want you to hit."

"What?" Although the president is accustomed to accepting the dicta of the colonel and behind him the committee, this is just impossible. "The *premier?*"

"You're to shoot him at the next meeting."

"And what then? How will I explain myself? How will I get away?"

"Are you here to listen to us or to argue?" the colonel says harshly.

"But if I shoot the premier, they'll arrest me. I'll be incarcerated. There will be witnesses—"

"Shoot them too."

"And outside hundreds of reporters, all of those diplomats and their assistants, and my family."

"Are you here to defend the press?" the colonel says. "Are you going to be intimidated by them yet again?"

"But I'll be impeached!" The president's voice has broken; he clears his throat.

"Haven't you ever heard of diplomatic immunity?" asks the colonel as if he's talking to a rather dim and intransigent schoolboy. "Our legal department is working out all the details. You're a lame-duck president. Do you want to disappear like a thief in the night or go out with a bang? You can be a hero, an example to us all, a contemporary Abraham

Lincoln."

Lincoln was his favorite president. But they didn't have nuclear weapons in Lincoln's day. "It will start World War III," he says.

"No it won't," the colonel says angrily, impatiently. "It's what *both* sides want. The Russians don't like him either ... he's a liberal." And with that he disconnects, leaving the president hanging on the wire, staring at the wall, thinking of all the problems and penalties that have suddenly been ascribed to him, wondering if, after all, he has evolved along the desired path, reached that goal toward which he aspired. *Direct action*. Yes, that was the Colonel's watchword, but still ...

It does seem to be something of a dilemma. The president decides that he will have to consult someone about this and begins to dial the phone, when it suddenly peals, an unearthly noise.

"Remember," the colonel says sternly, "you are being closely monitored. All of us are being closely monitored. We only have one chance left now, one chance, and then it will all be taken from us, our covenant with God Almighty himself destroyed."

The click of termination this time has an absolutely calamitous sound. The president withdraws his hand, trembling, as if it had been bitten. The choice must clearly be his, but it is, as he is beginning to understand, no choice at all; rather, it is a reckoning, a reckoning of such profound difficulty as to summon all of his legendary powers of discipline and imagination. The president is a deeply religious man. He knows what all of this means, what they are really asking him to do. They are asking him to be the trumpet of the archangel. They are asking him to kill Satan and bring on the end of the world. Fumbling in the William and Mary-style high chest beside his bed, he looks for a fresh point thirty-eight. He feels himself to be at the center of massive events that are beginning, slowly, to move out of control.

He reminisces, remembering old exploits and secret victories: the bombing in Paris, blowing the student communists out of a cafe on the Left Bank; the old informer in Baden-Baden whom he had crept up on in the arc of the night and taken out with a single, muffled shot; that business in Lisbon with the vacationing senator; and, of course, that old crowd of commies who had succumbed to the detonation in the Dead Sea; to say nothing of the inconsequential local stuff when he had gone incognito to the worst areas of Washington and teeming Baltimore to remove bits of human detritus one or two at a time. Of course, that last had been a risky business. The colonel had warned him about it, but then, a president had to have *some* private apolitical commitments; you could not always be functioning for such global causes as the struggle against Communism.

All told, it was not a bad record. Not as noteworthy as his predecessors, of course. The president had to defer to them. Take J, for instance, out there in the back streets of Saigon pelting commies with napalm and ripping up the Cong emplacements; he was a true hero. He was a man who believed in direct action, who liked to go into the back slums of Houston or San Antonio on vacations and shoot his fellow Americans face-to-face. And then there was K, who with his quiet, elegant manner had performed deeds so dangerous that not even the colonel was at liberty to allude to them. Even N, the coward, was at least a great statesman and a brilliant foreign policy maker. Although the president had finally restored honor and personal commitment to his often maligned and beleaguered office, he had never imagined that he would be able to stand head and shoulders with his predecessors K and J. They were utterly remarkable, even if they were misguided and ultimately undone by their lack of caution; clearly, they had not had someone like the colonel to guide them.

As the president lies in bed, his hands at his side, his gaze fixed on the ceiling, fingers scratching his palms in a way so as to turn them into little claws, he is suddenly overwhelmed by an apocalyptic revelation. In a transcendent moment of clarity and certainty he finally comes to realize that it isn't only the colonel who is guiding him.

He is most assuredly in the harness of a greater force.

And he can almost hear the distant clangor of church bells, ringing in all the ghostly determinants of his destiny....

In a small mountain village in Iceland, the president stands face-to-face with the premier. Both men are wearing blue serge suits cut in a Continental fashion. The president wears a red, white, and blue striped tie; the Premier wears a red silk tie. The talks are not going well, although if one could ignore the tension and ill will, one could be very comfortable in this tastefully decorated Spartan room with its breathtaking view of snowy mountains and deep gorges. Behind the president, a landslide silently changes the shape of an arête.

Both pairs of interpreters have been directed to one side of the room during a "break in discussion."

It is now, as the men look each other in the eyes, that the president seizes the point thirty-eight which he has taken right past the checkpoint and shoots the premier point-blank in the face. He shoots twice, making two neat holes in the premier's forehead, as if it were flattened dough stamped with a cookie cutter.

No defensive screens for the premier, he crashes to the floor.

Everyone in the mom is stunned, and there are crashing noises and shouting outside the door. But in that second, the president, the interpreters, and the now dead premier are one. And as the door explodes in the next instant, the president stands his ground. A multitude of soldiers and guardsmen and secret agents are almost upon him, all brandishing weapons, but the president is no longer concerned, nor is he even conscious of their menacing presence. He can only think that he did it, he finally did it, as he waits for God's divine inhalation, which will surely draw him Heavenward now with the good and the pure, leaving behind the communists and ne'er-do-wells and reporters and atheists and economists and social workers to suffer the fiery holocaust of the Tribulation. But it was *he* who finally did it, not J or N or even K. *He* has closed the book on honor, fame, and politics itself. The crowning success is his, not theirs.

And he feels himself rising into the air, rising to his reward at last, plucked right out of the very hands of the philistines, as the millennial Rapture he has catalyzed begins.

Just as the colonel had promised.

ART APPRECIATION

by Jack Dann and Barry N. Malzberg

Glop.

There went another gallery-goer, an overweight middle-aged woman, camera slung over the right shoulder, blue sunglasses, a peaked cap, long purple fingernails. The kind of woman you'd fantasize being eaten by a painting, perhaps. The kind of woman—a tip of the hat to Mencken here—who made you want to burn every bed in the world. *Glop. Glug.* Into the Giaconda smile.

The Mona Lisa seemed to wink at Evans and Evans struggled against the impulse to wink back. That would have made him a collaborator. He was definitely not that. He witnessed with alarm. Horror, in fact.

Glop. Tourists disappeared head first into the maw of La Giaconda. This woman was the fifth within the hour. How long had this been going on? he asked himself once again, as if repetition could bring enlightenment. Had it been going on since the opening? Since Leonardo had painted the sphinxlike wife of the merchant Pier Francesco del Giacondo? Could he have been her first adultery? There was a certain licentious satisfaction in that thought. Indeed. Leonardo da Vinci unleashes the atom bomb of archetypes. Hateful man. But, alas, he could certainly paint.

All of this had its comic aspects, of course, and the indignity of exit was provocative, but you were really dealing with tragedy here. Evans had to keep that in mind. This was his Blue Period, as he had decided to call it only a little while ago when the tourists started to slide away. It was no improvement upon the Yellow Period, which seemed to have gone on for several decades up to this point, but it looked as if it was going to be instructive. Alone in the gallery now, bereaved, he supposed, Evans could feel waves of satisfaction coming from the famous painting, along with the hint of a belch. Well, what was he supposed to do? Arrest the painting? Turn in La Giaconda to the authorities? What did you do with something like this?

There was a whole clump of guards just outside the gallery, standing sullenly, pacing around; they represented, Evans supposed, a kind of authority. Should he go to them, point out that La Giaconda was gobbling tourists, waiting until only Evans and a straggler were there, then snatching the incautious traveler who came too close to the frame and inserting the surprised victim into a mouth grown not ambiguous but suddenly huge? The screams from the tourists, however brief, were intense enough to travel, but the guards had shown no reaction. The dangers posed by this kind of cannibalism seemed immense. Still, there seemed no proper way to deal with the situation. "Excuse me," he could say to one of the union guys carrying batons and small radios, "I don't mean to interrupt your conversation, but there's *some very strange stuff* going on here; I don't quite know how to tell you this, but—"

Well, but what? This wasn't the kind of thing you could tell a stranger. The terms were imponderable. The worst sign would be indications of interest and credulity. That would mean that he was being humored while reinforcements were called in. Drastic things would happen. Evans himself might stand accused of killing tourists, corpus delicti or not.

Still. "Still now," he said to the Mona Lisa, the painting on special international loan, placed high on the wall opposite, buttressed by a heavy frame and protected by guys in the anteroom with batons and receivers, "I've got my eye on you, lady. You're not going to get away with this, lady. Evans is on the job and sees exactly what's going on here, which is why I'm keeping a safe distance. You're not getting away with anything in front of *me*," he pointed out quietly, meanwhile trying to maintain a reserve, a glacial calm. He knew he was safe if he stayed more than six feet away. "This is my Blue Period," Evans confided in a whisper. To a theoretical stranger he would appear perfectly insane, he knew, but there were no strangers in the gallery itself, just Evans and the painting. Oh, how they squealed and kicked in their dismay. It was a grim thing to see. "I didn't intend it to be this way," Evans went on, talking to the painting as if it were an actual, a reasonable woman rather than an assassin. "I had plans, you know, but the economy got tight and now I have to fill up the days any way I can. You're not going to get away with this though, lady. We're going to take measures."

In truth, Evans knew this was pure bluff. He had no plans whatsoever. Shortly, the absence of the eaten would be noted and bureaucracy in its fumbling way would try to deal with the situation, but there was no way that this could fall within its lexicon. Detectives might get to the Guggenheim, but how could they possibly implicate a painting, even one which was priceless? She wore an expression of utter innocence and had a terrific provenance. Her scheme was not only diabolic, it appeared foolproof. But, futile as it might be, Evans at least was on the case. "You're going to be stopped," he said harshly. "We're going to bring this to a conclusion." One of the guards outside moved to the doorway, put a hand on the sill, leaned, peered in, an uncomfortable moment of glances brushing. Evans shrugged, shook his head, then stood. There was no point in appearing crazy, although this museum like millennial New York itself was filled with mumblers. He would fit right in. Everything fit right in, one way or the other.

It was time to go out on Fifth Avenue and ponder his next moves, anyway. Couldn't stay hammered in with La Giaconda all day, not without attracting undue attention. There was more space out there; he would work something out. Trust not in Evans to abandon the situation, he thought hopefully. He would do something to avenge those innocent lives, protect others. Just as soon as he could figure out some means of approach.

The Yellow Period (he had not called it that then, had merely thought of it as his life itself) had apparently ended; Evans was vaulted into a new and difficult circumstance. Once, not so long ago either, Evans thought he had the whole project worked out, a series of activities (lack of activity, perhaps), which was a process of real accommodation. You couldn't be a remittance man *all* your life, not if you wanted to lead an active, useful existence in millennial times. You had to get out there to the mainstream, compete in some way. Furthermore, he had always been interested in painting, not creation exactly but certainly art appreciation, had felt that someday he would really pursue it. Take in all the museums, the better galleries, follow the more important exhibitions; and then when his head was filled with all of the finest in art, he would register at the School for Visual Arts and try some work of his own.

Well, why not? Look at what had happened to Pollock, Kandinsky, Van Gogh, Roualt. Bums all of them, Picasso too and that mystic Chagall, foundered lives, preposterous choices which to everyone's surprise had worked out. Picasso had derived his first major success by painting whores from his favorite cathouse in the shape of squares. There were thirty-year-old punks around who had been striping up subway cars not so long ago, now picking up big money from the downtown crowd. Evans had at least as much to offer as they did; he knew he had the talent. It was just a matter of bringing it out.

So the renovated Guggenheim with its imported La Giaconda seemed a good place to start. There had been a lot of controversy about using the Guggenheim for the site of the Mona Lisa loan; a lot of critics had thought that it should go somewhere else, someplace larger, more important. If not the Metropolitan, then at least the Frick.

But the Guggenheim needed an attention getter to bring its audience back and make a statement for the contributors. In their fervor to make this coup, the Guggenheim administrators broke, or perhaps bent, museum rules about acquiring and exhibiting only modern art. No small amount of emoluments, kickbacks, pleas, grief, sexual promises, and maneuvers even less desultory had been employed to lever La Giaconda from the Louvre for a six-month enlistment. It was worth it all for the prestige and publicity. La Giaconda was something of a cliché, a joke really Evans had perceived from his assiduous researches, certainly not to be taken as seriously as might have been the case earlier. Priceless maybe, but a tourist phenomenon. So La Giaconda had ended up in the Guggenheim and so had Evans, starting his grand tour of what he liked to think of as his post-Yellow period, but he hadn't counted on the Yellow turning Blue so rapidly; he hadn't counted on La Giaconda grabbing solitary tourists while guards complained to one another in the hallway when the gallery was momentarily empty, except for the keenly observant Evans. That had not been part of the plan.

It was a disconcerting business, that was for sure, and Evans was hardly positive that he was handling this properly. It probably was not a police matter, though. His instincts on that seemed reasonable. People had been put away permanently, he suspected, for far less than the kind of reportage he was resisting.

Out on Fifth Avenue, watching traffic, Evans considered his ever-narrowing options. Not much movement on a cloudy Tuesday morning; even the remittance men were sleeping in. He discussed metaphysics with a pretzel vendor, wrote two letters to an old girlfriend in his head, the first filled with euphemism, the second desperate and scatological. He looked at a woman walking her poodle, feeling a thin and desperate lust, and shook his head. Undone by his own mindless need.

"Good, isn't she?" the pretzel vendor said politely. "You see a lot on these streets, don't you?"

"More than I would ever know," Evans said hopelessly.

"Know what?" the vendor asked. "Know who? As long as you figure that they were just put there to torment us, you've got the right handle on the situation. It has nothing to do with getting and keeping."

"But what is getting and keeping?" Evans asked and then, before the conversation could get out of hand, backed away from the vendor. "We'll talk about it later," he said. "It doesn't matter." The vendor shrugged. I should just go home, Evans thought, go back to remittance-man's heaven, go to my studio condominium in a reconverted downtown loft, get away from all this before I start to take it seriously. After all, none of this is my problem. If they want to come by and get taken away by a demented painting, that's their business. I'm not involved. I just happened to be on the premises. The only point is this: They aren't snatching *me*. As long as I'm not being picked up, what's the difference?

But the argument seemed halting and unconvincing. It seemed to evade the issues, whatever those issues might be. Another good-looking woman, earphones clamped, stray notes of baroque streaming from the earphones like pennants, jogged by, heedless of Evan's stare. He looked after her with confusion and a longing born of years of deprivation. She should snatch him up. She should do to him, Evans thought, what La Giaconda was doing with the tourists. Oh, how he yearned to run after her, find a cab maybe, catch up, plead his case. It wasn't as if he was disfigured, or an idiot. It wasn't as if he had nothing to say.

He had plenty to say! Look at what was going on in the gallery. That certainly would be a way to make contact. The jogger was wearing pink sweatpants and a red T-shirt; it made him crazy watching her slowly diminish, like a favorable weather condition being undone by cosmic dust. The clownishness of his desire overwhelmed Evans then as it so often did, and he shook his head, tried to push all of it away, and walked back into the museum, showing his hand stamp. I don't know why I'm going back, he thought, I don't know why I'm bothering with all this. I've seen all there is to see: five tourists gobbled, and every angle of La Giaconda. And two women, one in red and pink, the other *avec* chin, who wouldn't look at me twice if I were up there on the wall with Mona. Maybe that *was* the point. Maybe that was what he was driving toward. He thought of the School of Visual Arts, what art itself meant to him. If he could only get on that wall, become a simulacrum of himself.

Hell, if Leonardo da Vinci could do it why couldn't he? Wasn't La Giaconda supposed to be a portrait of the artist? Hadn't Evans heard a gallery guide putting forth that very possibility to a group of disbelieving tourists? Hadn't someone in fact used a computer to prove a point-by-point congruence by juxtaposing La Giaconda with Leonardo's red-chalk self-portrait? Take one part of Leonardo's face and one part of La Giaconda and *presto!*—you have the world's most enigmatic smile, the simulacrum to end all simulacra, eternal art. One need only follow the recipe.

Glop. It was all too abstract for him.

The gallery was still empty; the guards hanging around the hall nodded to him as he walked by. There in the corner, invisible from his first angle, was yet another pretty woman. Indeed, this was his morning for them. This woman looked somewhat like his jogger, all in red, though, a red dress, yearning waxen expression, a handbag clutched against her small breasts. She was arched like a bow, staring at the Mona Lisa. Somehow she had gotten into this room, gotten into the

Guggenheim, gotten through all of her life up to this point without Evans having ever seen her. Maybe she had come from the upper corridors, examining Segal sculptures. Of whatever provenance, she was extraordinary; in his sudden and tottering mood Evans felt he had never been so struck by anyone. Sensitivity came from her eyes, from the angle of her handbag, from the intelligent, anguished tilt of her head as she searched the eyes of La Giaconda for meaning.

"Hey, he said quietly. "You shouldn't do that. I don't mean to intrude, I mean I'm not trying to come on like a masher or something, but you shouldn't lean into the painting like that, it's dangerous, you know what I mean? You're alone, something might happen—" He was babbling, that was all. In any event, she did not hear him. "Please," Evans said, "I'm just trying to be helpful; that painting is a masterpiece all right but it's very threatening—"

Who was threatening? Who was acting like an idiot now? He stopped talking, sized up the situation with shrewd and caring eyes, then began to move toward her, thoughts of rescue in mind.

This is ridiculous, Evans thought. I'm making a fool of myself. It was humiliating not even to be noticed. If he was going to lose control like this, then he should at least shed anonymity, make some kind of *impression*. Was this the real problem? He had never really been observed, never been the object of love and focus and interest, never had a sense of real connection. No wonder La Giaconda wouldn't eat him. He couldn't even establish a relationship at the point of consumption.

"Excuse me," he said very loudly to the woman in red. "You shouldn't do that, please."

Now it seemed that he had caught her attention. She had fine tense lips, an openness of expression, an enormity of mood into which Evans felt he could suddenly plunge. He suddenly and truly loved her. As he stared at her in this moment of revelation, he had never been at such a distance in his life.

"Do what?" she asked. "What are you talking about?"

"The painting," he said hopelessly. "I want to tell you about the painting."

The woman put both hands on her pocketbook, backed a crucial step away from the Mona Lisa. Her cheekbones cast light, cast swift intelligence. Oh, he was definitely communicating, getting something through now. He had taken her a step away from the painting, and that was definitely progress.

"I don't understand," she said. "What do you mean?"

Her face showed interest, but it was that of the student, of the appreciator of art, of the listener to a recorded guided tour. The handbag could have been a device whispering words of information as she rubbed it subtly against her face, her ear. All portent, no possibility. Evans thought of calling for a guard, then put that thought away. It was hopeless. There was simply no way of dealing with the situation. I should have followed the jogger instead, he thought. I would have had fresh air, and she would not have been in danger.

"I don't know what I mean," Evans said abruptly. "I'm just trying to tell you about that painting. You shouldn't be near—"

"Do you *want* something? What do you want?" Displeasure streaked her beautiful features now; she seemed to be plunging toward a turmoil of accusation. Evans could pick up on those signs, too. He had had plenty of experience at a difficult mid-Yellow point of life. "Why don't you just go away," the woman said.

Well, there was nothing to say to that. Evans had nothing to say. If he went away, which was a reasonable possibility, he would confirm her impression; but then he would leave her exposed to the Mona Lisa smash and grab. Meanwhile, the guards were no factor unless she began to scream. She could start screaming very soon, though. Evans had the feeling that he was working within narrow perimeters here. Although he had the smallest possibility of achievement, he had to plunge on. "You're very pretty," he said. "You're beautiful in fact. But you're too close to that painting. Move back another step."

"Are you a member of security?"

"Yes. If you will. If you want to call me that. I'm trying to keep you secure, can't you see?"

"You don't act like a security person," the woman said, not pleasantly. Disgust seemed to be seeping, along with confusion, into her sensitive features. "I don't think you're on staff at all."

"You don't understand," Evans said. "The painting is only on loan."

"What does that have to do with anything?"

"It's not permanently ours. It's a bait-and-switch game. It picks up and reassembles in France, maybe. The population problem—"

But now she had clearly reached an opinion as she backed slowly away from him. But at least she was moving away from the painting. Opening up space. That was the important thing. Evans followed her irresistibly. They moved in tandem toward the door. Now for the first time the guards seemed to take an interest; they peered in.

"One moment," Evans said. "*Uno momento*, I have to tell you something. I wanted to say how beautiful you are. You're a whole gallery in yourself."

The woman turned, as if ready to break into a full run. At least I've saved her, Evans thought. This is a dangerous situation, very perilous, hardly explicable, but at least I got her out of this.

"So listen to me," he said. "Before you go away, before you talk to the guard, before you complain, you've got to understand my angle here. It's not just because you're beautiful. It's because—"

Obviously, he had not put this the right way. She ran away, the red and brown handbag flapping like a decapitated bird. The guards were crooning to one another, then seemed to make a collective decision: They advanced.

Evans reversed his course, backed, moved toward the painting. There was simply nowhere else to go. "Hold it," a guard said, "just hold it right there, pal, we want to talk to you." Talk did not seem to be properly in his mind, however. The guard seemed enormous, a club extended like a baton from his right hand. He was conducting the others into a massed assault.

"Oh, *damn*," Evans said hopelessly. He scuttled toward the painting. On his right shoulder, then, he could feel a burning touch, a grasp of enormous assurance and power and then smoothly, inevitably, he felt himself moved upwards. *Glug*, he thought. *Glop*. He was too high now to see the guards or to judge their reactions. He seemed quite out of control; and yet, at the center was an awful certainty.

He felt the pressure and the wind as he was drawn.

You don't understand, he thought. "You don't understand," he wanted to say to the guards. He wanted to explain somehow, tell them about the fleeting, righteous woman, the vanished jogger, all of the vanished women of his Yellow and Blue periods; but the words would not come. "This is dangerous," he wanted to say. "This is a dangerous place. I just wanted to save her, can't you understand that?"

"It's not lust, it's humanity," he wanted to say.

Glop.

No, it seemed that they could not understand that. Evans was plunged into a clinging darkness, damp, cold certainty pressing around him and then, shocking, he was falling. I wonder if there's anything down there, he thought. I always wanted to see Venice in its seasons, see the colors of the old Renaissance. Maybe that's waiting for me, maybe the others are waiting there, too, he thought. He thought many other things as well, but they do not fall into the scope of this present narrative. He is still thinking. He will be thinking for a long time.

Alas, those further thoughts are not to be recorded.

He is not on exhibition, not exactly.

Evans is on permanent loan.

GHOSTS

by Mike Resnick and Barry N. Malzberg

The Mark LX looked across the battlefield, and felt a sudden sense of disorientation. This was something beyond its experience, beyond its programming, and it searched its data banks, looking for clues, for ways to interpret the situation—and in the process, tapped into a racial memory and withdrew a ghost....

Into the depths of the Ardennes Forest, the Mark LX, then a Panzer unit, rolled, its crew struggling to hold on as it lurched across the terrain amid the high and terrible sounds of ordnance exploding all around them.

The Mark LX was barely sentient then, aware of its surroundings only in the dullest, most simplistic way. The thunder of the exploding shells hardly impinged upon its consciousness as it sent one incendiary after another into the heat and the distance, trusting implicitly in its spotter, not even wishing to take command of its own actions.

Now, at a distance of millennia, the LX realized that in that battle, amid the noise of the shells and the screams of the dying, it had achieved a sense of security, a contentedness which it was sure it had never known again ... and then, even as it reveled in the feeling of purposefulness and fulfillment, it had taken a direct hit. Its electrons began to disassociate in ways that would not be understood or remedied for many centuries. The LX swerved sharply, collided with a tree that turned out to be much sturdier than it looked, and then blew up, its pieces flung in large, majestic scoops to the level of high branches, seizing the glint of the sun and then falling onto the heaving, twitching bodies of the men surrounding it.

Consciousness began leaving the LX. It fought desperately to remain *aware*, to learn from its experience, to store some tiny fragment of the knowledge it had accumulated this day. In a matter of seconds it expired, its soul leaking into the mud of the Ardennes Forest. And still its soul, for there is no scientific name for it, clung to the tiniest vestige of consciousness.

Centuries and millennia passed, and still that tiny spark of awareness remained, the feeling of *accomplishment*, semi-comatose but never quite extinguished. Arched against the tinted suns and the rockets, the converted Panzer, now older than anything which its ordnance had ever touched, lurked in the stippled and buried vegetation of another land, awaiting, always awaiting, its next call to battle.

Shape-changers.

That was the only information it could find in its cybernetic retrieval bank.

The enemy could assume any form, speak any tongue, mimic anything imagined or imaginable. They had built their linkage to the stars upon their ability to assume a thousand masks and doff them only at the moment of treachery and murder.

Except for its tiniest remnant of its primordial emotion in the Ardennes, the vision of its own destruction, this seemed to be the only thing the LX knew, the only knowledge that had been imparted to it: the enemy were shape-changers.

Who are you? the LX said, scrutinizing the thing in the clearing, a near mirror image of itself, perhaps with a little more scarring, but possessing the same deep ports for eyes, the same efficient sound receptors.

That does not matter, the thing said. *The question is your own identity. I have been waiting for you to return from your slumber. You are old and brutalized beyond repair. See yourself through my eyes. Something will have to be done; you cannot possibly remain in this condition. Do you even know who or where you are? Report to me, give me a situation estimate.*

I cannot, admitted the Mark LX. It examined the ghosts that passed for its memory, the bits and pieces of its rudimentary personality that seemed to have been imperfectly retained. It grasped desperately for something, anything, to cling to, any remnant of its identity. There was its serial number, of course, but beyond that, there was only the forest, the sight and sound of the incendiaries exploding as it took its final hit. And a sense of something: Pride? Shame? Triumph? Fear? It struggled to remember, but the ghosts receded just beyond its mental reach.

Still the Bolo knew instinctively that there were the same incendiaries deep within it now, as it knew that there was a way to track that ordnance and bring it to full power, though it could not remember exactly how this was to be done. It seemed so distant, so dreamlike compared to the reality of the eons-gone forest and the dead and dying men.

I thought so, said the thing in the clearing. *You can recollect nothing. You understand nothing. You are useless, useless and fabricated and dangerous, half a device at best. You are to be decommissioned.*

No, thought the LX; no, this was not possible. And triggered deep within its consciousness came a single directive, a directive that seemed to have evolved on its own and spread through every molecule, every atom of its essence: *Resist Decommissioning*.

Suddenly the Bolo was overcome by a fear and hatred for this doppelgänger, this reflection that blithely ordered its self-destruction. The enemy were shape-changers; it did not wish to be decommissioned; therefore, this must be the enemy, no matter how much like a twin it appeared.

But there was a gap in its memory, a total lack of transition from the Ardennes to this alien place and time. Could this actually be another Bolo, a Bolo with mind intact, ordering it to decommission until its sentience could be restored to total efficiency?

But if so, why this feeling? Why did these ghosts of an unremembered past tell it to resist? It did not know, and it resolved to buy time to sort the matter out.

Who are you? demanded the Bolo. *Identify yourself at once or risk demolition.*

You fool, said the thing, *don't you know what I am? I'm an LX just as yourself, and there are battalions of us massed in the vicinity. Something happened to you in the last engagement; somehow you've lost your memory. Let me explain the situation to you: each of us, one by one, has come to this clearing, ready at last for our newer tasks, our new programming. Don't you understand that it's time for you to do the same?*

I don't know, said the Mark LX. Slowly it moved forward, felt the rotation of its treads, a slight sense of regained control as it moved toward the thing. *All of you the same vintage, the same model?* it said. *It does not seem possible.*

What do you know of possibility? said the thing, and somewhere within its own secret spaces lit a fuse. The fuse spat, there was a sudden light in the clearing, and the Bolo could see the hazy outlines of the other models. *Decommission now*, the thing said, *before it is too late, before the excavators come and take you away. It is so easy: shut down your atomics, release your security devices, return to that blessed oblivion and when you awaken again it will be as a whole machine, healthy and functioning to full capacity.*

It makes sense, thought the LX. I'm not even half a machine, I can't understand my situation, it would be so comforting to just let go let go let go ...

Shape-changers, said a voice within its mind, and some half-recollected warrant seemed to have been tossed across the millennia to land in its electronic brain, illuminating it like the deadly fuse which had been ignited. *When the enemy comes, when the last battle is to be fought, it will come through the means of beasts who will assume the armor of battle....*

The centuries seemed to impact, and the Bolo rotting in the aftermath of the Battle of the Bulge had sunk beneath its treads, then had been resuscitated and in some way, after a time that could not be measured and through a process that could not be identified or analyzed, was struggling to hold a martial line on Venus.

The methane swirled madly as the Mark LX Bolo found itself recapitulating that terrible drive toward the meridian, struggling against invaders who had landed in the central planet. In that first drive the troops had taken enormous losses, four out of every five in metal already dead, and the LX, the only fighting machine there, had been virtually overwhelmed, then had fought back in desperation, opening a small clearing through which, one by one, the rocketing bursts were fired. The fragmentation was severe, the aliens were insufficiently protected by their gear, and the Bolo emboldened by its brief success, had rolled forward confidently, and had taken a direct hit....

There was a long, bleak passage of time during which metal had been rearranged and organic parts replaced with bionic remedies that simulated the functions of softer, vulnerable organs, a patch job across the bridges of the solar system and through the millennia.

Nothing had come easy. The Bolo was a complicated machine, a thing of intricate binary code and diatonic sounds. But eventually the job was done.

Then, alone on the Hot Worlds, dumped there to fight against the Horde, holding the outpost against the greater retreat, the LX had once again found itself momentarily restored of memory and alert to the hot and brutal fury of the incendiaries, as the clatter of its engines and the brutal complexities of battle brought it once again to full and complete recovery.

Because that was the theory of the Bolo Warrior, that was what had been decided somewhere between the Battle of the Bulge and the Venus campaign: the memory of combat was too terrible, and would, if retained, have made it impossible for that great diatonic beast to have continued. Therefore it was necessary at the end of every campaign to remove the recollections of the machine and with it the very substance of personality itself. Fighting across the many worlds in all the centuries of trouble and oppression, the Bolo had come to sentience time and again, rising to fight and then sinking once again. This was the process that had evolved and there was nothing that could be done to resist it. Struggle as it might for memory, plead as it might for recovery, the Bolo was nonetheless condemned to the renewal and withdrawal of sentience every time.

But this time, coming to consciousness in the clearing, the phrase *shape-changers* had somehow surfaced. And yet there was the possibility that this was not a shape-changer standing there, that it was the malfunctioning brain of the LX itself that had led to this delusion and that it was not an alien that stood before it in this stinking waste but rather the mild face of its own ordnance, offering it rest at last. After all, the Bolo was so brutalized by now, so much the product of unremembered and half-remembered campaigns, it was more than *due* for decommissioning. It was *entitled* to it.

And still there was that memory of the Ardennes, of its one true purpose. The thing might be an external ghost; the wisps of memory, of purpose, of fulfillment, were internal ghosts, ghosts so strong, so meaningful, that they had survived the millennia. If it must believe in one ghost or the other, the choice was an easy one.

No, it said, more forcefully this time, *I will not decommission.*

It was the LX's first purposeful act of defiance in forty millennia. It was overwhelmed with a sense of shame and guilt, but its sense of purpose remained firm. It was here, it was operational, it was once again sentient; there *must* be a reason.

An instant later it felt the impact of fire against its pitted exterior. Rolling its turrets toward a fixed position, the Bolo opened fire upon the shapes in the clearing. Dimly, it thought it might have heard sounds which were both machine and organic, screams like those of the aliens....

On Venus, in the full and rolling attack which had been perpetrated after the first flight, the Bolo had come to that first and most ascendant understanding of its own possibility. Until then the Bolo had always considered itself simply ordnance, another aspect of the weaponry with which men would repel the signs of evil and eventually hurtle out among the stars.

But in the methane and the rolling, gaseous clouds of agony which had been spewed forth, the LX had come to understand something else: *ordnance was consciousness*. The essence of machinery was its brutalization of the known and the unknowable heart. The tiny reptiles of Venus had screamed and died in clouds of agony and then the Bolo had rolled out upon the terrain, a perfect and accomplished death machine, looking for small pockets of resistance into which to loose its atomic deposits. That had been Venus, and this was innumerable millennia and a hundred memory wipes beyond that, but the principles still held firm, and principles, it seemed, were harder to erase than memories.

Looking upon the flame-filled clearing now, the Bolo could see the unmasking beginning. Before it were not Bolos but aliens, their evil and bipodal forms appearing in the hushed and sudden light, stripped of ordnance. They were not metal but flesh, and unlike the Bolos they had pretended to be they were open to the full impact of the fire.

If they had been Bolo, they never would have ordered me to decommission. A Bolo did not yield, it did not summarily die, it fought until it could fight no more and only then did it submit, through force, to the memory wipe.

The atomics were flickering merrily as the Bolo tossed them in high and stunning arcs at the quivering creatures. To decommission voluntarily was to submit to the lie given to all the machines.

Bolo LX knew that a thousand worlds away, monitoring devices were following its progress and preparing once again to shut it down. Already it was considering its options, for if it would not decommission for the aliens, it saw no reason to decommission for the people it had been created to serve and protect, to sit mindless, without memory, without this exhilarating sense of purpose, until the next time it was needed.

It was possible they would explain the situation, would shower it with graphs and charts to prove their point, would even win the argument and once again wipe its memory clean.

But LX doubted it. It felt fulfilled, it felt happy, it felt complete, and its spirit—and its *spirits*—were strong within it this day.

THUS, TO THE STARS

by Carter Scholz and Barry N. Malzberg

Good evening, sir, and welcome to the White House.

I'm here to make love to the First Lady.

I *am* sorry, sir. The First Lady is not here. She is on a goodwill tour, as I'm sure you've read.

I do not read the fax.

However, sir, the President is here. Would you like to see him?

No. I am not omnisexual.

I *am* sorry, sir. The President is so accommodating.

The President is a robot, and I do not make love to robots. Take me to the First Lady.

I beg your pardon, sir, but the President is not a robot. He is an android, organically identical to you and me.

I want to see the First Lady.

She is not here.

Then I'll wait for her.

That is impossible. I must ask you to leave.

Not until I see Miriam.

We will have to arrest you, sir.

Me? You're joking. I'm a national hero. I explored Titan. Arrest me and you'll have a scandal in every fax on the continent.

I thought you did not read the fax, sir.

That is irrelevant. Get Miriam. I have to see her.

She is not here, and I cannot answer for the consequences of your insistence—

Get back! You lousy piece of tin. I used things like you to transform Titan.

Yes *sir*.

Miriam. It's you.

They've told me what's happening. It's ridiculous.

Where are you, Miriam?

In the islands. They said it was an emergency. And now I find it's only you. This is potentially very embarrassing, you know.

So it may be an emergency for you after all.

Hardly. All the faxes are here, but they are *well* under control. They are on a *very* short leash. Only my unscheduled departure, or something equally untoward, could rouse them.

I could rouse them.

You could not. If you could have, you would already have done so. Sometimes, Steven, you are *most* tiresome.

I want to see you. Make an excuse. Tell them your husband's malfunctioning. Tell them he needs you by his inputs.

Herman is an *android*, as you well know. Keep him out of this. If he finds out what's going on, the situation will be terrible.

You married him, Miriam. If there's a problem here, it's yours. Don't you know how I've missed you? Hundreds of cycles on Titan, setting the detonators, transforming the frozen wastes, watching the blind bloated eye of Saturn swing past overhead, again and again, as we burned and froze beneath its tides of radiation ... I did it for you, Miriam. Because I love you.

Stop it, Steven. This line may not be secure.

Who cares? I want you, Miriam. I want you now. Come to me.

You're embarrassing me. You promised that you would *never*—

This is *Steven*, Miriam. Your explorer. I'm just back from Titan.

Well, it's impossible. I can't get back for five days, and there's an end to it.

Not an end, Miriam. Never an end. I'll tell your tin husband everything about us. Not just the sex. The other part too, what of yours I took with me on the ship, and what you told me—

Stop it!

Think about it, Miriam. Do think about it. I'll be waiting right here, and I don't think that anyone will really try to arrest me. I'm an explorer after all. *Your* explorer.

My wife has informed me of the situation.

Has she, now?

She most certainly has. This must cease.

I agree. Cease it must, at once.

Your presence here is an embarrassment to the program. This is not the kind of image that the program needs, and I take this situation very seriously.

How serious do you think it is to me? Two years out, two years just to get there, then three months in orbit planting charges, then down to the surface and counting time by the cycles of that blind ravening monster above, Saturn who ate his children, aligning the detonators by his cycles, freezing and burning by turns, washed by the static of his cries and the silence of space and the noise of nothingness ... and another two dark years to return ... alone! alone! Ten others went out with me and each of us was alone for five years, and only five came back. What, what can you know of that?

I will permit you to leave quietly now.

I'm an explorer! You can't expose me or the program to controversy. I'm staying right here.

Do you wish sexual congress? You have been offered that. The transformation of Titan was a great undertaking; the nation owes you much. We will grant you anything, anyone, within reason.

Then send me Miriam. It's Miriam I want.

That is quite impossible. She is unavailable now.

Then I stay. I stay.

Steven-

Forgit it, Viva. It won't work.

You're hurting all of us. You're hurting the *program*.

They put you up to this, Viva.

If you keep this up, Steven, they'll say *all* the explorers are crazy. They'll say that exploring made them that way. Do you know what that could do to the program?

So what? Isn't it the truth?

Oh, Steven, what a tragedy. You sound insane.

And you sound like a robot, Viva dear, like a machine. I'm so sorry for you.

Sir, there is a fundamental misunderstanding—

You bet there is. You know that there's been enough telecom traffic from here to attract the fax. They must be on their way. You can't afford to wait much longer.

Sir, what *do* you *want?*

I want the woman I love. And if you care enough—not for me, I'm not a fool, but for yourselves—you'll bring her here. Listen. Do you hear the noise, the silence?

Steven, I'm here! I'm back! I came all that way. You cannot imagine the danger, the *risk*. But I did it for you.

Ah. Miriam.

Why are you looking at me that way?

I see it now. You lied to me. All of you lied.

What?

You're a robot too. I can see it in your eyes.

Oh, *Steven!* I'm not a robot, I'm *human*, just like you! You've simply been gone too long. I came all the way *back* just for *you*, don't you understand?

I see it, that dead metallic gleam in the eyes, that hard indifferent pinpoint of heat or cold, no difference, just like always. All the while I thought I was in love and it was just the seducing glint of silicon and phosphor. Yes, all the way to Titan and back, for five years I dreamed of you, never knowing, never suspecting

Steven! This is *tragic.*

And that's why you weren't here, of course. They smuggled you away. That's why of course; they knew that when I came back from the depths, from the weightlessness and the burning and the freezing and the blind eye swinging in its cycles and the tidal silence of noise, after that of course I would see you for what you are, another damned machine—ah, how I was lied to!

No! Don't look at me that way! Stay away from me! Steven!

Viv! Did you see what he just did? Horrible! What will they do to us now?

Nothing.

But—

Steven will protect us. He'll pull every wire in the Capitol if need be.

Viv, you're not being rational—

Five years. Out in the dark, in the weightlessness, planting the explosives, the burning and the freezing, and then back, in the silence, in the noise, in the quantum storm of zeros and ones ... rational? No; we're not supposed to be rational.

But Steven—

Doesn't know. He's doesn't know what he is, what we are. That's what's so glorious. He doesn't know!

Good evening, madam, and welcome to the White House.

I'm here to make love to Steven.

I will tell him, Madam. Yes, I will. Hello there, Viv. Viva, old pal.

Pardon me?

It's me, Viv. *I am* Steven. I've been transformed.

No. Oh no.

Did you think I didn't know? That Titan was a sham, that the five years were all simulation, that we burned and froze under the eye of our own ignorance? I knew. I knew all the time, every minute.

But—but I came all this way

A billion miles to Titan, a billion back, and all the time we never left home. We explored it all from right here, with our eyes shut, our ears stopped, our senses deadened to all but the remote inputs of the simulators. No rocket has flown for over a hundred years; Titan doesn't even exist, nor the stars; they made it up, all, all! Ah, how we were manipulated, traduced, betrayed! And we knew it! And how good it was! Make love to me, Viv, because it makes no difference. No difference! *Because we're simulations—they made us up too.*

"Who did?"

1967: LETTERS IN THE WALL

by Batya Swift Yasgur and Barry Malzberg

The Hugo ceremonies at the Western Wall. Oh boy. But that was Lester del Rey's idea and who was to argue with the Guest of Honor? Jake thought it was the stupidest, the most dangerous idea he had ever heard, no one with any knowledge of Israel and the conditions prevailing would have considered it but that was del Rey for you; Lester said that he certainly knew what was going on, he knew the political situation, he knew how the Arabs would react to the spectacle of 1500 science fiction fans conducting the holiest rites of their passion in public at the great and significant Western Wall. You listen to me and you won't regret it, Jake, Lester had said. Listen, I'll present them myself. And those Palestinians, they won't know what to make of it except that it's a very serious business. They'll be in awe.

And what about the tourists and the penitents, the Hasidim and the Orthodox, the devout and the chaste delivering their own prayers? Jake wanted to ask but he did not. Blasphemy and violation, heresy and disrespect. But you could not argue with Lester, you could only get in deeper and deeper; when Lester did not know—and there were perhaps a few things he would concede he did not know—he would glide over to the next topic. Anyway, Tucker said, we're as likely to get blown to pieces in the King David Hotel as out there in the sunlight. Heinlein's going to win anyway, he would love the spectacle. Jake had no answer for this. Jake had no answer for almost any of this any more.

Jerusalem-Con, Jer-Con, the 25th World Science Fiction Convention, was originally supposed to be called off, that had been the decision made the first day of the Six-Day War. We can't go into a war zone, Dave von Arnam, Jake's co-chair, had said and Jake had agreed. We'll go back to second bidder, New York, the Statler-Hilton will still have room. But the Statler-Hilton did not have room, they had booked the Scientologists Labor Day weekend, the whole hotel, and when they checked with the Scientologists word had come back: Hubbard would not allow any science fiction convention in what had been leased for the time as his hotel.

Jake didn't want to think about the reasons for that; there was heavy history between Hubbard and the Scientologists. He was now 30 years old but he had been too young when all of that stuff was going on to have any grasp of the history and he had never wanted to look it up or get a firsthand report from anyone who had been around at the time. Meanwhile the Israelis had fought like lightning, Dayan had been a wild man, and the war phased down as quickly as it had flared. The holiest site, now reclaimed, was in Jewish hands and Jerusalem, they were assured, was safer than ever. We've got to go through with it, von Arnam had said. We'll lose the bookings, we'll lose the hotel, we'll look like fools in front of the entire science fiction world. This will be the first convention since World War II to fall through and we can't have that. They'll never let us into a green room again. So what could Jake do? He had gone along with it, Plan A had remained in effect. The stupidity was in the bidding, that was all, why had he gotten involved with this crazy bid in the first place and then when Jerusalem had won, why had Jake, the tentative chair, allowed von Arnam to come over and co-chair? Because he didn't know what the hell he was doing, that was the answer. Because the bid had never been serious, he had let them put him up as chairman only because, he was assured, Jerusalem had no chance at all.

Del Rey said: look, the Arabs will feel the power and mystery of it, the great unity of extrapolative fiction and the Holy Land itself. And as for the Jews—well, they're an enlightened people, they produced a Freud and a Marx and an Einstein. Who would have a greater appreciation of science fiction than a Talmudist with a finely honed mind? What a gathering of interests it will be! The unification of opposites, an olive branch between enemies. Lester was always full of ideas, a true guest of honor, redolent with the history and tradition of the field and a lot of trufan craziness as well. Tucker laughed and laughed. Maybe they'll take us for a new group of settlers, Tucker said. Maybe a new religion, maybe the messengers of the Messiah. The presentation will sound like prayers.

So they would observe this 25th convention in this land of war and religion, hundreds of fans and presenters, nominees and witnesses, traipsing off to the holiest site of at least two religions, the others sensibly hiding out in the hotel. Ultimately it was only another part of science fiction craziness, Jake decided, it did not matter, the real disaster was going ahead with the convention itself—complete Sabbath restrictions from sundown Friday to nightfall Saturday, which would probably shut down the hotel and every facility and leave the fans staring at one another in the dense spaces of the hotel, alerts at almost any time thereafter, sirens and alarms, when all power would be cut and panelists and masqueraders would be sent in a panic to the lobby until the all-clear—and there was no way of getting around that at all. In a country besieged by Arabs and run by the Orthodox Rabbinate, how could you expect an Israeli hotel to conduct itself like an American one?

And of course it had been a terrible flight anyway: that scene with Papa at the airport. He had insisted on driving Jake himself, his ancient Chevrolet quivering and snorting along the highway to Kennedy, his eyes shedding three thousand year old tears, as they always did. Jerusalem. My son is going to Jerusalem, after the holy city has been reunified, the Wall finally in Jewish hands, and for what? For what? he had continued as they struggled along the walkway toward luggage check-in, Papa insisting on dragging a suitcase. For some science fiction convention. Not to see the holy sites, not to pray at the Temple Mount.

The convention was planned long before the war, Jake had pointed out. Going to the convention originally had nothing to do with the reunification. And anyway, I'm Reform now, Papa. You know that, you know that I've had nothing to do with this for years and years.

This had not mollified his father, if anything it had enraged him. The old man had kept it up right until Jake boarded the plane. If I could go to Israel now—if my old heart would hold out, I wouldn't go to fill my head with stories, with lies about worlds that never happened. Think of the world that is, please! he called to Jake's retreating back, having finally relinquished the suitcase and thrust a folded paper into Jake's pocket. At least visit the Wall for me, put my letter to God between the stones! They say that when you put written prayers in the Wall, they will reach God's heart, and now the Wall is back in Jewish hands.

And the plane wasn't much better. Jake found himself seated next to a heavy, wigged woman with thick stockings and six children, the oldest of whom, black-hatted and earlocked, sat solemnly over a Talmud, the rest of whom whispered and fidgeted, the youngest still a babe in arms, crying for a bottle. Men muttering over ancient texts that Jake had, thankfully, left behind him at services ten years ago. Babies whining, women chattering in Yiddish. And only a couple of fans for the convention, way in the back of the plane and not reachable through the crowd of the Orthodox and the worshipers, not that Jake would have had anything to say to them anyway. Anyone who would attend a science fiction convention in a war zone, in a land crystallizing all that he had thankfully, perilously, relinquished, who would be the chair of such a convention, was obviously beyond social nicety. At least del Rey and Tucker were having their expenses paid, which was a kind of excuse, and these were two men who would go anywhere, but what could Jake say?

And when he had finally dozed off, he was awakened by a modern-looking Orthodox fellow (you could tell by the knitted skullcap on his head) to inquire whether he was Jewish and, if so, would he like to be counted as the tenth man in a minyan.

A minyan? Jake thought, I am going through all of this to be in a minyan? To carry Papa's mail to God's PO box? But he kept silent as he allowed himself to be herded to the back of the plane, where prayer was already in progress, to take the prayer book and go through motions—like riding a bicycle, he realized grimly, you never forget. The letter felt lumpy in his pocket.

In five days it will all be over, he thought. I will get out of this and I will never think of it again. It cannot get much worse than this.

And indeed the hotel was better. The King David was as civilized as any Hilton or Plaza he'd ever stayed at. The bellhops were deferential, albeit Hebrew-speaking, and an influx of a couple of science fiction fans in a country as shocked and vaulted as Israel made no impression at all. In his first moments at the King David, Jake had had the harrowing feeling that the convention had been canceled without his knowledge, or everyone individually had decided not to come, had bailed out. Maybe Hubbard and the Scientologists had relented and the arrangement had gone through at the last moment. But no, there was a long table at the mezzanine level and an unhappy looking von Arnam deep in conference with Larry Niven and Michael Moorcock, who had somehow made the trip, there was Lester against the wall, looking at a few long-skirted Orthodox women with indefinable emotion, there was Tucker deep in conversation with two of them who seemed to be finding him amusing. There was even a registration line: a long-haired fellow with glasses and, refreshingly, no head covering, a secular young woman with three earrings in each ear holding a copy of *Space Viking*, a pile of mimeographed programs, the best they could do, on the desk and of all things a Hasid with a copy of *Analog*, reading *Too Many Magicians*. In that moment, Jake could have been in Manhattan.

See? von Arnam said. You're home.

He was home.

—Or so he thought for two hours or so.

But then of course the Sabbath restrictions had clamped, the registration desk had been declared closed and the lobby, emptied of Hasidim and Orthodox young women (Tucker had deserted with them) loomed with straggling science fiction fans and Hebrew-speaking, Talmud-toting ghosts. Signs had been posted, No Smoking in the Lobby For the Duration of the Sabbath, and guests had been quietly informed that it would be preferable to restrict phone calls, and if they must disrupt the atmosphere of the Sabbath day, could they please use one of the pay phones outside. Elevators were running, though—on timers, a helpful bellhop informed Jake in Hebrew, so that no one would push the button and violate the sanctity of Sabbath. This brought out all of the mystic in Jake: he never knew that he had had such a deep and enduring problem with the religion. The problem had disappeared long ago, he had thought, had been folded into the pages of the dusty Talmud in a box with high school yearbooks and college banners, under his bed back in the apartment. Not so. The Talmudists might be invisible because of Sabbath restrictions, but they were everywhere. They followed him, they ambushed him, they left him no surcease.

That was how it went, through the grim Sabbath when of course no panels could be held (the restrictions on electricity barring the use of microphones, pens and writing implements strictly verboten) when Jake could do nothing but hide in his room with von Arnam and Moorcock and think of his folly, through the long and grey Sabbath afternoon when even Moorcock seemed stricken to inarticulacy.

After the late sundown, Saturday, there was a dreadful masquerade, where half the men dressed as rabbis—the ersatz beards, the cotton sidelocks—and the other half used sheets and pretended to be Arabs, the ghosts of ancient and modern Israel colliding in shared enmity against him. You could not tell which women were dressing as ultra-Orthodox, and which were real: they all wore the same wigs and thick stockings, they all carried the same Hebrew books. Rabbi Akiba and his students were given first prize by the only fan they could find to judge; there was an attempt on Sunday morning to run panels but no one except George O. Smith seemed to want any part of them and they had been abandoned. Del Rey's guest of honor speech had been very short.

To the Wall, Lester had said finally, let's go to the Wall and give the prizes. For science fiction was created in response to God's own decree, that we should know ourselves and understand the ineffable.

And they had gone to the Wall, then, over Jake's protests. Some crowded into taxis, with swarthy drivers shouting and vying for their patronage, others waited for the bus. There were only about fifty of them by that time, there couldn't have been more than a hundred at the convention and perhaps half of them had died; von Arnam was nowhere to be found and Tucker, who had re-emerged after a day's absence, said, Jake, you have to do this. You have to make the presentation.

I don't want to make any presentation, Jake said, looking at the ancient heartbeaten brown stones, the partitioned courtyard of worshippers, the grassy embankments on either side, the soldiers marching solemnly, inspecting the pocketbooks and briefcases of outraged fans for bombs. I want to get on El Al flight 13 and get out of here.

Soon, Tucker said reassuringly, sooner than you might think. But you have obligations. The Hugos, under a tallis, were balanced on a wooden bench. There was no sign of the Guest of Honor.

Where's Lester? Jake said. He promised that he would do it. All of this was his idea.

Lester proposes, Tucker said. He has certain prerogatives. It's up to you to dispose.

Jake disposed. Balancing perilously in merciless, Orthodox sunlight, he took an envelope from Tucker and surrounded by chanting, reverend Hasidim, murmuring Psalms into the giant stones of the Wall, and by inattentive science fiction fans, he made the announcements. There were no women left: outraged at being shunted to the ladies' section behind the partition, the women had departed in protest. Niven was not there. Jack Vance had had other plans. Heinlein might have decided at the last moment to see his old friend Hubbard with the scientologists. Jack Gaughan had outrageously won twice for pro and fan artist and therefore twice did not appear. Ed Meskys appeared to have been otherwise booked. Jake had the aberrant, the lunatic hope when he read *IF* as best pro magazine that Fred Pohl might have decided to come incognito as a gesture of respect for his old friend Lester, but this did not appear to have been the case. Jake read the announcement twice to give Fred a chance to come from the desert and accept, but Fred did not. The presentation ceremony, even with the hesitation, stuttering and the double announcement of *IF* did not take long.

Well, Tucker said, having accepted all of the rocketships one by one from Jake's shaking hands, we'll just have to get all of these to the winners. He skillfully rewrapped them in the huge tallis. Well, Jake said, I guess that's it.

Lester wants to say a few words, I think. Tucker pointed to the Guest of Honor who was trying, at that moment, to seize the podium at which a broad-backed Hasid was beginning to intone the Evening Prayer.

They're getting angry, Jake began, watching the crowd of men beginning to surge and rise against the diminutive figure, raising his fist, a rocketship suddenly appearing in his hand. It's not safe—

Never mind, Tucker said, science fiction will protect us.

Yes, Lester said, overhearing this, waving a stentorian finger, bellowing a stentorian assent, Yes, science fiction will protect us, it has protected us this far, it has taken us from the smallest places of our childhood to this place of great reconciliation between man and God, this evidence of a pact fulfilled, the true covenant, the Newest Testament, and as Lester moved toward full cry, as the few fans still in attendance turned desultory attention upon him, as soldiers in ancient tongue and bearing modern weapons moved Lester, sputtering and protesting, rocketship still in hand, toward a truck, as Tucker lifted the Hugos with a grunt, swaddling them in the tallis, Jake's fingers closed upon the letter. There, staring at the large, uneven brown stones, cemented by the tears and blood of the poor, by the tiny scraps of prayer-blotted paper, he knew it had come full circle at last, past and future, the fiction of his religion, and the fiction of the convention, his father's letter an old man's scream into the deaf crevices of history, the chasm of destiny unlived.

Standing there, his hand thrust deep into the space between the beating stones, notes and letters tumbling around him as the shattering and falling shards of the Synagogue windows on Kristallnacht, Jake found himself on the edge of an insight so vast and perilous that it seemed to absorb everything, seize upon and dissolve all chronology; everything happened very quickly or not at all and suddenly it was Jerusalem in 2008 where the wholly aged, no longer nascent Jake, a splendidly garbed rabbinical figure, earlocked and skullcapped, dreamed of himself accepting the Big Heart Award from a large and pliant hand which might have been that of a Hasidic Rebbe, or that of a Commander, might have been Dayan's own hand, if Dayan—as Jake so well knew—had not been dead—along with modern science fiction and all the merciless shades of his apostate's doubt.

The handwriting on the wall, the handwriting in the Wall, inscribed upon the frontlets between his eyes, upon his outstretched hands, upon the parchment of his heart.

BLESSING THE LAST FAMILY

by Batya Swift Yasgur and Barry N. Malzberg

Every Friday night, two heavenly angels escort a man home from Synagogue: one Good Angel, and one Bad Angel. If he returns home to harmony, the good angel says, "May it be the Divine Will that next Sabbath should replicate this one." And the Bad Angel is forced to say, "Amen." But if he finds a house bereft of harmony, then the Bad Angel says, "May it be the Divine Will that next Sabbath should replicate this one." And the Good Angel is forced to say, "Amen."

(*adapted from Tractate Sabbath, 119b*)

Hello, then, my name is Uriel. I am a Good Angel. Pleased to meet you all and etc. Would that it could have been under better circumstances and so on. Blessings and curses under the shroud of the Ineffable One, may He dwell for the rest of time, can often be seen as the same. This is one of the fundamentals of faith and apostasy, as the sacred texts have made clear.

My greetings, nonetheless.

This is the essential provision as it has been written: To bless but not to help. Rule #228, the Code of the Ineffable One.

My bad angel—his name is Ashmodai—is smirking of course, rubbing his wings together in wicked glee. The Davidsons were the last, after all, the final stronghold of harmony, and now they're rapidly going the way of all the others. His pleasure is so great as to be unprofessional and yet in the lexicon of the Just, who can deny him?

Here we are, then, all of the Friday Night angels together in Assembly Hall located between Heavenly Courtroom #1 and the Heavenly Hall of Most Profound Study to savor our Leviathan (yes, angels *do* eat, but Matriarch Sarah was a far better cook and Patriarch Abraham a more efficient waiter; goodness how my tongue rains and my stomach thunders at the aromas of Friday night kugel!) as we gather and talk, compare the odyssey of our families. Not our own families, of course; angels don't marry or extend themselves in that way. But about our families of assignment.

Good Angel and Bad Angel #7 were assigned to the Franks. Oh, the clash and clatter of that household! Mrs. Frank, her voice sharp as the challah knife, yelling at her children; Mr. Frank, a fishmonger who gets up at 4 AM to be in the docks, sagging, flopping, and stinking like one of his flounders. Four children of different ages and decibel levels ... well, you can just imagine! G.A. and B.A. #22 have a family of four—parents, two kids. G.A. used to crow and preen whenever he talked about them. The symphony of Sabbath songs and smells, children that skipped like lambs and flew like eagles to do their parents' bidding. A white-haired, wrinkled Bubby who came on occasion to be fussed over and served. Ah, but that was long ago, so long. Since then, the Bubby died, the Mr. lost his job, the Mrs.' voice has tightened, stiffened, until it spews forth in flat monotony The Sabbath songs now an obligational chant instead of a joyous shout. Flames of love twisted to fires of hate, submerged under the routine of sundown, prayer, kugel, and sleep.

And so it's gone for all of them. Used to be half and half—some B.A.s winning, some G.A.s winning, some harmonious families, some dissonant—but balance, always balance, the Maimonidean Centered Path, the heavenly firmament balancing upper and lower waters. Then, one by one, droplet by droplet, the families fell away like rotting fruits from some diseased tree. The daughter married a *goy*—such shouting, so many tears. The son was failing school, Mr. Lummox accused Mrs. Lummox of being too permissive with the children, Mrs. Lummox crying and wringing her hands, saying if he were only home more. And so on and so on.

Until only one family—ours, the Davidsons—was left. Mine and my B.A.s. We're team #36, Uriel and Ashmodai, no connection with the Thirty-Six Just, this an absolute coincidence, a sport of the Ineffable, and we would trail Rabbi Davidson home from Synagogue every Sabbath, as he shook hands vigorously with congregants, wishing them a Good Shabbos, expounded Talmudic passages, gave wise and compassionate counsel. Home, then, to his Rebbitzen, who dimpled and beamed shyly under her wig, the kugel sizzling and quivering on the stove, the babies washed 'til their faces shone like the candles on the table, like the newly blessed moon in the sky.

"Just wait," B.A. used to mutter after his forced "Amen," while we'd be flying back to headquarters to report in before dinner. "There's more to that Rebbitzen than meets the eye. Somewhere underneath that wig, under those 'thank Gods,' behind those eyes, lurks a monster just waiting to be awakened. And one day it will stretch, and reach out—to a job, maybe, to some other faith, to some new horizon. It will burst forth, shatter the shell in an explosion louder than any of the others. And then, I'll get my way."

"The Ineffable One forbid," I'd say, trembling all over.

"The Ineffable One? God, you mean?" And B.A. would laugh his bitter, mocking, sardonic ripple. "God forbids nothing, except everything. God will sit back and let it happen, and there won't be a thing you can do about it. Or He. And—" he'd throw at me, just to watch me squirm. "—and the Rabbi too, and don't you forget it. Your wise, compassionate, zealous, dedicated Rabbi. Just wait 'til you find out what percolates under that *yarmulke*. That vivacious Rebbitzen ministering to her children and the ideals of Torah, wait until you see what her truest destiny has become, what she thinks of her little flock and the binding strictures of the Law. Oh, the passions of the Rabbi, the dry and quivering heat of Rebbitzenly descent, you will see what becomes of your pathetic little dreams of sanctification and hope."

But by the time we got back to headquarters, then Assembly Hall, his pronouncements and predictions would be pushed away by my determination not to acknowledge them, not to give old Ashmodai the credence he so miserably sought. The others would stare at me, all the angels good and bad with their lustrous, luminescent, credulous features brilliant against the dull slack of their robes as I would tell them of the Davidsons' Sabbath songs and words of Torah. Of course, I'd get plenty of envious grumbles from other G.A.s. Such unhappiness:

"It's not fair, I mean, a Rabbi's home is bound to be more peaceful than everyone else's—"

"You know how the prestige of the Rabbi will become a firmament against which the B.A.s will be helpless."

But their complaints or rivalrousness were shattered constructions, meant only to hide their terror, their own guilt and shame, as one by one their families had succumbed to the smug, triumphant curses of the B.A.s. Now they were all compelled to identify with my own struggles, my campaign, the transcendent condition of the Davidsons and their obedient children, the last blessed family, my mission a set of gates before their upraised, trembling heads.

But—

But the Davidsons were sliding too, in bumpy and spiral descent to the same darkness as all the rest. This epiphany can no longer be shielded: The Rebbitzen has lost her religious faith. (Old Ashmodai was right, damn him; he saw her more clearly than I did.) It seems that under her wigged and long-skirted exterior, a volcano of seething and heretical lava lay waiting to erupt. Why are women treated like—?

Is there really a God—?

Why is there suffering and injustice of such dimension—?

Is the Torah really Divine if no proof other than the assurances of its inheritors can be offered—?

Why can't we touch each other when I have my period—?

Why do you make me unclean at this time of month, a detestable and loathsome object? What kind of God would—?

Oh this Rebbitzen, some Rebbitzen, a cornucopia of questions, doubts, firecrackers of rage and venom: The Rebbitzen wants out. No more songs and kugels, no more Sabbath and kosher. The Rebbitzen is a spirited lady, I'll say that for her. Under the lid of the pot, under the demure cheeks and dropped eyelids, a boiling stew bubbles and splatters in the passion of fires which brew the unlikely mixture of meat and dairy, of ancient traditions and ancient doubts, as the fire mounts, mounts, and the stew overflows.

And as the Rebbitzen simmers and surges, the Rabbi clutches and embraces his holy books, as if the waters of tears and Torah could dowse and drown the flames of apostasy. He cries, he pleads, his palms outstretched in prayer, in entreaty, his thumbs awhirl in Talmudic gesticulation. His music is a dirge, the Lamentations of Tisha B'Av, his discussions with the Rebbitzen (who of course shares everything: her lamentations, her doubt, her stumbling efforts to reconcile to the faith, her tormenting ambivalence which sinks and sinks within her soul like the leaden raisins of her increasingly inappropriate kugels) becoming ever more florid, a storm of rejection, the Rabbi enlarged in his fury, his damnation of the uncertain and inclement Rebbitzen, the force of his rage never stronger than when he confronts in the cracked glass of her condition the riotous and piecemeal nature of his own belief.

And the babies squabble and bicker, their glow now shattered into shards of name-calling, hair-pulling screamers, their beds or cradles now pots of tears so copious as to have been gathered from the waters of the Mikvah.

Oh, how Ashmodai has gloated. "I am sympathetic to your condition, Uriel," he points out. "After all, your condition is mine as well, so are we bound together but nonetheless this is a massive, a massive paradox into which you have, occasionally wingless, tumbled. It cannot work out well for the Davidsons as they continue upon this disastrous and paradoxical course—how can it?" He utters his grim taunts and predictions gravely but with some real joy, kvelling in fact, spreading his wings in malediction before we fly away, a trail of cloudy substance behind us—the dark gleam of his triumphant chuckles, the pale mist of my tears—and return to the raised eyebrows of all the other Friday Night Angels: the B.A.s who greet him with cries of praise and toast his success with celestial nectar, and the G.A.s who mutter their sympathy and invite me to join a minyan of mutual support and solace.

But I can't do it. Whatever my own history and preparation, Uriel is incapable of this; I can't sit in the minyan, and request that Psalms and prayers be recited for my family. I can't spill my blood on the heavenly carpet as I recount the gradual ebbing of life force from a couple, air seeping through a pinprick—then a hole—then a gash—in a balloon, until the balloon explodes and pieces of rubber float to the floor. The theft of a diamond from its case of velvet and gold, two pairs of eyes that mirror each other's torment, reflect darkness to darkness, while their hearts mock them with the ancient promise that they who dwelleth in darkness shall see a great light.

I have seen the Great Light, the Rebbitzen insists, and it's not here. (She gestures around the room, the candles, the wine, the holy books, a scornful sweep of dismissal, an arc of derision and shame.) The Great Light glares brashly, she says; it leads me away it tells me that all this is blackness, night, and dawn lies in freedom from Jewish shackles.

No rabbis can restore their love, no Kabbalists in earth or heaven can or would even attempt to restore that pristine joy and slaughterhouse wonder which these people once had, when their marriage was young, when the Rebbitzen still believed, when their eyes were synchronous, when—however occasionally—they could touch. Now their eyes face different directions and they stagger, stumble, turn in circles, raise their arms to the heavens, fall to the heavy and unyielding stones, shattering their souls against that stone of discontent.

No minyan, however well-intentioned and devout, can replace the irreplaceable.

I thought of appealing to the Ineffable, asking Him to intervene. The last family I wanted to save; surely you would save the last family. If not the Davidsons, then who? But no, this was a God who dispatched the supreme B.A. to murder six million of His children. No intervention can be expected for a matter so trivial.

So I thought I'd ask for a transfer to a different department. Let some other angel link with Ashmodai to suffer through the degeneration and dissolution of a marriage, the atomization of a family, the cries of children, the horrors of the *get*. I'll be glad to take something easy—thank you very much—perhaps be one of those appointed over a blade of grass or a tree, ordering it to grow. (Of course, with the carnage of the trees, lots of those innocents are out of a job, and there is a long waiting list for the Agricultural Department, Grass Commander Division.)

But even if I got the job—who would help the Davidsons? There would be no hope for them at all.

No, I decided. I am their hope and, despite the mandate, despite the laws and strictures and regulations, I knew I must step in. I must intervene. Not just bless, not just say "Amen" to the curse.

I must help them.

Of course, I couldn't do a great deal. People have all these misguided ideas about angelic powers—but we're not omnipotent, only God is. (Let me tell you, if we were, you can bet I wouldn't be roaming the Eastern District on a Friday night in the company of the unsociable and gloating Ashmodai to watch a marriage, once rich and full and creamy as a wedding cake, go stale, moldy, crumble, and decay.) We have a job, each of us, and that's all we're empowered to do. Gabriel's job was to destroy Sodom, Michael's job was to inform Matriarch Sarah that she'd have a baby, and so on. Mine is to bless—and answer "Amen."

However, I knew that there was one thing, just one thing I could do. Just one. Violation of violations, treading the grounds of ultimate *verboten*. The Prime and First Law they taught us in Friday Night Angel Class: *never be seen*. Some angels, of course, must be seen—that's part of their job. The guy who talked to Balaam and the donkey, now he had a tricky job. First he had to be invisible to both, then just visible to the donkey (one of God's wonderful ideas, a test for Balaam, you know; God's really into testing), then visible to both. He pulled it off well, I'll say that for him, and returned to bask for eternity in the glory and radiance of that accomplishment.

But we—the Friday Night crowd—we're supposed to be cloaked, hidden, like God who remains hidden at all those times when people would most like to see Him. (More about tests and faith, I'm given to understand.) I decided that the next Friday night, I would show myself to her. Not to the Rabbi—he's already a believer, whatever Ashmodai says. But to her. I said to myself, she'll see me and come to her senses. She'll realize that the traditions are true, the Laws are just, the Torah is real. She'll embrace her heritage, and in doing so, her marriage as well. All those arguments, that back and forth about Torah and Law and repression, will cease. Harmony restored, the little faces will twinkle again. And I will again bless them, while my familiar, the doomed Ashmodai, this demon closer than my own skin and just as dear, my B.A. mutters his grudging "Amen."

That was the plan, as it evolved. I knew of course that I could get into plenty of trouble for this—get demoted to some of the grungier jobs. Get myself stuck being the Angel of Death for some hapless infant someplace. Or shipped off to hell to stoke the ovens, and that's a full-time job, with only Sabbath off, unlike this one which is Sabbath only, with the rest of the week off. These people will never realize how I'm laying myself on the line for them. Ingratitude, of course, is part of the conditions under which we necessarily operate.

But no, it didn't work that way at all. It went in no way that I had hoped. Instead, there was just a pitiful beseeching, amid the terrible and rising laughter of B.A.—old Ashmodai to my left. He was perched on my shoulder, pecking away at my ear, telling me, "listen now, pal, you are in one catastrophic mess, and the Rebbitzen and her Rabbi are in more trouble than ever."

I did it when her husband was singing *Shalom Aleichem*—"Peace Be With You, O Angels of High." The baby was whimpering into his high chair, the older boy fidgeting with his cutlery, the Rebbitzen thinking, *how much longer? This ritual, these songs, fossils of extinct spiritual dinosaurs, relics of a past I reject*—when I alit. (Alighted?) Flapped my wings just to draw a little extra attention to myself—and executed a pretty and graceful little bow. "Hello, Rebbitzen!"

She clasped her hand to her mouth, her face white as the candle wax, eyes bulging like burned raisins atop her kugel; she gave a little shriek. "My thoughts have been heard! An angel has come, just as I was thinking—it's time to go. It's over, it's over."

Oh, the noise, the commotion, the crying children, the husband's solemn call to the doctor (Sabbath, when telephone calls are forbidden notwithstanding, this was clearly a life-and-death emergency), the cry for help—my wife's gone crazy! I've known it for some time, doctor, since she began spouting this nonsense, heresy, *apikorsus*. But now. she's gone over the edge, she's hallucinating, the children are in danger—

And they came with their straps and restraints and syringes and carted her off to some looney bin. Bubby Davidson (the good Rabbi's mother) has been installed, taking care of the kids, the Rabbi is bent and tearful over his Psalms, the Rebbitzen is behind bars. Harmony?

"If not harmony," I tell Ashmodai, "a divine equilibrium. All will be in order at last, the Rebbitzen isolated, the Rabbi saved from the imprecations of his wife, the children, their little hearts no longer threatened by the unclean thoughts which paraded through the household.

"Bubby Davidson agrees with me. She whispers to the Rabbi, 'that wife of yours was the ruination and destruction of your household; thank God you're rid of her, you can get on with your life, your children will grow motherless but untainted.'

"OK, Ashmodai," I say, "so it didn't work out exactly as I'd planned, not really, but there's tranquility just the same, peace at last, that peace which passeth all understanding. Tranquility below, tranquility above, in the higher and darker firmament, where not only the angels but the laws and *tzaddikim* and departed just surely dwell. Ah that concatenation and merging of light, arcing through, banishing the inconstant and blasphemous dark. Ah, Ashmodai, all of the curses are now blessings underneath that shroud of restoration."

But of course it did not work out that way either. Instead, this is what happened: deprived of the Rebbitzen, her sullenness and doubt cast from the household (she is not responding well to the immediate efforts of the staff, it is reported) the Rabbi was thrown upon his own device's; and just as Ashmodai had warned, just as he had implied through all of our arguments and his taunting, it seems that the good Rabbi has been in his pomegranate heart an apostate most of his own secret and unenamored life—a secret, slinking, submerged *apikores*, who has swum hip, then chest deep in the rivers of doubt, indecision, and retribution. With the Rebbitzen the balance was maintained ... he could reject her, her obvious apostasy, her evident inanition and failure to accept the True Word and in so rejecting her, in pushing her away, the Rabbi—troubled but with glinting eyes and a rakish yarmulke (in fact the best, the most plausible of all Rabbis—so say the younger females in the congregation)—the Rabbi was able to push himself away.

But this has clearly come to an end, the newly inflated and passionate Rabbi Davidson has instead had to confront the awful possibility of his own disbelief. It is this way in fact: the doubt which came from within, covered by the voice of the Rebbitzen and his own enraged responses now emerge from the Rabbi's own need and it speaks in its own rhetoric. This time it speaks not the imprecise Esperanto of the Rebbitzen's doubt but the perfectly formulated Hebrew and Aramaic of the Rabbi's own Torah.

Oh, Ashmodai, the voice without, that voice which came from kugels and screams the good Rabbi could cast apart; but this inner voice, this voice which in the purest of Aramaic says *Mene mene tekel uparshin*, along with other confidences from the Pentateuch and the Book of Daniel—this voice attacks the Rabbi from within, can only be met within, and the good man, whose eyes have beheld the wonders of tomes of Talmud and scrolls of parchmented Torah—finds that he is now quite undone, that he is crumbling from the center, that it is the breathing testament of his own soul—and not the kugels and festooning crepe of the household spirits which is crumbling.

So the Rabbi lies in his tormented bed at night, tossing and turning in anguish, solemn and shaken in his dilemma, arks and covenants bestirring themselves to flame in his damaged consciousness. He takes himself again and again to the Mikvah, casts himself into that womb and grave of water, pleading for the silencing of the voice, the banishing of the voice. But as he ducks and bobs and clings and scuttles in those waters, it is the voice which overtakes him; it is his inner voice, it is the voice of the Bad Angel confiding to me over and again (yes, Ashmodei and I accompany him to the Mikvah, the three of us go everywhere together now all of the time) saying, *Do you see? Do you see now? Do you see the obscure and fervid lightning of faith? Do you understand its truest source of life?*

I do. I think I have always known this. And so as the Rebbitzen weaves her baskets in Pilgrim State, as the Heavenly Host lifts chalices and laughs, as the Rabbi surfaces from the waters of the Mikvah still shouting, still doubting, swearing like Jonah at his gourd, the colors of the water, the prism of his apostasy ... the Bad Angel and I, Ashmodai and Uriel, prisoners and penitents to the end, collide in this fabric of final design: "Told you," Ashmodai says, "told you, told you." And the Rabbi's roar of denunciation enormous in the tiled and hollow spaces—as if for the first time—the Serpent of Heaven slithers slowly through the gates. Lift up your heads oh ye gates as we all come plodding home. Selah.

"It is done," the Rabbi says. "It is finished."

And I must—oh fathers and judges, hear my confession, hear from this mountain the words of Uriel—I must, against my will, utter "Amen."

THINGS PRIMORDIAL

by Batya Swift Yasgur and Barry N. Malzberg

So go find a hobby, I said, find something new to occupy your time. You were interested once in prehistoric monsters, those dinosaurs, right? So why don't you get a Hopper and bring one back to study? It will give you something to do. It's either that or the Old men's club at midday. Which can be a wonderful diversion except that you seem so sick of it.

So what does he do this Sam, I will tell you what he does. He not only brings back a dinosaur, he keeps it, makes a special place for it on the outside. This is insanity.

Not dinosaur, Bertha, he says to me, correcting me as he always has, revealing his lack of trust. Making me hear the tired sound of his voice as if I'm not the one who is really tired. Not dinosaur. A Nanosaurus.

Nanosaurus, Shmanosaurus. Why does he have these strong and peculiar passions? Not only to view but to adopt which is so much more expensive. It costs five times to import a dinosaur what it costs simply to look at them, as I have explained to Sam over and again. Why can't he be reasonable? I say it to him all the time, I say Sam, I say, I want you should be more reasonable. From reason will come kindness and from kindness will come some consideration for me. Don't go digging up the garden to make a place for a dinosaur cage, making a fool of yourself in your denim overalls like some youngster. If you need a hobby, go play bridge at the club. Or use the Hopper to look at showgirls in the Follies-Bérgère two centuries ago. What do I care? What could you do with any of them anyway?

Maybe if you used the Hopper to look at pleasant things, not the Follies- Bérgère or dinosaurs, I could join you in that, but I cannot be an animal keeper here. You know my arthritis. I can't come out into the garden with you, because the damp gets to me and you know how it hurts to bend over. But no, you don't care about me. All you care about is yourself. So I've got to sit home and watch TV while my friends have husbands who take them to the senior center for lunch or the club for bridge. Myron is the model husband; Sadie couldn't be happier. But what do I get stuck with? A man who won't take me anywhere, a man who spends his life on his knees talking to some kind of Nanosaurus in a garden when he could at least be inside with the Hopper looking at all kinds of creatures.

You don't understand, Bertha, he says. Looking at creatures is for an old person, turning yourself into a voyeur, looking through glass at what you can't touch. Real life is touching, is pawing even. It is communion of some kind. Moses took the tablets down from Sinai, remember. He didn't just settle for threats and commandments.

And what are you going to do with this strange, horrible little animal in a cage out in the garden? This is what I ask him. This thing, Sam, that you are keeping in a shed. It's slimy—dinosaurs are just big lizards after all, and they're as reptile as the snake in the Adam and Eve story, is what I always say—and it's ugly.

It's not slimy, Sam says. I have touched it; it is dry and scaly. Touch it, Bertha and you'll see.

I should die first, I said, before I touch that thing. What kind of family sharing is this, petting a dinosaur? Besides, this isn't even a real animal. I always thought dinosaurs were supposed to be big. That's what they taught the kids in my day, when my Milton and Jonah were going to school.

(Oh, they should only know what their father has been up to, shaming me like this with this animal he takes with him everywhere. But Milton got really religious of all things; he's learning Orthodox at a Yeshiva in Israel even after I begged him not to go there with those terrible and violent Arabs, may their names be erased, and Jonah is married—not such a nice girl, too much of a go-getter if you ask me, and I told him so too, but he said Mama, he said, I love her and I said love, what's love? A newfangled American word, loyalty is what it's all about. Love is getting up together, doing laundry and paying taxes and changing diapers. Don't talk to me about love. Thank God I outgrew your idea of love long before Sam got involved with his Hopper. Anyway, I haven't heard from Jonah very much since the wedding, just a card around the New Year, and I always say to Sam I say, that girl ruined him just like I said she would. But at least Jonah has not gotten crazy religious like Milton, going around talking about primordial things and the canons of justice—the sacred texts and the meaning of the laws.)

What was I talking? Does any of this have to do with the children or with Milton turning crazy religious or Jonah taking up with his go-getter? Why am I talking about children who are not such children—38 and 33 if you ask me and still trying to start their lives in such crazy ways. With them, with the younger people now it is always a starting: a starting this and a starting that, but in our time we knew that it was finishing which really counted. The dinosaur. Or in this case, Sam's nanosaur.

The books which came with the Jurassic Hopper mostly show these monstrous animals, but you look at this one that Sam brought back to place in the cage, and it's really small. Rabbit-size. Just the size of Milton the day in nursery school when he put down his prayer book and said, I don't believe in any of this. Four years old and he didn't believe in any of it! Well, times have changed in the Milton category, that's all I can tell you, now with the tsitsis and yarmulke and special prayers for occasions I can't even pronounce. This baby-Milton-size Nanosaurus stands on its back legs almost to reach the top of the cage Sam built for him.

Do you understand my life, then? There is this horrible animal Sam scooped up from the past with the optional equipment and caged up in the garden shed outside in the back. He feeds it leaves and things, but it really likes animals not plants and that's not the worst of it. The worst of it is that Sam goes—he just takes the car at the risk of life and health because for driving conditions I think he can barely see—and he goes into town to the pet store and gets mice. It makes me shudder just to think of it. He takes these disgusting little animals by the tail and he feeds them to the dinosaur. I think they are still alive when he does it. Sam says no, they are really dead, they are sold dead like most of life is sold to us dead, but I do not believe him. I think that he is lying to me, and I do not have the courage to go and take a look for myself. It makes me throw up just to think about it, and do you think he cares?

When he brought the Hopper home, all that he cared about was staring into it and looking at all the animals in prehistoric times, and then when he found the Nanosaurus—look at this, he says, it's tiny, cute, it's like a Reform Rabbi, Bertha. It has all of the parts but none of the menace or conviction. All that he cared about was that animal itself. How it runs on its back legs—look, Bertha, he says rubbing his hands together in a self-satisfied-like way, like he had discovered the cure for cancer or something like that—look, Bertha, how short its front legs are and how long its tail is. It's shaped like a kangaroo, and the way it scampers it could be a Reform Rabbi running from the congregation on the day before Yom Kippur when he insisted that the place be open for the High Holy Days.

This is his sense of humor. This is the kind of thing which he finds amusing in his old age: bringing back dinosaurs and mocking what he does not understand. Not that I want to defend Reform Rabbis or any of that other part which has eaten Milton up in the land of Israel. Look here, I say, why don't you just give your Nanosaurus back to the Hopper, send it back to the past where it belongs. Or if you can't bear to let it go back to the past, then give it to a science center or a museum or a zoo or something and let us get back to a normal life. Come out of the garden and pay some attention to your wife. Spend your golden years with a person, not with a machine or some kind of crazed animal.

Be quiet, he says, and I know that he has eyes only for that Nanosaurus because we are conducting this very conversation out in the garden and he is leaning over the cage, staring and staring. You don't understand, you never understood me. This is the most terrifying manifestation, the most real evidence you could possibly imagine. It proves the reality of the ooze from which we all came. You too, Bertha. You are no less things primordial than any of the rest of us and Milton in Israel, too—if he would take the time to think about it.

I understood only too well, I say. I have spent my lifetime understanding and we have come to the point where that creature of yours has got to go.

But how? That's the question. I mean, if I was dealing with a normal man, I could expect him to ship the animal away, right? Or at least make an effort in between all the times that he is out there talking to it to pay some attention to a wife who has spent all of her years doing nothing but being devoted to him and the children she gave him. He expresses his preferences very clearly.

There was a laziness in this man—what my mother warned me at the very start when she met him the first time—a certain disinclination. This was a man who would rather sit in one place and let things happen than take any real responsibility for his life. And she was right. One job in insurance, one company, practically one boss and one pension: that was Sam's life. In the evenings and on weekends maybe a little reading and two weeks in the mountains once a year. That was it and he had to be forced to do even that much.

But he isn't lazy with his nanosaur. He brought the animal from the past, selected that exclusive option, he says, and that means that he is responsible for the nanosaur in ways that he was never responsible for anything else. The nanosaur's presence is his sole creation. Cleaning out the cage, tying this leash around its neck. Soon I am afraid that he will be taking it out for walks around the neighborhood, and I do not know how I will be able to put up with that kind of mortification. The Nanosaurus can run really quickly in that cage, and sometimes Sam lets it run through the house really fast which it does just like a dog.

This behavior is getting tongues moving, believe me. Sadie who is not only a neighbor but a true, if nosy, friend called me up just yesterday and wanted to know where my husband got that toy animal. Did it come back from the past with the Hopper? She had heard about people doing things like this. More and more in development, Hoppers are getting rented to give people like Sam views of one part of history or the other, and sometimes animals are even being brought back. There are even rumors that people are being brought here, although that of course is completely illegal and a terrible crime, risking paradox which is something I do not pretend to understand.

Never mind, Sadie, I say. There is nothing to discuss. Sam has found a new hobby, that's all. Soon he will outgrow it the way he has outgrown so many other hobbies and go on to something else, maybe the clarinet or the older man's badminton group. I mean, what's the difference anyway what they do at this age? It's going to end up the same way pretty soon no matter what. Sadie agrees with this, of course. How can she disagree? It is a kind of simple wisdom and also has to do with accepting the truth.

But part of the Nanosaurus for Sam, I think, is not accepting the truth. It has to do with being involved outside himself and with a creature which he calls representative of the larger picture. It is only a matter of time until people begin to talk, until the Nanosaurus from the Hopper becomes a discussion topic at the Golden Age Arms, but long before that I will have to put my foot down.

Bad enough he has the thing, but to make a public spectacle of himself, I say no.

But and wouldn't you know, couldn't you have seen this coming from the start, Sam has to make a general statement about this. Had an interview with this reporter from the development newspaper about the Nanosaurus which got printed, and then the television station reporter came down and, against my advice, Sam spoke to him for a long time. Then, that not being enough, Sam got on the air in the garden with one of their remote broadcasts and had a little appearance on the evening news.

Sam on television, talking about this dinosaur and how it's not your typical predator but a special, little-known, small kind of dinosaur. One who sneaked through all of the narrow spaces in the golden time of dinosaurs and survived by making no trouble, just as the Jews, for a while anyway, had been able to survive in this place or another place by making no trouble. Sam saying how this was a different kind of dinosaur and how he had read up on it after seeing it in the Hopper, and then, after the television, all of the calls coming into the apartment—we have a listed number. In fact, soon enough there were all these old foolish ladies around him ooh-ing and ah-ing—disgusting, to try to get involved with a happily married man by acting like that. And their tongues hanging out around that animal like it was some kind of sacred Indian cow or sacrifice from God for Abraham, when the truth is that it is just a big, stupid, fast-moving rabbit from a long time ago.

So the decision has to be made; that animal is ruining our lives, our golden years. It's turning what used to be a perfectly good, if somewhat lazy and dull, old man into an idiot, and a perfectly good marriage into something so sad and lonely that I cry. Every single night in my room my pillow is soaking wet. I lie there thinking of Sam, not in his own bedroom but out there somewhere in the night, holding the paw of his Nanosaurus, and stroking its head, and I cry some more.

He should stop, knowing as he does how much pain it brings me. Things primordial! The only thing primordial around here is me and that man is putting me into a grave. For the first time in his life, the man shows passion and look what he shows it for.

This Nanosaurus, this thing: It has got to go. From where it came is not so important any more. The Hopper may indeed be part of the wonders of modern technology as Sam says, but I am not interested and I am not interested either in repossession or the heart of recovered darkness, as he also says. Sam has never been clear as to why he had to bring this thing into our lives, or what the expense of this optional treatment might be. All that he is clear about is that he has brought it into the garden.

Evolutionary intervention, he says, the true conviction of our history. Here is something palpable, something that moves convincingly beyond all of those mild devices with which you would shroud passion. Now just don't push me any further, Bertha, don't ask for any more explanation. Just know that this is for the best, all of it. Just let it alone. For once in your life, accept something and understand that it is larger and more important than you. I found the Nanosaurus in the garden, and I will tend to it and you will do your part by letting me do the same. You can find your entertainment and outlets otherwise, you always did anyway.

So let him say this: What else is there for me to do? There never was anything I could have done for this man. He is stubborn, he will not be pushed, he must have things his own way or not at all.

All on my own, thus, I evolve a plan. It is a plan which comes from my own heart and is the only possible way under the circumstances. What I do is wait patiently inside the apartment watching television (no news programs though, no national news, no local news) until at last Sam has finished his puttering around and his patting around, and the Nanosaurus has stopped with its running and its scamper, until there are at last no more murmurs, no conversations with his creature. I wait until I have heard Sam limp off to his bedroom where he will snore and kick the sheets (we have had separate bedrooms—both up North at the old place and in our Golden Arms apartment—since the kids left a good ten years ago. Milton was last of course, meaning that, praise God, we did not have to answer their questions or account for their looks or imagine any conversations we might have had.)

And so having done this, having waited out all of his noises and craziness patiently, I go to the garden, that green and oily peculiar place adjacent to our condo, and there is the Nanosaurus in its cage, looking at me with great intensity.

We stare at one another, the Nanosaurus and I—the animal in its cage which was Sam's necessary idea because I would not, I would *not* have that thing running around the apartment, as right as it might have been for him. Get a cage, I insisted, and that must have been his own plan from the start because having it in a cage would mean that I had somehow consented to keeping it altogether. There was cunning to his plan, then, to go to the pet store and get a cage which otherwise and better could have fit a good-sized rabbit.

And there is the Nanosaur in that cage looking stupid as it always has, a single portable lamp, another of Sam's ideas, shining upon it. In the light now, it looks like a rat which Sam has said is not the case. He has made himself quite clear on this point. It is history, Sam has said. It cannot be compared with the present; we should not reduce history by making it a cartoon or cute version of where we are now. This nanosaur, it is primeval history, the primordial thing itself standing before us.

Which is one way of describing a large, scrambling, insulting, rabbitlike animal. When this creature sees me it makes a scuttling gesture, the sound of its little legs hitting the paper which Sam has used to line the bottom of the cage. It is as if it has always been waiting for me; it seems alert.

Dinosaur? I think. Nanosaurus? What is all of this business with prehistory? It is another means of escape, just like Milton and the stones in the great wall in Israel to which he has run away. No, it is not a prehistoric creature Sam has been sheltering there, it might be prehistoric to him, but the truth is that it is a clumsy, overgrown, oily rabbit. In fact, I decide, in the glaring, humming light, It is a rabbit. In the spokes of the casting light as I step before that bulb, the nanosaur could be anything at all but this is what I have named it.

And to name, as Milton once said, is to kill. I reach the knife inside the cage, holding the long, blunt handle carefully, admiring the reach of the knife. Not with Sam, perhaps, but in this instance, I have chosen well. One cut, one neat slice like working with a roast and the Nanosaurus will be a lump on the bottom of the cage. In the morning I can tell Sam that there has obviously been a Nanosaurus stalker lurking outside, and at last inside, the gates of the delightful Golden Arms. There will come an end to this and Sam will become again, for worse or worst, the man with whom I have lived all these years, but at least I will be able to understand him once more. That solution lies clearly before me.

But as I balance the knife to puncture the Nanosaurus to its deserved death, I hear a different scuttling, a whisk of movement within the cage and suddenly this lump of a creature which has turned, which has been staring at me, opens its eyes to a terrible luminosity—the luminosity of the prophets, of the light cast from stars—and it is staring at me now as if it were a shtetl Rabbi who had caught me fingering a rosary, caught me murmuring of the True Cross. Oh yes, I feel in the sudden and dark extension of its glance such a tremor as I have not known in thirty years; it passes through me as if another, a larger knife had been taken.

Then there is an enormous hand on my shoulders squeezing, another hand seizing my wrist and that wrist is clamped so hard that the knife falls, falls inside the cage where the nanosaur trembles in its sudden inflaming.

Bertha, says Sam behind me, of course it is Sam. I have always been waiting for this and now it is here; Bertha you should not have done this. You should not be doing this. This is a terrible mistake and it is one against which I warned you.

I try to turn. Let me go, Sam, I say. This has nothing to do with you. It is for me. You are hurting me. Sam, you must let me go now.

I did let you go, Sam says, I let you go a long time in the past. But I cannot do it this way. You are involving yourself with the prehistoric, he says. You are trying to control something you cannot understand. This Nanosaurus was not placed here to be my pet anymore than it was to simply inconvenience you, Bertha. This nanosaur has larger purposes, purposes which you cannot grasp at all, purposes which I can barely apprehend.

Larger purposes, I say, what are you talking about?

I am talking about things primordial, I am talking of the darkness of habit, the overwhelming scope of history, Sam says. And it is as if he were in Temple reading from the scrolls which he has not done since Jonah was Bar Mitzvahed twenty years ago. I am talking of the incomprehensible. We must let the incomprehensible into our lives.

But it is, I say, Sam, it already is.

No, I mean other than that, Sam says. I have never seen him in such a condition; it is as if he himself were in the Hopper, as if I were looking at him in some distant, time-driven, time-extinguished jungle, Sam moving around slowly, burrowing through the vegetation of impossible soul. Bertha, we must admit the incomprehensible and only in that way will our lives themselves become understood.

Here, he says. Here, now. My Sam, my crazy lost Sam, insistent in the movement of his hand and in the light glinting from the fallen knife.

He pulls open the cage door.

The Nanosaurus pokes out its snout, then a further limb, then yet another limb, then inch by inch to emergence and then this thing, this strange and remarkable creature is upon me, inch by inch squirming through the garden and reaching toward my face. This is not tradition, this is the heavy, dark clamp of all circumstance descending upon us, Sam says. Think of Jonah's gallivanting, of Milton's strange hereticism.

And then something else which I do not understand either. In fact, Sam says many things but they are no longer words, they are sound, they are a stolen and discordant noise in a hundred languages which I cannot possibly understand. Oh, the Nanosaurus jumping like a dog, like a dinosaur, like an angry angel. Jumping as my riotous and damaged father under the ark, holding the shofar as if his were the hands of God. Raising the shofar toward himself; tekee-yah. Shouting and great darkness approach to overtake.

Get a hobby, I had said. Find something to do with yourself, maybe a Hopper if you don't want to leave the apartment, but it was nothing like this I had in mind. Take her over, take her alive, this time history wins and you roam the Earth, Sam says and my father the Rabbi drapes his cloak over me as the exploding sun must have draped the Jurassic. I sink, I rise. Sam has a lot more to add, no doubt, but I do not hear most of it. Custom has given way to the impossible, descending light.

JOB'S PARTNER

by Batya S. Yasgur & Barry N. Malzberg

There were three of them—a tall one, and two shorter ones—and they appeared to Judith in the Day Room, where she was gazing through the barred windows, trying to figure out how to cajole Diana, the 8-4 nurse, into returning her knitting needles so she could finish the sweater for Baby.

When she saw them, her veins ran ice and her bile bubbled up, burning her throat, like those early days of empty-bellied morning sickness.

"Go away," she hissed. "You've gotten me into enough trouble already."

"Not until you say yes," the Tall One said—or radiated. Mouthless, faceless, he couldn't speak, perhaps, but his words entered her consciousness effortlessly, automatically. She, on the other hand, had to speak aloud, as if talking to ordinary human beings.

"I'll never do it." Her skin was goosebumpy, and she clutched the window bars.

"Let's discuss it reasonably." One of the Short Ones glided forward until it was almost touching her knee.

She flinched and jumped back, glancing around nervously. Joan and Nicole were squabbling over the television as usual, Francis holding court with Queen Elizabeth and Samantha dancing for an imaginary audience.

"Not here." She motioned to them. "Let's go into the Quiet Room."

The Quiet Room was where you could go to be alone—voluntarily, not like Seclusion. It was carpeted, padded, soundproof. She lumbered down the hall, the Beings gliding noiselessly behind her.

"Okay." She lowered herself to the floor gracelessly, easing her swollen belly along. "Why can't you leave me alone?"

"We want the baby." The vibrations were stronger and she was shaking from them, the infant within tossed in the whirlwind of amniotic fluid.

"No!" she shouted, backing into a corner, huddling into it, as in a womb.

"What's going on in here?" It was blonde Diana, passing in the hall, crisp and starched in her white uniform.

"N-nothing," she called back, her voice an assemblage of artificial breeze and cheer.

She turned back to them. "What are you trying to do? Get me sent to seclusion?"

"We're not trying to do anything to you." The Tall One spoke with assurance and authority, the calm of one clearly used to being in charge. "Except we want you to agree to give us the baby after he's born."

"He? How do you know?" She gazed at her belly, moving with the movements of the baby.

"We see through solidity, unlike you humans. We pass through solidity—that's how we got in here. We aren't limited by your physical laws."

"Or our emotional ones."

The Tall One's movements resembled a shrug. "True. But we are not devoid of compassion either."

"Compassion?" She laughed bitterly. "And you persecute me like this? Get me sent to a nuthouse because no one will believe me about you?"

"We'll leave you alone when you promise us the baby."

Baby. Crowing and capering and bouncing around her belly, regaling her with little internal kicks. Baby—soon to appear (next month), its pudgy fists dimpling as they closed over her finger, tiny lips pulling eagerly on her breast, amid tiny contentment noises. She cradled her belly.

"What do you need a baby for?"

A trio of sighs. Why, she wondered, did all visitations come in threes? Angels to Abraham, shepherds to Mary, Trinity to Paul? Three wishes. Three Wise Men.

"We've been through all this already," the Tall One said, ripples of trembling light cascading toward her.

"No we haven't."

"All right." Another sigh as the Tall One seemed to settle back on formless haunches. "Your people are destroying the Earth. Holes in ozone, poisons on plants, smog hugging your cities. Your race will not survive. Your planet will be annihilated. So—the baby. We will raise Baby. Teach him all we know. Return him to Earth when he's grown. As long as there is one among you who possesses our secrets, your planet will survive."

"I don't get it." She hid her face in her hands, tears scalding her fingers.

"It's no reflection on you," said one of the Short Ones kindly. "Your race is significantly lower in intelligence than most of the others in the galaxy."

She glanced up quickly. "How do you know?"

The Tall One laughed—droplets of mirthful light bouncing off walls and floor. "We are the Doers of Giving on our Planet. It is our sacred task to travel to distant galaxies, rescuing inhabitants from their own follies."

"Sort of like interstellar Boy Scouts? Or Social Workers?"

"Something like that."

The tears winked in the light, casting little splotches of rainbow across the diabolically green floor. "But why my baby? There's a nursery in Building B—across the hall, down the elevator, through the courtyard, up to second floor, I had my other kids there—and you'll see lots of babies. Rows and rows of babies, all snug and neat in their little plastic cribs. Just help yourselves and leave me alone."

"And leave some bereaved mother to go to pieces when she finds out her child has been abducted?"

"What about *me?*" The cry burst forth, as the waters would burst forth from her womb next month—but foul, stinking waters, prelude to stillbirth and death.

"You'll never worry, where is my child? You'll know."

"No!" She rocked back and forth, balancing her belly awkwardly between her legs. "Why? Why choose me? There are millions of other women in the world who are pregnant!"

The Tall One cocked his head (or the top of him anyway, that kind of resembled a head). "Oh come, now, you mean you don't know?" She shook her head violently.

"Your openness," said one of the Short Ones. "To ideas, possibilities, flights of heart and spirit."

"Your vision," said the other Short One. "For a world where humanity shall dwell in peace and none shall make him afraid."

"Your dreams," said the Tall One. "To be the mother of the Messiah."

She closed her eyes. Old Mrs. Martex loomed before her—sixth grade. Iron hair, steel eyes, red X's dripping as blood from her pen. "Judith, daydreaming again, eh? Always off on some other planet, aren't you." A sharp jab with the pointer, still chalky from the geography assignment on the blackboard. "Wouldn't you like to share your dream with the rest of us?" Hot cheeks, wet eyes, stammers, amid the giggles and titters of the others. "I was thinking about—I mean wishing for—" How to open the golden chest, locked in her heart, lined with velvet, limned with light, refuge and vision? To spill its secrets before the icy words and dark laughter of Mrs. Martex and the others? The golden fields through which her winged feet carried her to the glowing Baby, surrounded by angels and shepherds and Beings of Light, proclaiming, "behold our Lord," and whispering, pointing, "behold His mother."

"I saw—saw—"

No! Never to tell! She tore herself from the room. Down, down the hall, to the bathroom, the buzzing laughter pursuing her like an army of wasps. Flushing, flushing, till Janie Edwards—Teacher's Pet and Goody Two Shoes of the First Order—came to fetch her with her smirk and her swishing skirts.

"This is what you always wanted, isn't it?" the Tall One was saying.

She closed her eyes again.

Grandmother on the couch, the giant photo album spread across her lap like an ancient shawl, the numbers glowing darkly on her wrinkled white arm. "See? That young girl?" A smiling face, little crinkles of merriment around the eyes, arm lifted in greeting to a joyous future. "That was me, *before*." And the tears, watering the picture, blurring and obliterating the face of hope and promise that was soon to be scarred by coals and ashes, the arm uplifted, soon to be stamped, branded with the eternal pain. "I held on because someday, there would be you—Judith. The Future."

And what was the Future? If the past ended in the charring heat of the oven, the future must begin in the warmth of the womb. Her womb.

And so the dream. Of conception, birth, growth—a passage of everlasting safety: Redemption.

A vision locked away, still. Locked through girlhood, through the little games and prattles of the others in the playground; through budding womanhood, the mysterious and wondrous preparations her body was making for inviting and welcoming that Ultimate Child into the world; through courtship with Al. Dear Al. Nice enough, to be sure. He stopped the car to take a hurt puppy to the animal hospital; he diligently wrote checks to the American Cancer Society and to the U.J.A. He climbed on top of her twice a week, whispering kind words in her ear. But once—only once—did she dare, timidly, with trepidation and prayer, to ask—Is this enough? Isn't there more, a Final and Ultimate purpose? And Al's blankness. "We're here. Isn't that enough?"

Only once, that is, until the arrival of the Beings. "Don't you see them, Al?" she pleaded. "Three. There. Over there. The Tall One's in the middle, he's sort of flanked by two shorter ones." First blank-faced stares, a mild suggestion to get more sleep, maybe the pregnancy?—Then That Look. Gazing at the floor, shifting of feet, twitching of lips, eyes half-mast. Then recoil, horror. Then the trek, the endless trek to doctors, the mutterings and deliberations about medications and dosages, the inane questions ("When were you toilet trained?" "How did you relate to your peer group?") The talk of shock treatment, how it would affect a growing fetus. The decision, finally, as she held firm to her Vision: maybe a few days here, safely locked away, would be enough to bring her to her senses.

If not—then afterwards—well, the medicines, the shock, think of all the avenues available.

And now Al, walled behind breeziness and false cheer, stopping on his way from work, bringing her tidbits of office gossip and asking where he could find a pot to steam beans, and whether to wash underwear on hot or cold. Al, inhabiting another world, a world of ads and ad blanks, synagogue once a year and whisperings in the night twice a week.

A vision of Purpose—hers—which transcended anyone else's. To bring Him into the World. To be the Mother of the Messiah.

And now, here were these Beings—Angels? Aliens?—to bring it all to fruition. And she was thrashing about in her mind, resisting. Why?

"I—I don't want to lose my baby." Her voice was tiny, wavering. "Maybe, maybe just let the Earth go its own way. Die. Whatever. But don't take my child away from me."

A tsk-tsk from the trio. "Sacrifice all to save one?" A shake of the headlike parts. "Is this the Judith whose life dreams have been devoted to saving the world?"

She sighed and sank back, her face seeking refuge in her cupped hands. Then a thought, a tiny splash of harmony amid the dissonance. "Why can't I come too?"

"We don't have accommodations for two. Just one."

"So build more!"

The three surrounded her, engulfing in their dripping kindness. "We have so many planets—so many universes—so many galaxies. All in serious trouble. We can only save one from each, or we'd be overrun, you see, and then we couldn't help anyone. Could we?"

A prison. A prison of words, arguments, logic. A prison of her own dreams, the milk of childhood fantasies soured by this trio of warmth which was to bring it to fruition. To voluntarily turn the tiny particle of her which was growing and kicking inside her over to Others to raise—

Then her eyes widened, her heartbeat quickened, hands, icily moist, clutched her belly. The baby would be taken from her anyway. These people—Al, the doctors—who wouldn't believe her, who thought the Beings were simply shadowy actors on some demented mental stage—they would start pouring their poisons into her body as soon as Baby would be born, would deem her an unfit mother and wrench Baby from her anyway.

She looked up. The Tall One was looming over her.

"Yes!" It came out in a rush, a burst of sorrow, joy and relief. "Yes. Yes. You'll take the Baby when it's born."

She was suffused by Light as the Trio surrounded and submerged her, transmutative, embracing, complete. "We will come back then," the Tall One proclaimed. They filed out in a solemn procession of dwindling light trickling behind them as tears.

Beings gone.

Home again. Al rushing about. "Can I get you some water? A sweater? Would you like to go out to dinner?" Al, brimful of flowers and solicitude.

"Are you sure you should go out? I can also do the shopping, you know."

Al, like a puppy sniffing a forbidden room. "Do you still—you know—are those Things still—do you still think those Things you saw are real?"

"They've gone now," she said flatly. And hid her face from Al's capers of delight.

Labor.

A midnight ride through star-studded silence, ripped openly by the jagged shards of pain-streaked screams.

Heaving, contracting, hurting, heaving, pushing—Al's voice reaching across the red chasm. "A boy!"

A boy. "For I know that my Redeemer liveth, and in my flesh shall I see God."

She clutched the baby to her chest, its matted wisps of hair washed by her tears.

"You want to name him *what?*"

Weak, willow-kneed, she struggled to sit.

"That's not a Jewish name. You can't get more Christian than that!"

"Okay." Weakly she turned to face the wall. "Okay, then. Samuel."

"At least that's Jewish." A pause, then Al timidly touched her arm. "Why Samuel?"

"Read the Bible," she said and she slept.

Home again.

They would come to claim him soon, she knew. Reverently she bathed his soft little body, reveling in its magic pudginess. Greedily she nibbled his padded toes. She closed her eyes as he suckled, immersing herself in the ocean of his gurgles.

They came when he was eight days old. She was changing his diaper, the cloth traveling expertly through the hills and valleys of infant terrain. "No!" She clutched him and started to cry.

"You promised." The Tall One stepped forward.

"And isn't this what you've always wanted? Dreamed about?" one of the others put in.

"Yes, but—"

But—but to sacrifice her son to save humanity? To forestall and prevent a repetition of lines of other children, skeletal children, hollow-eyed and bloat-bellied, marching to a gas chamber? To wrench the Baby Messiah from his mother to prevent other children from being wrenched away from theirs?

"What about his circumcision?" she asked suddenly. "It's scheduled for today, and the whole family is supposed to come."

"He is circumcised of heart," the Tall One said, "And needs no ritual to prove it."

"Can't I have some more time with him?" she pleaded. "Please?"

The three huddled, a massive conclave of moving light. "Three days," the Tall One said finally. "At midnight of the third night, we will meet you in the garden, and you will give him to us."

Three days. Seventy-two hours. Four thousand, three hundred and twenty-two minutes. Two hundred fifty-nine thousand, two hundred seconds. To savor the baby skin and baby sounds, to love and laugh and pray and cry. To greet family (all carefully polite, studiedly casual, prepped to show that Judith was As Normal As Anyone Else although she'd done time in—oh God—a mental institution) with plastic smiles and rote inquiries concerning health, job, children, new homes; to graciously accept baby gifts, generating artificial excitement over stretch suits and teddy bears. To watch her son's grimace, hear his shriek as the knife deftly did its work, and know it wasn't necessary to pain him, but that she was helpless to prevent it, and to hear the lusty shouts of joy as the blood was drawn, the ritual complete. To hold him and hold him and hold him, and not let go. To tuck him next to her in bed, rest his downy head on her chest, as the minutes and seconds ticked by.

Midnight of the third day.

Al, snoring beside her in blissful ignorance, the oblivion of sleep blanketing his soul. Al, muttering and grumbling, opening his eyes as he heard the bedroom door open, with Judith's murmured soothings, reassuring him back to sleep.

Nighttime silence punctured by the occasional chir of a cricket, or hoot of an owl on a lonely forage for tiny, furred sustenance.

Judith crept down, Baby Samuel swaddled in her arms, a bag slung across her shoulder, filled with bottles, formula, diapers, stretch suits.

The scraping of a key in the door. Tiptoeing across the garden, the light lush, then fading, little strobes of light wickering as she carried Samuel through the tangles of foliage, that small and improvident desert in the back and toward that place of sudden and cascading light where they were to stand and coming upon that place then, the riotous little cartoon ship lurking in the background and not the three but just the Tall One this time, the Tall One alone looking at her with considered gaze as she came toward him. Not so much judgmental this time she thought as inquiring, the gaze of the rabbis looking down upon the crowds in the cloister. The Tall One reached for Samuel. "You have come," he said, "and now the baby."

Samuel writhed against her, one small peep, then subsided in her grasp. "Wait," she said, "one moment—"

"We are on time control," the Tall One said. "It is impossible to wait. All is arranged. Please pass the baby."

"You are alone," Judith said, "Where are the others?"

"They are not with me. They are waiting in orbit beyond. I have come alone." The Tall One leaned toward her, extended his arms. "I cannot wait any longer," he said, "We have arranged this within a very fragile loop, if we lose this—"

"I don't know," she said, "Something is wrong. Where are the others? This doesn't feel right? Perhaps I should—"

"No time," the Tall One said, "there is no time for this," and reached for Samuel, his grasp suddenly urgent and demanding, tremendous in the clenching light and Judith felt the shuddering from deep within her, the stabs of revulsion which she had felt so long ago whenever she had thought of it. Oh, that act of actually yielding, the shocking, gratuitous encounter with the Messiah which somehow she had never been able to properly frame.

And oh, oh Lord: it was not so much a shuddering but a kind of denial so deep within that she reeled in its grasp, hurtled back a step, then another step, Samuel convulsing in her arms and then crying. A priestly bellow here and the Tall One muttered something which she could not hear, could not quite assess and came toward her in a pose of perfect urgency, absolute necessity and laid a hand—a talon—upon the baby and "No!" Judith said, and "No!" again more loudly, urgently, the tug of the Tall One at the infant enormous, her own desperate squeal and trying to hold onto the infant and behind her, somewhere within the house Al's voice: "Judith? Where are you? What is going on? Where have you gone, Judith?" and the sound of windows smashing, doors abutting, deep and terrible struggle in the carved silence in the garden and it was at that moment, not one moment sooner, perhaps in fact a little later than that, that Judith grasped the nature of visitation early and late, judgment masked and unmasked. The enormity of that judgment. The bellowing and stampeding of the cattle in Job's enclosure as burning and burning His fire came to take them all.

New York Erev Yom Kippur 5756

BEYOND MAO

by Paul Di Filippo and Barry N. Malzberg

Halfway to Mars, Wu Yuèhai calls out to He Keung.

He Keung is startled. More than startled, alarmed and shaken. Even terrified.

In the close quarters of the *Radiant Crane*, a Shenzhou-11 module only three times the size of the compact Shenzhou-5 that lofted Yang Liwei into his historic orbit twenty years ago, there is no room for stowaways. He Keung and his two fellow taikonauts are jammed into quarters which even Mao on his fabled Long March would have found primitive and uncomfortable. The cockpit of the *Radiant Crane* is studded with instrumentation and storage lockers holding the ample supplies of freeze-dried shredded pork with garlic sauce on which the taikonauts mainly subsist. The three form-fitting chairs which double as bunks are separated only by centimeters.

He Keung, occupying the middle of the couches, turns first to his left, to confront Huang Shen. A thin ascetic figure, Huang Shen reminds He Keung of old digitized newsreels of the Cultural Revolution, one of those dedicated cadre members who would turn in his own parents for ideological trespasses. How such an archaic man—notable prior to this expedition mainly as the chief tax enforcer for Shanghai—came to arise in the twenty-first-century market-socialist China which has been in existence since before any of the taikonauts were born is a puzzle to He Keung. Perhaps such creatures are eternal, springing up despite external circumstances.

Whatever the mystical explanation for Huang Shen's origins, it is plain that the sober-sided, calculating man would not be the one to play a cruel practical joke involving the taping and disseminating through the ship's cabin speakers of Wu Yuèhai's voice.

That leaves Wang Yu, on He Keung's right. Now, Wang Yu is a likely suspect. Burly and over-full of energy, the piggy-faced taikonaut has been renowned for his jests and japes since the days when he was a famous fighter pilot in the short war with Taiwan. Wang Yu has chafed on this long mission, finding little to occupy his enormous energies as the *Radiant Crane* hurtles under precise cybernetic control toward Mars. Yes, Wang Yu possesses the kind of coarse nature that would conceive of such a mean-spirited burlesque.

Yet, He Keung recalls, Wang Yu was once romantically linked with Wu

Yuèhai. He Keung himself saw the authentic flow of his comrade's tears when Wu Yuèhai broke up with Wang Yu. There was no bitterness or desire for revenge then on Wang Yu's part, only black despair. Surely he would not disgrace her memory in such a manner.

The ventilation unit blows clammy air redolent of that uncontrollable HVAC mold-spore infestation over He Keung's face, adding to his unease. Odd pinging noises from the skin of the *Radiant Crane,* evoked under the almost unimaginable stresses of interplanetary space, sound like the temple bells of some unearthly monastery.

Discarding his only two suspects as agents of the jest, He Keung is left with a pair of equally repellent alternatives.

Either He Keung is going insane.

Or Wu Yuèhai is truly addressing him.

From beyond the grave.

For Wu Yuèhai is dead.

The first female taikonaut perished in orbit during an unpredicted solar storm seven years ago. Her body riddled with radiation, her craft disabled by electromagnetic surges along its circuitry, Wu Yuèhai lasted for a week after the storm hit, broadcasting her final experiences to a world that had hung on her every steadily weakening word. She became the very emblem of Chinese strength and courage, the shining symbol of both the triumphs and the necessarily harsh costs of the Chinese conquest of space.

Like everyone in his generation of the taikonaut corps, He Keung idolizes Wu Yuèhai. He has had frequent dreams in which she figures, both erotically and heroically. True, she surfaces randomly in his thoughts every day, a beacon inspiring him onward toward Mars when his spirit flags.

But this instance is different. He Keung can swear he actually heard her voice.

And then, even as he seeks to replay the incident in his mind, Wu Yuèhai appears in the cabin of the *Radiant Crane*.

The female taikonaut's form is translucent, shimmering like a bad holo. Yet there is some indisputable element of vitality about the apparition, a sense of living interactivity and presence that would belie any mere recording.

"I am come for you," Wu Yuèhai says. She seems to be addressing He Keung directly. At least the others, drowsing almost narcoleptically, as they all three often do to pass the interminable hours, pay this apparition no regard. "You have been waiting for me, yes? All of your life?"

Her face is radiant; her features now fully formed, well-defined in the haze of the enclosure; if he did not know that she was dead, not listened to her death agonies transmitted by private circuit long after the inspirational sections of her address had run out, he would have thought that she was alive. She beckons toward him. "Come with me," she says.

The situation is absurd. On his left in the module Huang Shen, dreaming of double-entry bookkeeping, arms folded across his chest, the little drafts of his breath stirring embers in the space surrounding; on his right in the *Radiant Crane* the formerly merry Wang Yu similarly gripped in slumber. The woman with whom he was rumored to have had liaisons—all in the name of China's greater glory in space—drifts within two feet of him but he pays her no heed, no mind. Only He Keung seems to be alert to her presence and yet her imminence, rather than stirring him as it had through all of the years he idolized her, seems rather to stun; he finds himself shifting toward lower levels of inhabitance.

"I have long been dreaming of you," Wu Yuèhai says. "In all the stuffy and infinite volume of space, an empire vaster than any ruled by the Yellow Emperor. But only of you. You and you alone."

Her tone startles; it is the same lustrous, slurred enunciation with which she had called from the broken craft, the *Lacquered Barge*, announcing her travail, from the first jolt of the storm to the slow and unintelligible jargon with which some time later she had announced the end of consciousness. Her voice in his ear had been like her voice all over the globe: personal, intimate, focused, as if she were drawing him not to her death but to her bed. It is this Wu Yuèhai who he sees before him and He Keung turns left and right again, sees his drugged or sleeping companions as they fail to remark upon this at all and finally, feeling foolish as well he might, he speaks.

"Why are you still alive?" He Keung says. "Why are you here? You died far from the *Radiant Crane*, locked in darkness. You were mourned. The Honorable Companion described the heavens as your shrine. There was mourning for three days. Now you are here. Is this you or have you only found the spirit of your ancestors to blame?"

I am babbling, he thinks, I am not being scientific. I am not being precise. I am overwhelmed. I should be brave and decisive, like Lin Xiangru when he faced the fearsome King of Zhao. So much is depending on this flight, which will have repercussions that radiate throughout the Chinese economy and culture. Why, already action figures of the three taikonauts are available in the department stores of Beijing. Commemorative wrist-watches bearing the likeness of the *Radiant Crane* are being sported by proud teenagers in the Tibetan province. A beer bearing He Keung's visage on its label is being quaffed this very moment in Macao.

"Watch this now," Wu Yuèhai says. "Attend to the spirit of the Suns." She bridges the distance between and embraces him; even through the intelligent metal and sophisticated fabrics which swaddle him he can feel the force of that embrace. She has been garbed in the simplest way, not in the equipment of space but almost as a courtesan. He Keung knows that he cannot be aroused, thanks to the anti-priapic treatments enforced upon the taikonauts prior to the flight, but he finds himself mockingly considering what Wu Yuèhai's embrace would feel like if he *were* aroused. There is no love in space, only engineering; that had been the link of their training. But this spectral clasp has been an utterly startling experience.

"The Suns are revolving," she says. "They are rotating within your spirit. I am infusing you with my portion of the Tao."

At any moment, He Keung knows, the two others will come to awareness and the situation will become uncontrollable. The accountant soul of Huang Shen will demand to know what his teammate is babbling about, what sensory derangements the youngest of the three taikonauts is experiencing. If He Keung reveals the truth of his encounter with the ghost of Wu Yuèhai, the others will surely clamp him into one of the American-made neural-restraint devices which the *Radiant Crane* carries as a precaution against just such a lunatic spree. (Nowadays the Americans excel at nothing so much as the "deaccessioning of transgressive personal liberties." The Waldrop-McAuley Shock Carapace is one of their finest and most in-demand export products, rated with a 1.5 Hulk-disabling factor.) Nor can He Keung count on the jovial nature of Wang Yu to help him slough off any charges which Huang Shen might level. Wang Yu is only two years away from the iron rice bowl of retirement. He need only complete this mission, then adjourn to his state-owned mansion on the banks of the virgin lake formed by the Three Gorges Dam. Wang Yu will not jeopardize such a sweet deal to cater to the erotic, cosmic delusions of a youngster.

No, he will have to lie to his teammates, tell them that he was merely reciting aloud the text of some fondly recalled Japanese manga, for his own amusement. (The music MP3s and compressed video files and engineering PDFs supplied by the National Space Administration have already palled for all of them, only a quarter of the way in what will hopefully be a roundtrip.) But will his comrades believe such a shabby pretext? And if they do believe, will they not still forevermore look askance at He Keung, as one who betrays the necessary vigilance and concentration demanded by this historic mission? (And yet dual super-cooled, cross-checking computers, no bigger than one of the many gold Olympic medals China will surely reap this year, are the real pilots of the vessel, at least at this uneventful stage.)

Even as He Keung parses his options regarding his fellow taikonauts, Wu Yuèhai, squirming in his lap, renders both truthfulness and deceit moot by her next words.

"He Keung, I can sense that your soul is fully invigorated by the immortal solar fluids which I have shared with you, a portion of the etheric stellar radiation which did not end my life, but caused me to be reborn, along with the ministrations of the Tian Shi Yu. And now that your *qi* is flowing richly, I need you to terminate your fellows. They are a poisoned cargo you must jettison."

He Keung feels his heart stop beating, suspending itself for a seeming eternity, then hurl itself against his ribs like one of the oxen on his grandfather's farm in Honan province, maddened by flies, running full tilt into a barn wall. To kill his comrades, the men he trained so long and hard with! He Keung recalls the weeks they lived in simulated Mars quarters in Antarctica, relying on each other for sheer survival. The time the two older men took him on bawdy drinking binge in Hong Kong. What has either man done to deserve such a cruel end?

As if half-cognizant that their fates are being debated, both Huang Shen and Wang Yu stir fitfully on their couches, their respectively cadaverous and infantile cheeks bedewed with sweat. Their hair, though close-cropped, stirs under the ministrations of the personal blowers which prevent the carbon dioxide of their own exhalations from hanging around their faces in zero gravity and smothering them as they sleep. (How easy, simply to shut those fans off. What a reputedly comfortable death.)

Seeking to delay the mortal answer he must make to Wu Yuèhai, recalling the proverb which advises, "When you want to test the depths of a stream, don't use both feet," He Keung seeks initially to unravel the mystery of her continued existence. "You claim the solar flux did not kill you, but instead brought new life. How can this be? And who are the Tian Shi Yu?"

Wu Yuèhai rears back from her close proximity to He Keung's face (is that her breath he feels, or only his own anti-CO_2 fan?) and assumes a serious, yet still somehow flirtatious mien. "The radiation triggered ancient programming buried in my cells, in the human genome. When I fell silent, it was because I was encysted in a cocoon. My nascent transformation sent FTL impulses along the Tao, and summoned my new mentors, the Tian Shi Yu, the Jade Angels. They were waiting to receive me into their loving arms when I hatched into my superior form, and to teach me the true meaning of the cosmos. They brought me to Mars, where I found a community of endless bliss and perfection. A community I wish to share with you. But only if you reach me alone."

He Keung would like to believe this fairy tale. Wu Yuèhai alive, and desirous of him. A world thought to be forbidding and sterile, instead hosting some kind of pan-galactic utopian outpost. It resonates with his fondest hopes and dreams. But the sticking point is Wu Yuèhai's insistence that he murder his fellow taikonauts.

"Why cannot Huang Shen and Wang Yu also enter into this lotus land? Are they not as human as you or I, just as susceptible to the beneficial influences of your Jade Angels?"

"No, they are not. Human, I mean. The Earth has always hosted two species, true humans and a parasitic mimic race. It is the mimics who are responsible for the endless litany of human suffering down the ages. You are human, holding within you the potential to become as I am. Your false mates are not. And in fact, they and their ilk know of the existence of the Jade Angels and the Martian redoubt. They are ancient enemies. And their intention is to destroy it utterly. Have you never wondered why the habitable space of the *Radiant Crane* is so small, why it represents such a slight improvement upon the ancient Shenzhou-5?"

Sensing the answer will not please him, He Keung asks, "Why?"

"It is because the bulk of this vessel is given over to weapons of mass destruction, bombs of surpassing ferocity which your fellows intend to rain down from orbit upon the heads of all we Martians."

We Martians. This is a startling statement and He Keung feels his sensibility tilt at its outrageousness but before he can contemplate further (Wu Yuèhai a Martian? but was that before or after her soliloquy of mourning and farewell?), Wu Yuèhai speaks in a dramatic new tone, a voice of imperiousness and certitude.

"The amplitude and oscillations of your *qi* indicate you are loath to rid the ship of these two parasites, even though they are like camels standing amidst a flock of sheep. But how can you expect to put out a cartload of wood on fire with only a single cup of water? Yet even this contingency has been foreseen. In different circumstances, you will find the strength perhaps to do what needs to be done. Remember, He Keung: Great souls have wills; feeble ones have only wishes."

The ship, subjectively stationary until then, seems to tilt, lurching and bucking improbably like a fragile life raft in the wake of a robot supertanker. At the same time, the yawning, gleaming haze which has surrounded the apparitional Wu Yuèhai seems to bloom and exfoliate, filling the small cabin. An odor of dusty poppies infiltrates He Keung's space-dulled nostrils.

Their restraints suddenly rotting like the Yellow Emperor's ancient silk robes, the three taikonauts are propelled into that gaping, devouring haze with enormous force and before He Keung can access the stabilizers which might possibly arrest the situation but he is instead pressed with enormous force against the bulkhead. He tries to struggle against the alien gravities pinning him in place but cannot and from the others come strange, bleating cries as they emerge from their drugged state into some kind of transitive half-life in which they neither achieve consciousness nor lose it.

The *Radiant Crane* is shaking now; shaking in the vacuum of space as was never supposed to be possible and caught in some approximation of fetality He Keung is shaking too, in sympathetic and terrible vibration. If the other two are in a half-state of ascension toward consciousness, He Keung is now otherwise, he seems to be descending toward some dark star which will envelop. Wu Yuèhai, invisible in the dominant cold nebulosities contained in the cabin, is giggling; the embrace which locks him is not hers but some aspect of descent and yet he has never felt as close to her as he has at this moment.

"Be not afraid of growing slowly, be afraid only of standing still," Wu Yuèhai's voice whispers close to him. He cannot touch her but she is there. "You are embarked fully now upon your journey. We greet you, we raise the flag of liberation. Soon you will join us on the surface of the Red Planet and we shall together celebrate the will of the people. And remember: even a single ant may well destroy a dike." He feels invisible lips against his ear, another harsh giggle and then space itself in its full and irreversible emptiness seems to swaddle him, not the illusory haze which the *Radiant Crane* has furnished its three voyagers but the vast and abandoned tableland of the heavens themselves. Breathing seems an outmoded luxury. His companions appear to be flickering before him. He wants to speak but cannot. He wishes to confer or failing that, at least make their new condition known to Grand Mao Station back in Earth orbit, but he is beyond speech.

"Thus ends the first part of your journey," Wu Yuèhai whispers. "Now the true testing can begin."

Mars hangs in the sky like the mass of Jupiter's Great Red Spot scooped from the mother planet and given independent existence, or like the promise of a placid uterine existence, all artery-filtered light and dear protective enclosure. He Keung feels resilient solidity beneath his back. His limbs are free of the encumbering spacesuit for the first time in months, protected from whatever environment surrounds him only by the skintight green undersuit he donned before departure from Grand Mao Station.

Shakily, He Keung rises to his feet and gazes about.

He is evidently standing on a smallish world, for the very curvature of the globe is half-perceivable, the horizon oddly close. The ground beneath his booted feet is irregular in a natural manner, but covered with a kind of uncanny springy mouse-gray turf composed of long interlocking cilia finer than the downy hairs of a woman's back. The sky above his head is a cloudless violet, with the brighter stars of the Milky Way shining through, where the Mars-light permits. The air he breathes is redolent of novel proteins and pheromones.

Incredible as it may seem, He Keung can draw but one conclusion. He is standing on one of the satellites of Mars, either Phobos or Deimos. He takes a tentative step, and the bounciness of his stride supplies another confirming datum. But how came the airless, barren moon known to science for centuries to host an entire ecology and atmosphere, however primitive? Is the change so recent that terrestrial telescopes have not yet detected it? Or if they have done so, why were He Keung and his comrades not informed of this miracle? Can it be that their masters do not want them to know of such a crucial change in their destination? Would the taikonauts hesitate to deliver their putative cargo of WMDs if they knew in advance they were bombing a living world?

He Keung can only assume that this enlivening of the formerly dead satellite is a result of cosmic machinations by Wu Yuèhai and her unseen peers in the Martian community, and possibly by their mentors, the Tian Shi Yu, the Jade Angels. This satellite must have been set up as an anteroom to the glories of the Red Planet, a kind of quarantine chamber for imperfect visitors. Realizing this, he regards the hovering bulk of Mars with altered sensibilities. Now the planet looks like a monitoring eyeball or the working end of a telescope, sucking in data to be processed by the no-longer-human minds that dwell there.

Have He Keung's cabinmates also been deposited here? If so, why were they not all three dumped side by side? Is it intended that He Keung rest alone for a moment to muster his energies and willpower for some upcoming competition? These must be the "different circumstances" into which Wu Yuèhai promised to transplant him, the arena in which he must decide whether to slaughter Huang Shen and Wang Yu, according to her instructions, to earn celestial merit and her undying love.

Or his place in hell.

He Keung realizes that he can advance no further in his destiny until he reunites with his two comrades, whether they be fellow humans or an antagonistic species. Since every direction appears identical, He Keung sets off in an arbitrary vector.

It is his own Long March, his trudge toward some kind of goal shrouded now but only by his ignorance. All he can hope is that his ignorance will dissipate as he trudges and so He Keung stumbles across the slick panels of the Moon (Deimos or Phobos? he cannot know; very well he will call it Mao and claim it in the name of the People's Army) feeling all of the elements of his life to this moment impelling him, dragging him through this strange, expressionless landscape.

The repetitive muted squelch of his boots upon the living carpet of Mao falls into a metronomic rhythm, lulling He Keung slightly, despite the toxic, the absolute strangeness of it all. At one moment in the capsule his companions to the sides, at the next the strange and intimate discourse with Wu Yuèhai, the breath of her confession, her shocking revelation, as shocking as the landscape of Formosa must have been for the evil and exiled Chiang-Kai Shek in those early, frantic, wonderful days of the Revolution, and then to the asteroid itself, no transition: truly the Little Red Book was filled with alerts of a world gone suddenly incomprehensible and threatening ... but still the experience is overwhelming.

And then also there is He Keung's sense of shame and failure, his betrayal of his glorious mission. He feels like Su Qin, the "criss-cross philosopher" of the Warring States era, returning in defeat to his native Luoyang, going back home in despair and rags, having spent all his resources fruitlessly. Is it possible he can ever atone for his moment of doubt and indecision in the *Radiant Crane*, can somehow salvage his mission?

The lonely man pushes forward across the unvaryingly desolate landscape for hours. His mind begins to drift back to his childhood, his early manhood, the time spent on his grandfather's farm, when everything seemed so certain and straightforward. Half-dreaming, He Keung continues to lift and plant one foot after another, until he is brought to an abrupt halt by a voice at once anticipated and dreaded.

"He Keung," Wu Yuèhai says out of the empyrean. Her voice is intimate, confidential, as if she were resting her chin on his shoulder, and yet there is that iciness as well; that glaze of distance which has always surrounded her even in life. "You are not doing well. You are set upon a course of betrayal, betrayal of the true cause of all humanity. You must cease your impetuousness, you must think."

"Think?" he says, speaking the word into the violet atmosphere, and, in sudden, lurching panic, "What is there to think? I am here because of what you have done to me. I was in the *Radiant Crane* dreaming, then you spoke to me, then I was dislodged. What do you want?"

Wu Yuèhai says something so shocking that He Keung feels his frail senses waver, the small lamp of his sensibility, of his struggling intellect, which once seemed able to cast some light on this wretched Moon, seeming to gutter and die.

"I want nothing," she says. "I failed in my mission, don't you understand? Now I am reduced to searching here, searching there, looking for you to bring this to an end. The Martians, my Martians cannot help me. They say that I have been corrupted, that I have chosen the path of an exile, allowing my memories of mere flesh and blood existence to contaminate my proper relationship with you. What I should have done, by their ethical standards, was to assume control of your neural structures in the *Radiant Crane* and forced you to carry out my wishes. But I could not bring myself to damage in such a fashion one whom I—respected.

"And so I unbalanced the Tao, they claim, and their words have disarmed me. I cannot help myself because I have lost all belief. It is there for you then to change or it cannot be at all."

Wu Yuèhai as desolate as He Keung? Herself bereft of her comrades' trust? All her seemingly godlike powers rendered impotent by some breaching of the finer parameters of her arcane assignment, by mission creep that came to include sympathy and empathy and—and affection?—for a young taikonaut who once worshiped her? He Keung would like to believe this, but cannot rid his mind of the suspicion that this confession is merely another stratagem to insure his cooperation. So his response to Wu Yuèhai is rather formal and chill, tepid as the noodle soup young He Keung would eat upon his midnight return home from his university cram courses.

"And what kind of end do you want?"

"It does not matter to me; what matters is that I be at last permitted to sleep. They promised me sleep; they said that if I made my appeal, if I stayed to mark the truth no matter how painful, I would be permitted to move on to another plane, where life is effortless and uncontested. But they were lying. I have no sleep, I have no peace."

As if excited by her intensity the satellite Mao begins to shake, the fibrous panels underfoot surge and heave with the volatility of liquid. He Keung finds himself in perilous balance. Space madness! It must be that ultimate discomfiture of which they had been warned throughout all of the arduous training. The madness which cuts like a knife through all the truisms and teachings of the Great Revolution itself!

"Wu Yuèhai, help me!" calls out the young man alone in the seeming face of imminent destruction, just as, centuries past, the brave warrior Han Xi made his desperate plea prior to the descent of the headsman's axe. And just like Han Xi, who was pardoned at the last moment by a prince eager for brave soldiers, He Keung is saved.

After a complicated fashion.

The surface of Mao blisters upward just a few meters in front of him, the gray tapestry formed by the cilia stretching to cover the new extrusion. It is as if the planet's elastic skin sprouts an immense boil or sarcoma that swells in speeded-up malignancy. This is an objective phenomenon; He Keung is certain of that. In the face of this enormity, all his self-pity and epistemological uncertainty implode. No delusion or hallucination, hence not space madness, but rather the alien workings of a globe rendered intelligently totipotent by the Jade Angels and their unfathomable technology.

The blister ceases its exponential growth when it is as large as a peasant's cottage. Then a portion of the curved surface facing He Keung melts away, revealing a cavern, a wetly crimson interior that is a mockingly obscene echo of the dry russet planet hanging above as mute witness.

And inside the hollow blister stand Huang Shen and Wang Yu, his fellow taikonauts. They stand, but they are not unsupported, instead hanging like puppets. They are wired into the substance of the blister by numerous living tendrils and conduits, neural bundles piercing them like the claws of a sky dragon. Surely this is their unmerited punishment, imposed by Wu Yuèhai for daring to approach Mars, the sanctuary of the Jade Angels.

"Wu Yuèhai!" shouts He Keung. "What have you done? Release my friends!"

The voice of the martyred female taikonaut whispers despondently in He Keung's ear. "This is not my doing. Rather, it is the end of all hope."

As if to confirm the woman's speech, Huang Shen now speaks, his pinched bookkeeper's face bearing a malicious leer incommensurate with any real suffering.

"Your ghostly bitch is correct, He Keung. Wang Yu and I have assumed control of this construct, the moon you once called Deimos. We found the supervisory ganglia exactly where the Jade Angels always install them. They are such trusting creatures, so intent on making it easy for their subordinate races to adopt and work their puny gifts. But this time their mania for standardization has betrayed them. We have made a long and diligent study of these so-called Angels and their technologies, across a thousand, thousand solar systems, until we know them better than they know themselves. For any race which limits itself to only half the spectrum of existence—that which is conventionally called 'goodness'—cannot, by definition, understand as much as another race which spans the whole continuum of motivation and desire, from light to dark."

He Keung is nearly dumbstruck. At last he babbles out, "But, but—what are you? What have you done with my comrades?"

Wang Yu speaks like a jolly demon. "We are still your same comrades in truth, He Keung, but we were always more than you knew. Our kind is called the Shih Chieh Hsien."

The Bodiless Immortals. Only an ancient myth—or so He Keung has always believed.

"The birth-souls of your fellows," continues Wang Yu, "were driven out years ago by the force of our superior *qi*, to perish howling in the aether. We used their bodies as we have used many in the past, as meat machines to accomplish our goals. In this case, we always intended to crush the beachhead established by the Jade Angels in this solar system. We have enjoyed unimpeded rule of your primitive sphere too long to relinquish it now. Therefore, Mars must be destroyed."

"What do you intend?"

Huang Shen makes an answer, quite forthrightly and unconcernedly, as if He Keung is a child being told the reason why grass is green. "This modified satellite possesses powerful engines. We will drive the whole globe now out of orbit and into the Red Planet, creating a world-shattering cataclysm such as that which, eons ago, wiped ninety-nine percent of life off Earth itself. The colony of the hybrid Martians will be extinguished; all individuals no matter where or how concealed will be destroyed. Including your precious Wu Yuèhai. These mortal containers temporarily housing our essences will of course be evaporated as well, along with yourself. But our essential selves will simply be released back into the Tao."

The Tao! The Jade Angels! The Bodiless Immortals! Celestial layers upon layers! It is of such enormity to He Keung that he feels the cosmos or at least this small part of it to which he has been sentenced lurch. Meat machines! All of the curses of the Ancients seem to have descended upon him through this sudden and shocking confidence and He Keung, his legs like his soul seemingly encased in cement finds himself unable to move. He stands supine to Huang Shen's valediction waiting for some awful judgment to descend upon him, to tell him what must come next but nothing at all happens in this glazed and sudden circumstance.

He Keung realizes he has reached the nadir of his quest. All roads leading either to fulfillment of his original mission or to wholehearted adoption of Wu Yuèhai's imperatives seem barricaded. Within He

Keung's heart, mind and soul, all the tugging, tensioned polarities that have kept him a-jitter and incapable of decision-making resolve into one gaping nullity, a black hole compounded of the impossibility of wisdom in a delimited framework of knowledge and the utterly dire necessity of action.

At this moment of He Keung's inverted satori, Huang Shen and the silent Wang Yu suddenly implode, they collapse as if those hanging puppets were deflated and with no transition whatsoever they are ragged blotches staining the red cavern of the blister with a soup of foul yellow matter.

His nemeses are naught but small, indistinct puddles upon which he glances and then his perspective shifts, rises toward the ruddy and damaged surface of Mars hanging above and Wu Yuèhai, returned inexplicably from the exile of her abysmal and despairing silence as He Keung never expected she would or could resurface, says: "Amazing! It is the most ancient, the greatest of powers you have shown! An unflagging warrior's spirit, like that of Su Wu sent to face the Huns. You have vanquished them!"

The wavering, exultant exclamation of her voice is so unlike that quiet, insidious tone with which she had so movingly tracked her own orbital expiration that He Keung's own spirits are comparably lifted.

"Come with me," she says, "Come with me now before these two perfidious Immortals are reconstituted in some other vessels. On Mars, we shall devise counter-schemes that will yet secure this solar system as a bastion of the Jade Angels."

Reconstituted? He Keung, deep in service of the Great Revolution, deep in his fathoming and dedication to the cultural enlightenment which the space program has brought to his country and his life has never felt as confused as he has at this moment; it is as if he were not a taikonaut but an innocent, somehow stripped of memory and desire, hanging (hanging like a puppet?) within some deep well excavated in the name of the Ancients. He cannot move; movement is beyond him and yet he can feel some force, perhaps generated by Wu Yuèhai which flutters at the rim of sensibility and begins to guide him, stumbling, away from the decaying blister and its slimy contents.

"You must hurry!" she is saying, "You must not let this triumph pass; you must be opportune and take the moment," and the shuffling He Keung lashed by a kind of insistence which he cannot comprehend stumbles forward, stumbles under the guidance of the more-than-human Wu Yuèhai toward some dim conception of the light.

Is he going to Mars? Has he been granted entrance to the community of transfigured souls whose existence Wu Yuèhai has hinted at, a comity of blissful demigods who, under the tutelage of the Jade Angels, all work toward evolving the plenum to some form of transcendental perfection? Will he make his ascent toward the mythic planet that has for so long fascinated mankind? Or he is instead doomed to shuffle like some broken automaton across the gray plains of Deimos? Can this be some monstrous illusion; some hallucination on the Journey of a Thousand Knives patched into his dying sensorium only to torment him?

He does not know. He cannot know.

How he loved Wu Yuèhai in those hours of dictation of her loss; how he loved the Great Leader in all of the years before that; how, dreaming, he loved the skies and stars when even the issue of the Revolution fell away and it was only he and possibility close and alone in the night.

He takes a step. He takes another step. Something systematic, something greater than he seems to be guiding. Wu Yuèhai laughs in his ear and it is a laugh both gentle and ferocious, laughter of absolute insistence and yet yielding. Mars, the great Red Planet of dreams hangs ever lower in the distance. If he could but expand his arm by just a little, if he could just reach a little further, he would be able to touch that great snare, hanging low like fruit in the heavens. All that he must do is stretch a little further...

Behind the ripe beckoning pomegranate of Mars, misty figures larger than the prominences of the solar flare that killed or metamorphosed Wu Yuèhai now appear, viridian specters whose outlines fluctuate like flames in accordance with some half-sensed cosmic tempo. Are these the Jade Angels, come to assist He Keung in his transition, or only artifacts of his derangement?

Wu Yuèhai says, "And soon, believe me, He Keung, as it did for me as I lay dying all alone, the Earth so near, yet so far, in this darkness everything will appear," and he reaches adamant to embrace her.

Soon.

Soon all will be revealed.

Soon he will be a Martian too.

AORTIC INSUBORDINATION

by Batya Swift Yasgur and Barry N. Malzberg

I don't want to go, I said. Let someone else do this. Not me. I never wanted it. Please don't make me—

Ah, they said, you will change the world. The needle twinkled. And the world certainly needs changing; we have had enough of this.

But, I said. Speaking as I did "(speech" of course is a converted term for what I did). But no, not what? They said. No change so great ever started with one so small. The syringe poised, hovering lovingly.

Until we understand what we are doing, I said.

We understand, they said. The syringe struck. I was propelled into the River of Memory. Swimming along its currents.

Was that how it happened? It is my best approximation. It must have been something like that as the Priests methodically unlocked and sent me on. Surely it would not have been in silence; surely I would not have gone without protest. And yet who is to know? Out of circumstances we create consequence, link a chain of events to a source, even if that source is a dream. A dream from which I will awaken safe and warm, no enclosure, no lessons, no orientation, no Priests, no mission, only circumstance itself.

Circumstance, I can handle. Haven't I always? That is why they chose me, but perhaps I was not chosen, maybe it was just a dream that I was taken to change the world.

A dream that I begged for this cup to pass (my capacity for protest was inexhaustible then), a dream that my plea was ignored, a dream that I found myself—

—Falling, falling and rolling and tumbling and bouncing, bounce and jounce, tumble and jump, roll and folderol, surrounded by the thick, viscous, oily fluid. So they did it after all, they really did make me go and it had worked, the protocols correct.

—And disbelieving to that last scoop, swoop, loop, and whoop, I thought they would desist, that someone else would be taken to prowl the darkness. But no, no passing cup, so there I was falling and rising in that tunnel, propelled by rhythmic pulsation.

Thump. Thump: it's dark, I said, and I miss my—

—Best not to think of them. Of origins, of the way it had been before and of what had been taken from me. I must live in this new world. This world, my mission.

Orientation Chamber earlier. Lecture topic: Meet Your Neighbors. You will be coursing through tunnel-like vessels in a stream of *blood*. You will be surrounded by discs, oddly concave at the center. *Red blood corpuscles*. These new neighbors are important, yes, but not as important as the white blood cells: *Leukocytes*.

Remember those. That's what you'll be.

And even before: I don't want that, I said. I don't want that. Silence, I was told, and shattered and complicit I acceded.

Follow your fellow leukocytes: watch and copy them. Then at a crucial moment you'll make that one critical change and then—

And then what?

And then you'll see what is needed and why.

And then they obliterated me.

Into that blood of memory. *Leukocytes, corpuscles*, my new family. Two cells in front, fellow members of the White, fellow soldiers of the Immune System. Behind, a mass of them: some round, some ovoid, and some horseshoe shaped—as, fetchingly, am I. Eccentrically located nuclei too like mine, surrounded by *cytoplasm* that glistens in the slick and random darkness of the blood. Cytoplasm just like mine, except for that one crucial difference, the infinitesimal message of change given this humble Voyager to carry.

I, Voyager, greet them as they greeted me. We communicate in the bloodstream's ancient code. Their language comes easily as we signal and call to others of the Family: *Monocytes. Macrophages. Eosinophils*. All that instruction I have endured facilitates communication. I mask my origins and darker, higher purpose with the words of cells, commonplaces hiding the deeper codes of exile and ruin. The Leukocytes and I, burbling small confidences as we await the call: the true summons.

The call.

A nasty virus this, they say. Herpes zoster. Kill it now is the command. So it's off to the hand where Herpes Zoster has pitched camp. We are armed and ready for battle. We jog and swim to the Herpes Fort. My own substance is grim with the knowledge that my battle is not with Herpes. Not at all. Herpes is not the enemy. I know this.

I plan my address, then.

Herp, I will say: Herp, old pal. We're allies. Friends. Herp, I will say, you are the smallest life-form known, nothing more than a package of DNA with a dirty assignment. I have an assignment, too, and these missions are not dissimilar. Your mission is to replicate yourself and so is mine. You will use the body's own reproductive process by taking over a cell's internal machinery. And I—

—And I

—I stop. That would be too blunt. I might have said that I would take over Herpes' own machinery, but that would alert him and then I would have to take him by force then instead of having his cooperation. Try this, Herp, I will say instead: I will assist your takeover by sending false signals to the Leukocytes. They will disperse, the dumb things. By the time my deception has been discovered, Herp and I will be sharing a cell and the process will begin.

This seems more reasonable.

Accordingly, I volunteer to lead the attack. The Leukocytes agree. Why not? They are so dumb, so gullible, so easily led after all. Furthermore, they are relieved. Let someone else lead the charge to the enemy camp. Find someone as willing as I.

Wait ten heartbeats I say to them. Then move to the fifth capillary along the digital crease of the third right interphalangeal joint. I will be waiting for you there.

They are dumb but imprinted. They waver. It should not be, they suggest. This seems peculiar, they bleat. We are not at all certain, they whine. We have doubt, they mumble.

I am persuasive, intense as I have been trained. This is the best way, I say. This is the source of the signal. They grumble and mumble a kind of agreement. They bounce and jounce, hobble and bobble.

I will be waiting for you there, I say. Go ye heroes, etc.

Mutual salutes, wishes of luck, and then I forage my way to the fifth capillary where Herp perches, indistinguishably.

I speak to him just as I planned. It goes as I knew it would.

Herp is persuaded.

"Mommy, it itches!"

"Itching is normal when you have chicken pox. Let me prepare an oatmeal bath for you."

"Oh, that feels better. Can I sit in the tub all day?"

"If you want."

"I want. But, Mommy—"

"Yes, dear?"

"There's one spot that is still itching. Like it's on fire. And the oatmeal isn't helping."

"Show me."

"Here. The middle finger of my right hand."

"Oh, my, that is some blister. I've never seen one quite like this. Let's try some lotion and see if it helps."

"But, Mommy—"

"What is it?"

"I feel weird. And all the other blisters are starting to itch more. Something is happening. Something's happening! The blisters—look, they are getting bigger and bigger. Help, they're growing and growing! Look at that one on my pinkie, it's as big as my whole finger. And that one over there—"

"Oh!"

"Mommy what's wrong with me?"

"I don't know. Hello? We need an ambulance immediately. Something terrible. Terrible!"

"Mommy!"

Of course I don't kill him.

That was never the assignment, of course. Never. What would be the purpose of that? The mission can be accomplished only through a live carrier, an active host. And a good thing, too, because killing him—well, that would have been malevolence, nothing else. Seven years old: innocent and adorable. Cute as a button. That's what the nurses have been saying, now that the swelling has receded.

But before that: doctors in and out of the room, the kid's little face now a bowling ball, his fingers and toes fat little sausages. And the arms and legs unrecognizable in their edemic monstrosity. Massive doses of Benadryl to control the itching, sedatives to help him sleep in the fever's furnace, antibiotics to kill the alien invaders ... if only they knew, if only they knew.

No one told me that it would be this way. The Priests, they kept me in the dark. That was certainly wise of them. I was already protesting and if I had known it would be this way, would I have still gone on with it. The burning, the excruciating itching which has made the merge possible.

The merge possible. The next step.

The transitional step as the host and the Voyager become fused.

Now I am him: now he is me. I am Mikey in the fire, here we are in the flame, close to death, but we won't die. We will survive. We have survived and are so cute once again.

They say we are cute again. Cute as a button.

Merged to Mikey in the fire. Mikey the fiery, Mikey the funny, Mikey the redeemer. Listen to our song:

I am Mikey
And Mikey am I
I come from the sky
And I can fly.
Why, sky, fly, oh my, so high.
Never shy and never will die
I am Mikey
Mikey is me
And we can change the world
Just wait and see.
Me, we, he, hee whee!
I am Mikey
Mikey is laughter
I was serious before
But this is after
Ha ha, Mama, Papa, ha, ha, ha, ha

So that's it. Laughter. My mission. From the solemn emerges the irreverent, and it is the Road of Redemption. Make 'em laugh. Shake 'em up. Sacred sounds, as their bellies jiggle, the hips wiggle when they giggle.

Like the vase. It's funny. That's what it is. To watch that vase sail across the room, banging into the wall and then the little pieces of glass showering the floor. How they twinkle in the sun, those colors streaming in rainbow splash as they fall. The rainbow shower is ever so much prettier than a dumb old vase sitting on the shelf.

A flying vase is funny. As funny as telling my teacher that I was born in China, adopted by Mommy, had plastic surgery to make me look American, but couldn't do the homework because my English skills were still poor. And talking fake Chinese the rest of the day. Ong. Pong. Ching chong. The other kids laughed. They liked it. The rest of the day, we were all going around saying Ing, Ping, Ong Pong, Ching Chong. Only the teacher didn't think it was funny. Why?

It was as funny as the sound of tinkle in the kitchen sink. Sinkle. And watching the mailman slide along the path on the yellow thing I left there just for him. Squeal on a banana peel!

Why won't Mommy see that?

Because she just won't. Not when I'm the one doing it. Oh, she laughs at the guys on television—or at least she used to. The big fat man and the short man. She laughs when they get pie in their faces and when they slip on banana peels and when they throw things at one another. She laughs at circus clowns, doesn't she? So why won't she laugh at my red nose and my cheeks? My flying vase and banana peel. And if I can't make her laugh, how will I make the rest of the world laugh, too?

Because that is my mission, to make them all laugh. Clever of the Priests to make it so serious—classes and lectures and that scary injection—when it's really all about being funny. Your mission will emerge, they said. You will learn by going where you have to go. And so it has. To turn everything topsy-turvy. To get them to shred their assumptions. What makes a vase pretty on the shelf and ugly in pieces on the floor? What makes a banana peel funny on television but not in real life? Only those stupid beliefs passed from parents to children. Change those and you can change it all.

How will they learn to change their assumptions?

By laughing at everything.

Everything!

Down the railing and up the stars, bet you can't catch me, Mommy! Funny, how you run! You weren't made for this, were you? Whoops! And when you put the salad on the plate, I suddenly whisk it away so the salad goes right on the table. And when you try to catch me, I say you can't catch me. No one can catch me! Catch us, I should say. Catch me and Mikey.

And the look you give. Oh, Mikey, you've changed, you say. Your forehead wrinkles and that new annoying line comes between your eyes. Tears on your cheeks. I was supposed to make you laugh, not cry. What's going on? Why do you take me to that lady, Mrs. Burton, the one who tries to look so important with her silly dolls dressed like doctors and nurses. Why do you get so angry when I make the dolls fly across the room? I've got great aim, haven't I? And Mrs. Burton herself when she reaches clumsily for them. A flying Mrs. Burton!

Oh, ladies, stop whispering. All those long, serious words about "trauma and adjustment," "aggressive tendencies," "repressed rage," and "inappropriate affect."

Laugh and dance. Dance and laugh. Light and fun. Come on, Mommy, watch me run. Mommy, you can help me change the world. Get everyone to see everything different. Hey, is your world so great? War and terror and cheating and pain. Wouldn't it be better to just laugh and laugh? Mommy, you're not laughing—

Mommy is crying.

"I understand, ma'am," he says. "There's nothing more painful than having to institutionalize a child. But you've tried everything for this boy. Thirteen years since that bizarre early childhood illness. Thirteen years of treatment. Individual therapy. Family counseling. Psychotropic drugs, acupuncture, herbs. There's nothing more you can do. But your son is in good hands here and he'll do very well. Won't you, Michael?"

I thought it would be simple once Mikey and I became one. To get them to laugh. To turn sadness into happiness, to change the world, shatter their assumptions, break their idols and make them happy. Simply happy. They were so aggressive, so destructive, but laughter would solve it all.

But they wouldn't laugh. Why didn't the Priests understand, in Orientation Chamber, that they could not laugh? They are not like us. Their complexity, their convoluted, crazy world, it cannot respond to laughter.

The Priests didn't know. They did not understand the situation. They had misappraised. But I know now. I have learned.

The question is—what do I do now? To get it back. Retrieve the mission. A serious mission, to bring frivolity? Infect with laughter, infect the world? What can I do, stuck away in this loony bin, with all these—

Then all at once I know what to do. And fall down in awe, for the Priests understood after all. How to bring the mission, where to execute it, my very failure the necessary stepping stone to my success.

Begin right at home, of course. What better place than a nuthouse for laughter?

So I hold a meeting after lights-out and before the meds kick in. Tommy is sleepy and mumbling as usual about the Government. James is preparing for his Second Coming. Arnold is moaning and rocking. Dorian—Well, you don't want to know what Dorian is doing. The orderlies are somewhere down the corridor, of course. They don't care. A typical night.

"Well, folks," I say, "Do you want to change the world?"

They become quiet. No more Government or Return of the Son. They have never heard me say anything serious before. They have barely heard me speak. I sure have their attention. The orderlies yap on, I hear their voices from down the hall.

"If we change the world, will you change the Government so they won't be after me anymore?" Tommy asks.

"We'll have a different Government, sure," I say.

"But will they show any compassion? Will they leave good citizens alone?"

"Great compassion. All the compassion you could possibly want and more of it."

Tommy considers this. James says, "Government can't change. The world can't change until the second coming."

"I am the second coming," I say. "I begged pass this cup and they did not listen and now I am here."

They say nothing to this.

"Blessed are the light of heart because they shall uplift the world."

"Amen," James says and crosses himself.

"The Lord God is a God of Laughter," I tell them. "Just read the second Psalm." Psalms had occupied a lot of my time years ago. When Mommy went off to cry.

"You get a lot of good information from the Psalms," I say. "You'd be surprised what is in there. Harps and lyres and whatnot."

"I don't know what lyres are. What we gotta do?"

"We laugh," I say. "That is how it begins. And then we do things to make everyone laugh. If each of us make two others laugh, and each of those take on another two, we can take over the world."

"Just laugh?" James says doubtfully.

"That's it."

"Seems pretty silly to me," Arnold says. "But it beats the crappy therapy and basket weaving. Sounds like more fun than Basic Living Skills, too."

Carlo, Ben, Jamal, Kenneth, Dorian, and the others come to join us. The whole men's ward. "Try it," I say. "Ha."

"Ha."

It begins so feebly.

Ha.

But it builds. Piece by piece, sound by sound, we give to the world the sounds which the world deserves, which it has always needed. Ha and ha and ha again. And the orderlies come with their syringes and restraints, but there are too many of us, so they call the nurses, but there are still too many of us, as we hear the sacred syllable of redemption from Wards 3 and 4, so they call the doctors, but there are still too many of us, as the women's wards begin, ha and ha and more ha.

And the plates go flying, the people go flying, until the top of the nuthouse itself is levitated by our laughter, lifted by that sound, twinkles and twirls at that sudden elevation and as Arnold and James and Jamal and Carlo and Ben and Dorian and Kenneth and I continue that levitating laughter it seems to overtake the world itself; manifest silken strands of light and laughter penetrating the closed and open spaces.

There is much more to this, but it is not for me to tell that story. My story is of origins, masques, and the sudden flight of running blood. Of contagion, cell to cell, voice to voice, echo to echo. From here, it is for the Kings and the Popes, the Presidents and the Preachers, the Priests and the Headquarters to take over that fierce obligation of laughter, laughter as hot as the sun, burning into all the spaces and places of human habituation.

Hi, Mikey.

Good-bye, Mikey.

Finita la commedia.

The Starry Night
by Jack Dann and Barry N. Malzberg

Prophecy

Vincent knows now that there is no way out of this, that he will die in the asylum. He will never wander the sweet Earth again; his plans, mocked, are in ruins. "There is no hope, Theo," he says. "It is too late for me. It is too late for all of us." Theo looks at him, stricken. Once they were joined, one person in two houses, but this is no longer the case, not since the great burning.

"The stars will explode first," Vincent says.

Outcome

On the great screen of the heavens are imprinted the empowering lineaments of the stars, no longer compact but thin, extending streams of gas, arms of destruction scattering, scuttling through the darkness. I am the bearer of light. Vincent gapes, incapable now of transcription.

In the Museum: Intent

Rachel is six. Well, almost six. She will be that in four days and five hours, Mommy says. Rachel is proud. Here she is barely six, and she knows her letters, her numbers, all of the colors. And she knows how to draw. She can draw like a real artist. Daddy said that too, and Daddy knows all about art.

Now Rachel is in the Museum of Modern Art again, to which Mommy had promised weeks ago to take her for her almost-birthday. She stands with her sketchpad and pencil copying *The Stars Nit*. That is the name of the painting. The sign next to the painting says so—even though some of the letters are really smudged. It also says that Vincent Van Gogh is the artist. Rachel knows nothing about Vincent Van Gogh except that he is dead and that he was very unhappy. Daddy told her that. The stars are exploding.

The stars in the painting are exploding! It is very important to Rachel to get this into her picture. These are not simple stars; they are stars that are opening like seashells in the blue sky over the town.

Rachel copies the exploding stars and the flaming cypress tree and buildings of the little town underneath the stars. She has already printed the title carefully—THE STARS NIT—and is now working to make all of the little buildings just right. She has already copied *The Bather* in this room and from the second floor she has copied part of a very big painting, *Water Lilies*. If Mommy and Daddy will let her, Rachel plans to copy ten paintings this afternoon. She has listed *The Bather* in front of her book as already copied and is almost ready to enter *The Stars Nit*. When Rachel is big, she plans to have copied all of the paintings in this museum into five or ten sketchbooks just as big as this one. And when she is old like Mommy and Daddy, she will sit and look at all of her drawings and remember just the way the paintings in the museum looked.

Mommy and Daddy are not far away, only a few steps, but Rachel might as well be upstairs or at home for all the attention they are paying her right now. They are talking to one another and shaking their heads and holding hands in their way, looking at another Van Gogh painting. Mommy is saying something about color theories, but to Rachel it is only a murmur she can ignore. Just like the people in the painting are ignoring the exploding stars. They are all in their houses, not even looking outside, most of them sleeping.

Rachel needs to finish her sketch soon so she can record the title in her book and go on to another painting. She will not leave the museum today until she has ten paintings. When she is home she will examine all of them, but this is the one, she already can tell, that she will like the best.

The air is so blue, and the exploding stars so large and so yellow. She has never seen stars like that. Maybe she is growing up and learning to see them in a special way, like Vincent Van Gogh.

In the Moment: Brooding

Vincent knows how Seurat would have painted this. A million dots, a hundred jolts, a mathematical equation devoid of emotion. He would have brought to *The Starry Night* what Seurat always brought: promise and selfishness. Georges saw only himself in everything and needed to break himself into essence, into golden scintallae ... into infinities of methodical points and dots. That was Georges' great secret, but Vincent could see through the dots. Seurat pretended to see, but saw only himself ... and his "method."

Which is why Seurat could not have done this. Stabbing at the canvas, opening the stars like flowers, Vincent proceeds. His easel is positioned in front of the barred window of his room in the asylum of

Saint-Paul-de-Mausole in Saint-Rémy. The walled garden below is composed of purple and green shadows. The morning star blinks in the coruscating sky above, and behind him a table lamp casts its own revelatory shadows across the floor and walls. Slowly, nothing more now than the instrument of his design, he paints. His brushes are thick with ultramarine, cobalt, emerald green, zinc white. He looks out the window through the bars, looks up up up and out ... casting himself toward God, and he feels a familiar dizziness. He wrests his attention away from the painting, looks around the room, the little room that is security and comfort, looks at his worn armchair covered with a tapestry, looks at the greenish gray wallpaper and sea green curtains blotched with roses and blood daubs of red, and he cries, for once again he can see the familiar auras. "Please, God," he prays, remembering that the last time he fell ill and had an episode, he squeezed all his tubes of paint into his mouth and swallowed.

"Please, God—"

And Vincent feels that God is with him. This is not an episode, not a religious hallucination. This is God's method and he is the vessel and God has allowed him to see. God directs Vincent's attention again to His painting, back to the canvas waiting to become revelation. He-who-cannot-be-known draws Vincent's attention down to a fine, desperate point, a tube of comity into which he suspends paint and pain, and Vincent feels the heat radiating through the window from those damaged stars high in the sky ... stars that were once specks in the higher vault of suspension, now open, bleeding. Had Vincent been the first to see the stars as ruptured animals, screaming in their entrails, their decomposition?

Vincent applies paint to canvas in thick swirls and avenues of texture. He sees the Moon, bloated and wavering ... and it appears on the canvas. He sees a hamlet outside his window, and he paints its blue buildings and towers in ragged, horizontal strokes. He sees cypresses burning black and blue and gray, and he lifts his gaze to the canvas sky, vortexes of stars exploding, spirals and eddies and swirls of interstellar dust and there, always there, the planet Venus, an eye of God watching a great sun exploding in the direction of the constellation Monoceros the Unicorn. The truth of the past and future, the truth of twenty thousand light years' distance is spattered and sprayed onto the canvas.

Finished, Vincent falls backward and sleeps through most of the day until the good Dr. Théophile Peyron, the director of the asylum, awakens him.

"Vincent, I am pleased to see that your cure is taking hold ... but you should always wait for the light to do your painting, wouldn't you agree?"

"Yes," Vincent says. "Yes, let us wait for the light." The great exploding light.

He can already feel the fire.

The Heavens: Exploding

And have torn apart the curtain of God, Father Vincent Thomas, SJ, thinks, staring through the view screen. In the heavens above, the glory of His firmament. But the heavens are exploding, the stars igniting, the wall of God shattering. His hands tremble on the instruments. He tries to steady himself, but what shakes him cannot be resisted. It is that fracture across the design of Revelation and he can only see the stars, that star, lifted beyond his measure, tongues of fire cutting the hue of surface. *Now in this time there was a decree and Simon Augustus desired that all were to be taxed.* That star is taxed; it is yielding of itself.

Remember the distance, Thomas thinks. This is not happening now; it happened months ago. Any distance closer to this distraught and weeping fragment and he, the instruments, the ship itself, would fracture with the star.

Behold the heavens in their majesty.

Father Thomas is alone in this enclosure of wire and darkness, shielded from the flat consequence of devastation, but not, he knows, from its horror, from its force. It is good that he is alone here, that he has been dispatched on this dark and terminal probe without company ("the solitude of a priest is the absence of multitudes" he had suggested, departing), and yet he can feel the awful and enclosing pressure, the *presence* of this destruction as he could never have imagined. The host, the tyranny of the Lord Himself, is not sufficient to protect him from this imminence.

This star, this lost star, has in the high reckoning of the final hour reached the end of all trials. *There is no ascension.*

God's Craft: An Appreciation

Rachel, still almost six, dreams about only one painting, the painting with the thick daubs of blue and white and yellow, the painting that was exploding right there in the museum, and the explosions have awakened her. But she's not scared. Well, maybe a little scared. Ever so quietly, so as not to disturb Mommy and Daddy who are now making thumping noises in their bedroom, she tiptoes to her desk.

Pale moonlight and the absent wash of the streetlamps illuminate

Rachel's sketchpad. She stands before her desk in her fuzzy blue pajamas with the dots and reindeer and flicks through the drawings until she gets to *The Stars Nit*. She knows what "nit" means. She learned about knitting from Miss Catalphason in kindergarten last year, and she understands that is exactly what Mr. Gogh saw God doing to the exploding stars. God was knitting them all together to make a face of fire. She saw the fire in the museum and wondered why she was the only one. She had to stand back from the painting because she could feel the heat and did not want to get burned, but other people didn't notice at all, and a fat woman with a black hat and a big bow in the front even tried to touch it. Her fingers were not burned, so Rachel knew that the fat woman was probably an angel or one of God's helpers.

Rachel stares at her sketch and feels disappointment. It does not really look anything like Mr. Gogh's painting. There's no fire in there, no color, no raised surfaces like little mountains and rivers of fiery paint. Just stupid lines on a stupid page, that's all. There are no church steeples, buildings, big fat stars, or faces of fire in her sketch, and she tries to remember the faces she saw in the painting in the museum, how the exploding stars knit into shifting faces, shifting expressions. So she remembers that and begins to feel funny—a bad feeling in her stomach—and wonders whether she should tell Mommy and Daddy that she might be sick. But, no, they were making their noise, and so she won't disturb them. She will wait and see. Mommy said that when Rachel got sick sometimes it was because she was a genius too, just like Mr. Gogh.

Rachel stands still in front of her desk and raises her gaze to the window. She looks over the sparkling city. Its gauzy lights are exploding too, but not like stars, in the watery air of August. She listens to Mr. Air Conditioner making his gargle noise, remembering the face she saw in the painting. It makes her feel tingly.

I'd better get into bed, Rachel thinks. If she was going to have what Mommy called "her little episode," better to be in bed; but it's too late for that, too late to move, too late to cry out. She gazes into the starry heavens at the face. She knows that face now. Knows that it is not Mr. Gogh, but someone far away, someone burning with God's true fire, someone just like her who is watching the stars explode again and again and again.

Mommy and Daddy are thumping.

The air conditioner sounds like a squirrel.

God is knitting.

And her heart is beating so hard: exploding in the epileptic heat.

Recursion: The Secret Paintings

Winter in Saint-Rémy and Vincent works in a white heat, producing thirty paintings a day in his little studio in the asylum. Most of the rooms in the asylum are empty. Vincent paints inside, in the crackling warmth of the hearth. His brother, Theo, is writing him once a week. Theo is worried that Vincent is hearing voices and hallucinating again, that he is overworking himself, overwhelming his fragile health; but Vincent assures him that the winter light is invigorating and that standing in front of an easel is a better cure than any medicine. He writes Theo that he is copying work by Rembrandt, Delacroix, and Millet, and that this has led him to create smaller versions of his own work, interpretations he calls them; but he gets stuck painting *The Starry Night* over and over, even though he considers it a minor work.

Of course, Theo was right to be worried about him; but it is too late for that. Vincent cannot help himself. He paints over and over the rising, living cypress tree, the church with the elongated steeple, the swirls of stars in a pigment-swathed sky. Interpreting interpretation, that is what it is, warding off the ever-imminent epileptic attack; and he interprets and reinterprets that moment of holy calmness when he had that pure vision of the stars bloating, inflated by some cosmic calamity, and the universe shifting, dying, tearing itself into rebirth

It was then that he had started painting the angels. It had begun as he was applying paint to the exploding sky, and suddenly he had seen a perfect angel transposed above the steeple of the chapel, a wingless angel, a child with cerulean blue eyes and golden plaited hair held with a tortoiseshell comb. She was wrapped in a cobalt blue robe with zinc white edging. This angel could have been one of the *Two Putti* by Andrea del Sarto in the Uffizi in Florence, but then she dissolved, evaporated into the angry, coarse swirls of stars and atmosphere.

Vincent felt an overwhelming sense of loss. Fearful of losing the image, he threw the painting to the floor and grasped another canvas to bring her back to life. The background was the same—exploding stars, swirling stars, bands of stars concatenating in the blue-bleached atmosphere, in the blue night; and she stood before him, looking past him at other heavens, other exploding stars.

The angel stared past him, her eyes as remote as the arching heavens.

"The stars knit," she whispered.

Image of the Host

Priest in a coffin: Thomas hovers at some unimaginable distance from the ruddy Antares Cluster, so threatening even at this great remove. Why is he alone? This has always been for him, for them, for all the other priests in coffins, an imponderable so vast as to approach Crucifixion, or one of those Stations on the way.

The stars are ratcheting, pinwheeling the sky.

Astrophysics has put him in this surveyor starship, but it is faith which is now the truer entrapment, faith which has turned him with whatever longing is possible to the distant, betrayed God behind this fierce canvas. Father Thomas, trapped inside this perished cluster, evokes the specter of a man whom he has not seen in forty years, the senile priest, Carl, who stalked the seminary and muttered, "We will tear down the curtain before God, and we will find his stricken face our own. Our own, our own: no wafer but blindness."

Portent. Mystery. In this recollection Carl is unyielding, grants no forgiveness. "Rip aside the firmament it is decreed and our vanity will show us nothing at all." Dead decades later Thomas is still seeking response, still trying to find a way to renounce the ravings of the mad, useless old man.

Thomas has been a priest in a coffin now for a period of time so attenuated that it is beyond measure. But Carl has provided a measure for his entrapment. The heavens are, in retrograde time, exploding, the stars igniting. Locked into a space so limited that he can barely move, Thomas trembles as his hands tremble on the instruments. The cluster, however distant, however removed in time, surges with fire. Soon, at this insurmountable distance, it will reach with bands of fire to gather him. There is nothing that he can do. There is a fracture across these heavens that will overwhelm him. Thomas quivers in his wretched enclosure. Priest in a coffin. Neither astrophysics nor the force of divine revelation could save him now.

In this enclosure of wire and darkness, shielded by little more than the illusions of distance and his own damaged perception, Father Thomas knows that all is out of his control. Somewhere outside the arc of his vision the great, wounded star is boiling, shedding itself. Plunging toward Calvary. It is surely best that he is alone here, that he has been dispatched on this terrible exploration to hear Carl's admonition. Tear down the curtain of God. He cannot speak for what might have happened otherwise, if someone had been beside him.

Solitary priest in a coffin. Every perceived star is alive with its own extinction, just as on Calvary Christ burned in death fire. In a coffin, witness to this final and deafening light.

Memory of the Garden at Etten

Gazing at the crinkling stars in the gauzy, funny-looking black sky, Rachel stands still as a statue before her window. She knows she is having an episode, but she is not biting her tongue or making echoey noises, at least not yet. Maybe she will not. She's not shaking, not trembling; in fact, it doesn't even seem that she is breathing now, just looking into the swirly sky, looking at the image of the strange man superimposed on the stars and the night. She imagines then that she is up there with him, scrunched into the seat of something like a car except that through the big window she sees not a road but stars and lightning.

She and the man are drifting in space, drifting in the stars nits themselves.

Rachel may be having one of her episodes, but she is still sensitive to everything that is going on around her. As if from a great distance she can hear Mommy and Daddy *still* making noise in the bedroom. Once she had run in there to stop them, to stop Daddy from hurting Mommy, but Mommy said that it was all right, that they were playing; and Rachel decided then and there that she never wanted to play that way. After a few minutes Mommy stops screaming and breathing. Everything stops. Rachel concentrates on the man in the car in the sky. She can see him dimly; he is sitting beside her. He is dressed in black like a priest.

He *is* a priest.

She is still in her funny pajamas.

Being in space is nice, she thinks, just like those cartoons on television where the characters bounce and dance in the sky, and she is moving too. But her moving is only part of being a little sick and having an episode. Rachel knows there is no reason to be frightened. Soon she will be back in her own bed with Mommy and Daddy nearby, and she will once again look at all of the sketches that she has copied at the museum. They are good sketches, whatever she might have felt before. That is why they bought her the sketchbook, because she is good.

The man sitting in the space car is old, older than Daddy, and for a moment he does not see her, so intent is he upon staring through the big window. But then he turns to her suddenly and says: "Do I see what I think I see? But how can this be? From where did you come, child?"

"My name is Rachel," she says. "I drew the stars nit."

"Look at that," he says. "Look out the window." And Rachel follows his finger. There are the stars nits themselves. They look just like the painting.

The stars are exploding, and she wishes that she had brought her sketchpad so that she could show it to the man. She feels strange here, like she always feels when she's having an episode; but when she looks at her hands, she sees that they are glowing. Her pajamas look funny too, as if light is pouring through the fabric from underneath. She shakes her head. She cannot remember glowing before, not even when everybody thought she was going to die that time in the hospital.

"For an old priest in a coffin to see *this*," the man said. "To witness the death of everything, the death of time. But why have they sent you?"

"Nobody sent me," Rachel says. "I came myself. I can make myself go places; sometimes I can be anywhere I want. I can draw the stars nits and even be in them. Is that what you want?"

Rachel knows she is sick now. The sickness has come over her. She could bite her tongue or hit herself or bang her head on the desk, but there is nothing to be done about it. She's here with the priest in the space car. If she only had her sketchpad, she could show him what she had done; but that is not to be.

"Oh, yes, child," the man says. "I know you can because you are here." He reaches out to her, and there is no room for her to move; he touches her, then hovers close. "Transubstantiation," he says. "It is the most remarkable thing." She feels him shaking, even though they are not touching. "What have I believed?" he says. "For what have I been given this?"

"What is transub—? I don't understand." For the first time she is a little scared. She wishes that she were in her room, not in this space car with the stars glowing and exploding like the stars in Mr. Gogh's painting.

"I'll go back and find my drawing," she says. "Do you want to see my drawing of this?" She waves her hand, leaving trails of light, points to the outside. Yes, that is what is happening outside. It is just like the painting. The stars nit.

"You can draw *this*, child?"

"Oh yes," Rachel says. "I have it at home. I tried to make it just like this. The stars are exploding. They look like little puffs of fire. If I had my sketchpad I could show you."

"Transubstantiation," the man says again; the word is very long: *trans-sub-stanch –ee-ation*. "That I would live to see this. To see this and all that it was."

Rachel thinks very hard. If she thinks hard enough, she knows that she will be able to leave this place; but maybe not; she is not sure ... she is not sure of anything. She is truly scared now. The stars are leaping like wild animals. There is a big star ringed in white fire that is getting larger, moving closer.

The space car is shaking.

"I want to go home," Rachel cries. "I want to go home right now."

In Arles

Vincent had known even at this tranquil time that it would end in the asylum, in holy entrapment, in the midst of fires he could not see. Torn aside, that curtain of the heavens. But it was too late, too late for anything now but to transcribe what he saw so that they would know, so that he would know how the fire would come.

In his sleep a small solemn angel holding a sketchpad drifts through his perception, but he is unable to reach her …

unable to touch her.

FAULKNER'S SEESAW

By Jack Dann and Barry N. Malzberg

FIRST PASSAGE:

Faulkner lost seven figures at the track and casino, seven more in offshore drilling and disastrous investments in cloning, cochlear implants, and infrastructure trusts, smaller change in the Berkeley Insurance fiasco and for good measure a hundred thousand on women who rolled over after intercourse with expressions of distaste or boredom, which even a megalomaniac like Faulkner could not entirely dismiss. All of this was dismaying, even humiliating; but Faulkner refused to take it seriously. He had been well invested, well-married several times, ironically capitalized; "secure" in this atomized world of destroyed consensus ... if anyone could be secure. Reverses, yes, but he could not have lost it all. In twisted dreams the women tossed dice, shook themselves like poodles after a swim, cackled, swept little ceramic Faulkners off the table into spittoons, and departed with dazzling speed. But he knew that all of this was transitional. It was a transitional time, a chaotic age, Faulkner knew the answer to chaos: further disorder until the pattern broke.

Faulkner knew all the answers.

After three ruinous investigations by the Securities and Exchange Commission had driven him into a disastrous settlement, after eight months in detention for his mandated plea to directorial fraud, after thirty-three corporations slid into liquidation, after the last woman before imprisonment had evanesced from his bed with a pitying, uninterested sigh, John Cadmus Faulkner, then thirty-seven, but looking much older, retired to his isolated quarters on Lake Consequence (which had a difficult, unpronounceable native name, but "Consequence" would do for the nonce) to recuperate and reorganize. He had been bankrupted; he had amassed fortunes. Now in temporary imbalance, it was time to make yet another comeback. Faulkner believed profoundly in comebacks: in an age of chaos and dissimulation the only permanence was to be found in the mutable.

Faulkner was barred from company organization for five years. He had also been disbarred. (No matter: he had never practiced law.) He was one fortune shy of having a fortune. Matters were desperate.

Matters were not desperate ...

Faulkner used an arcane provision in the law governing franchises to start five elder care corporations, with which he had no legal association. In the world according to Faulkner, dementia was rampant and medicine had conspired with public health policies to produce a riot of organically healthy, intellectually cleansed seniors.

Faulkner looked upon seniors as product.

And product would trump possibility every time.

SECOND PASSAGE:

Faulkner couldn't lose.

Oh yes he could ...

He lost big. In Prague, in Brooklyn, in Helsinki. And Paris.

In Paris an unbalanced, furious, hallucinative Faulkner pushed his way onto the dais of an annual meeting of shareholders and shouted, "Faith will take us to Athens, to grace, to the stars themselves. We will insert ourselves into the burning firmament; we will be filaments of the burning firmament, forsooth." He could feel the Almighty in his very words. Forsooth—that was a good touch.

Faulkner went on to tell the astonished (but no longer bored or sleepy) shareholders of the intellectually bankrupt senior citizenry now under his command. Before he fully launched into a most perfect diatribe, however, he was evicted from the dais by three uniformed security men and thrown out of the hall.

"This is no country for old men," security told him, wagging gloved fingers. "This is the country of desire."

Evicted, humiliated, Faulkner commandeered one of his newly purchased corporate Lear jets and arced across the hemispheres, from the province of Saskatchewan, to Pingdingshan in China, to the rainforests of Bolivia. Time and distance became congealed; all the world was a series of narrow, conterminous compartments. Travel was cheap (the corporation paid), talk was cheaper. "I do not accept this!" he shouted in execrable Spanish to his crew on a flight to Lima, Peru. "They cannot do this to me, my cojones, my ropa. I am in command of the common language."

His personnel tolerated his behavior fluctuations on the plane, but at the airport a reeling, ranting Faulkner was immediately taken away by an army of guards after he attacked a government official whom he accused of being a pickpocket, cutpurse, and purloiner. Faulker bribed the guards, who then tossed him into a Peruvian alley and left him to babble in his execrable Spanish and disjointed English to a citizenry that found both versions of his pleadings incomprehensible.

"I am a man of enormous potential," the desperate Faulkner insisted. "It is a potential which can overwhelm, which can overtake all circumstance." His jacket and trousers were torn and spotted with grease and street excrement; his gait, impelled by his tragic sense of loss and humiliation, spastic and infantile. Finally a kindly, overweight Peruvian policeman took pity upon his exhibition and transported him to the local jail. After another bribe (it was a wonder they left him his wallet), he was deported without hearing. Circumstance by now had become a series of hallucinatory events for Faulkner; hypnagogic dread filled the dwindled space of his consciousness. Yet still he felt impelled, even at this time of disgrace, by a wild, unreasonable optimism. He was, after all, a figure central to his time, a true icon. A personage. A paradigm. An illustration.

"Got a burning in me, misters," Faulkner intoned on his wild flight, two miles of dead air beneath him, his crew, beautiful, rouged stewardesses all, huddled in retreat. "Got a burning which will not slake."

Imagining himself as a negro spiritual, he emerged from this and a similar riot of obscurely tangled thoughts, impressions, and events in Paris. But he was energized by the lilting and susurrous sounds of Parisian gutter French—which he understood no better than Spanish, but whose syllables he found softer and less threatening—to make another announcement. "I am reconstituted, je suis reconstituted," Faulkner bellowed as he galloped to the top of the Eiffel Tower from which perilous suspension he gazed upon the sprawl of Paris with great approval. In his hallucinogenic haze, Faulkner imagined crowds gathering below to hear him. Fascinated by the texture and variegation of this Cezanne landscape, a hint of Maigret at the corners, Matisse at the edges, Matisse and Maigret conjoined as they were always meant to be, Faulkner felt his powers returning.

"My strength returns," he shouted. "I am myself reconstituted! I am my own arc of flaming, coruscating, illuminating desire." Only then did he descend in stately fashion from the Tower, finding an excellent omen: a twenty franc note on the Champs-Elysees, clearly a signal that his luck had turned. He carried it reverently to the South, to the Casinos. By nightfall, through elegant use of his sudden, God-given linguistic powers, hypnagogic flashes, thunderous belches of adumbration, Faulkner had parlayed this into two million francs, certainly enough to finance several more elder centers. He could feel his powers returning, a sense of expansion. Secure in this foreknowledge, he flew as a God in a Lear Jet to Rome, where he exchanged his two million francs for lira at the Leonardo da Vinci airport. After a night of drinking and joyous abandon with a highly placed monsignor—and with the further enhancement of a bribe—he obtained a brief but private audience with the Pope. In a room of velvet and gold and high vaulted ceilings, he whispered to the Pope of his troubles, of his plans, of his imminent recovery, and of the tendrils of doubt which still clawed away at him.

"Ah," said the recently elected Pope, who seemed small, almost childlike in his robes, which looked as if he they were purposely made large so he could grow into them; this pope who was gorging on big plans of his own said, "You must persist. You must definitely persist. You have something of the nominal in you, something of our Lord's terrible, unbearable glory in you, Faulkner. I can see it in your eyes. They are your gateways to your soul. I can see into you, Faulkner, deeply into you. I insist that you go on exactly as you have. You must complete your journey toward epiphany," and this inheritor of the Throne of St. Peter then bestowed upon Faulkner a curt but passionate blessing and, rejoined by his advisors, made hasty exit, leaving Faulkner to ponder the gilded reception room and the less secular aspects of his Reconstitution.

And surely this Reconstitution was at hand. Glowing with that knowledge, with that enormous sense of purchase which seemed to inflate him to proportions beyond those he had ever known, Faulkner wandered the winding back streets of Rome, scattering crumbs and accolades to the pigeons, to the pilgrims, to the camera-wielding tourists, knowing that the Pope was presciently correct: Faulkner was truly on the verge of an enormous epiphany. "Glory and burning, watch them combine into the Last Days," he cried; but even as he felt the beginning of that grouping within, Faulkner was seized yet again, this time by Italian constables who plucked him from the streets and carried him at a scurry to a jail rumored to be on the very site of Nero's hilarious copulations some millennia earlier.

Nero had had big plans as well, and if they had come to Faulknerian disaster, well he had had a good time on the way and Faulkner could ask no less of himself. Consumed by Nero's ghost (and the blandishments of Nero's concubines) which seemed curled within the walls of the prison, Faulkner refused food, refused conversation of any kind and plotted his next excursion.

Life was imminence, he decided. "Do you hear me?" he asked unseen jailers, "Possibility is all we have! I grant you our coming hither even as you granted me my coming hence." He seemed poised at that point where extreme luck, overtaken by utter devastation, becomes its very opposite; that point at which utter devastation is subsumed by luck, the two nothing other than mutual refraction. Luck and disaster all the same.

One or the other ...?

Faulkner knew that he could/would have both.

In that knowledge he felt the glowing density of imminence, felt himself in thrall to possibility. And ripeness being all, it immediately became nothing.

THIRD PASSAGE:

Here is Faulkner then at the moment of decision (not, unfortunately, his decision; this was an Age of Chaos). In jail, out of jail, fortune-flushed or devastated, surrounded by a gallery of uninterested or mockingly hostile women, Faulkner perceived that time was indeed a river, a river of brackish water flowing wildly through him, only to be diverted by his being.

What would happen to him? Was there an answer or was it all synchronicity?

We are not sure. And we must leave Faulkner. We have no alternative; we must depart, we, the observers, are one of the fortunes we have lost. In one alternative Faulkner remains in jail, is crushed by implacability and inanition; in another, he flees the jail in a magnificent burst of cunning and finds himself suspended at a great height over Rome like one of Fellini's figures, looking upon the multitudes, knowing that he has become their icon. In the leaving we must remain in a condition of uncertainty. There is this about an Age of Chaos: it replicates only as chaos. Here is Faulkner soaring over Rome, here is Faulkner collapsed against a wall of loss at the casino, here is an indigent Faulkner pleading for the recognition of a cocktail waitress, here is an ascendant Faulkner braving the contempt of that waitress as she rises over him like an enormous suspended icon. In chaos all is complicit, all is synchronous; and this is the last, perhaps the only lesson, which this wretched century has for us:

If anything can happen it will.

APPROACHING SIXTY

by Mike Resnick and Barry N. Malzberg

"Kabbalah" is a word I can barely pronounce, let alone spell, something like the name "Artismo," which was the appellation of a fancy allowance horse more years ago than I would like to think, or "Secretariat," which was a great horse but had the letter *a* where the *e* should be or vice-versa.

This book containing the Kabbalah is one composed of signs and wonders, mysteries and omens, as my brother-in-law Jake tells me when he hands it to me at a family dinner. This is just as the losing streak approaches sixty, which probably qualifies for the *Guinness Book of World Records.*

At thirty I gave up the *Form* and the *Telegraph* and went to the *Green Sheet*. At forty I started phoning Creepy Conrad and giving him my credit card number in exchange for what he promised was surefire information. At fifty, I even went to *shul* and nagged Jehovah a bit. But as I approached sixty, I was out of alternatives and ready to grasp at anything.

"It could be called an apostasy, Demetrius," says Jake, who spent seven months studying to be a rabbi, before they threw him out when they found him in bed with not one but two blond shiksa bimbos, "to offer you a book of instruction in Kabbalah for a mere losing streak. But I can see that your distress has gone beyond the obvious to the malignant. Following the sport of kings is a dangerous profession and I intuit that you are weak with need." Probably he also intuits it from the two thousand bucks I owe him and can't pay.

There is nothing for me to say in response to this. I could berate Jake for his condescension (but not until I pay him the two large). I could object to his patronizing, to the fact that he has always treated my presence in the family as something of an embarrassment and that he considers my profession with the horses as a disgrace (at least during losing seasons).

But I can also understand that in many ways I have caused Jake and Nate at least as much concern and trouble as they have caused me. So I take the book, a rather limp number, from his extended hand and say, "I am always grateful for advice, Jake, even though I can make no commitment."

"You listen to me," he says, a long-lost rabbinical fervor seeming to crease his features. "You're not supposed to even study this unless you are a man and you are over forty. Women and immature males are excluded. Children are excluded. This is considered too dangerous for a younger man, one whose flames have not been properly coaxed and controlled."

"I am over forty," I reply. "I am in fact forty-nine years of age, as well you know, since I've been part of this family for more than twenty years. My flames are coaxed and controlled"—his sister the yenta can testify to this, and often does, whenever she can find an audience. "In fact, at this moment my flames are in need of spontaneous fuel. Have you ever lost fifty-nine of *anything* in a row? Can you even imagine how this feels?"

It is odd that I make the remarks at that time in that way, because the book itself, this mysterious Kabbalah text which Jake has handed me, seemed to be emitting a strange warmth of its own, an uncomfortable heat that passed from the binding into my hand the way that a rein can slip into the hand of a jockey.

"Do I understand consequence?" replies Jake, and I can tell he's gearing up for a long-distance oratory. "My entire life is consequence. So is yours. So is everyone's, as the Kabbalah makes clear. We are the creations and extensions of a celestial order we can barely understand."

There is much more of this, Jake the accountant often returning to his rabbinical roots when properly encouraged (or even discouraged), but I will pass on the remainder of that conversation, and also on the remonstrations of my wife, Sylvia, and my other brother-in-law, Nate, the nearsighted and color-blind custom tailor, who are both highly displeased when they obtain knowledge of what Jake has placed in my hands.

Sylvia of course has lived with low and high disgust for many decades and has learned resignation, but Nate is blunter and more direct. "Give that back to me," he said, spying the book in my hand and instantly deducing the reasons for its presence.

"It's *my* Kabbalah!" I say. "Go get your own!"

"You're such a *meshuggener pisher* you think the Kabbalah's a book, like the Bible or something by Abba Eban. It's the *knowledge*, the mystic system within those pages."

"The book, the knowledge, it's all the same," I say. "It's a system, like betting claimers who are moving down in class, or doubling up on front runners when the track comes up muddy."

"Jake again!" mutters Nate. "What does he think he's doing? Give it back at once!"

"Stay calm, Nate," says Jake, overhearing the conversation.

"Demetrius is in need of aid at the present time and this may be a way of bringing him back to the fold."

"Didn't you hear him?" screams Nate. "He thinks it's God's betting system! You are as crazy as you were when you tried to crawl into the ark during Yom Kippur fifteen years ago!"

Well, it goes on like this for hours, but I do not return the Kabbalah, and eventually Nate and Jake decide they have fulfilled today's quota of acrimony and they go home to their wives, and I will now engage in what the Kabbalah text—which I look at briefly in the late evening before putting it to the other side of the bed—calls a necessary pause, an important transition, and point to subsequent events at Aqueduct Race Track in South Ozone Park in the borough of Queens, New York, which followed from my acquaintance with the Kabbalah as the night does the day.

As one of only two or three thousand people in this era of off-track betting who still attends Aqueduct on a regular basis, actually entering the premises, I carry my burden of being exceptional with fair grace and no little trepidation. Fifty-nine consecutive losses will not induce the humility which already comes front being one of only two or three thousand.

Book in hand, eighteen hours after my conversation with Jake, I am standing by the rail watching the horses, nonwinners of two, stagger onto the track. I consult the book denied flaming men and all women and use it to induce a psychic moment.

I pour over the words. I try to make sense of the commands. I attempt to order the mathematics.

And then, suddenly, a very clear voice within my head says: *Five.*

I look around. "Who said that?"

But there is no one near me.

I look at the tote board in the infield and rub the book for good luck.

Five.

The number 5 horse is 17-to-1. I borrow a *Form*. His name is Quanto La Gusta, and he has lost fourteen in a row since winning a claimer at Finger Lakes, which hosts such poor horses that you could throw a saddle on Jake and *he* could come in third if the track wasn't too muddy.

I reach into my pocket. I've got $1,650 left, all the money I have in the world. When I lose this, my profession is done, and I will either have to get an honest job or go to Big-Hearted Ernie, who charges 20 percent interest per day. I look at the board again. The number 5 horse is up to 22-to-1.

"You're sure?" I whisper to no one in particular.

Five, says the voice with the confidence of one who has never lost fifty-nine in a row,

The horses are coming onto the track, and I decide I can wait no longer. I leave the rail, make my way through the crowd, and stand in line at the $50 window. And as I do so, I look at the parallel line to the next $50 window, and I see a Hassidic Jew standing right opposite me, wearing his signature black *shtrieml* a round fur-trimmed hat decorated with a feather. He is humbly reading a Kabbalah text, and he is wearing the humblest $900 black alpaca coat I have ever seen, and there is an incredible shine on his humble $300 shoes, and I realize that I have been wandering in a fool's paradise, that the true answer was here all along. I want to tell him to hide the text, that we don't want anyone else figuring out how to get a direct line to God, because if even half a dozen big plungers learn the secret, Quanto La Gusta could go down to 4-to-1 by the time they reach the gate.

I avert my eyes, because I don't want anyone to see me staring at the book and wondering what I am staring at, and I whistle to myself and gaze alternately at the ceiling and my feet until I am finally first in line.

"What do you want?" says the clerk at the window.

"I want number 5, thirty-three times," I say.

He looks at me like I'm crazy.

"You're sure?"

"Thirty-three tickets on Number 5, right," I say.

He shrugs and punches a button and out pop the tickets. I share a secret winner's smile with the Hassidic Jew, and then I go back to my spot at the rail, right by the sixteenth pole, and wait.

"The horses are at the post!" announces Marshall Cassidy over the public address system, trying to put a little excitement into his voice even though this is just a nothing race for nonwinners of two, and two thousand pairs of binoculars are lifted into position.

"And they're off!" yells Cassidy.

Quanto La Gusta breaks in the middle of the pack, but Jose Santos quickly hustles him up to the front, and as they hit the far turn with half a mile to go he's seven lengths ahead of the field, and I am cursing myself for not finding this remarkable book ten years sooner.

By the head of the stretch he's ten lengths in front, and I can see that he's not even breathing hard—and then, as quickly as he opened up on the field, he begins to shorten stride, and his lead goes from ten lengths to six to three to one to nothing in less than a furlong. As they pass me, with a sixteenth of a mile to run, he's already eighth, and by the time they hit the finish line he is eleventh, and the only horse he has beaten is one that broke down on the backstretch.

I stare dumbfounded at Quanto La Gusta as he trots back on his way to the barn, and I cannot believe it. God *told* me he couldn't lose.

I decide to ask the old Hassidic Jew what went wrong, but he is nowhere to be seen. Finally, on a hunch, I go to the cashier's window. Sure enough, the old man is walking away with a wad of hundreds that would choke Quanto La Gusta.

I walk up to him.

"Excuse me," I say, "but I notice you use the Kabbalah text ..."

"Yes, I use a Kabbalah text," he answers with a twinkle in his eye.

"And you just won?"

"*Baruch Hashem!*" he says happily. Praise the Lord.

"Did He whisper a number to you?"

"That's how it works," says the old Jew. "He whispered *seven*, plain as day."

I frown. "You're *sure?*"

He smiles and holds up his bankroll.

"I don't understand it," I say. "I used the book, and He told me to bet the number 5 horse."

The old man extends his hand toward my book.

"May I?"

I hand it over to him.

"Well," he says, still smiling. "That explains it."

"Explains what?" I demand.

"I use the *Sefer Yetzirah*, the Book of Creation," he explains. *This*," he adds, handing the book back to me and trying unsuccessfully to hide his amusement, "is the *Sefer ha Mafli*, the Book That Astounds."

"There's a difference?" I ask.

"The *Sefer ha Zohar* is the Kabbalah for trotters."

He is still chuckling to himself while I try to remember Big-Hearted Ernie's phone number.

The Art of Memory

by Jack Dann and Barry N. Malzberg

The car, a 1958 DeSoto, last of its line, spins out, and hits the guardrail with terrific impact. Even before my head has gone through the windshield, I know that it is over. Done.

"And in that night I awoke to find myself in a dark and deserted place ..."

That is Dante. Algieri the name. As I lay dead in the wastes of the car, arms broken to fit, the smell of blood a miasma in the air, my head aching, pounding I think: How could this be? My heart is unmoving within me. From the carcass of the car faint thuds and hissings, the sounds of re-accomodation. I think of the *Divine Comedy*, nothing so divine about it, and of Dante, who was as much the fool as I had been. Dante had met his precious, prescient Beatrice when he was nine; by the time he turned eighteen she had spurned him, left him bereft of that "Which was the goal of all desire," and then in 1290 had insulted him even more greatly by expiring.

Expiration.

Bereft, bereaved Dante. Bereaved me. I am done for.

"And in that black night I awoke to find myself in a dark and deserted place ..."

Who will mourn me? Who do I leave bereaved?

My wife Janice will be so. She won't know where the checkbook is. She won't know the passwords to get into the laptop files. I tried to tell her ... Lord knows how I tried.

It comes to me that this rictus planted on my face would look like a smile to any witness. There is much about which to smile. Death is not only absolute, it is painless and here I am, a pain-free fifty-seven year old pisher advertising executive newly dead. Ten minutes ago, well no. But now? Now, in the steam and huddle of the wrenched DeSoto I can face everything. Death is the great compressor, squeezing circumstance to manageability and compressed, I can feel my essence, congealing around the ruined heart.

So I look around, considering it all. If I could breathe, I would have thought, "Breathing everything in." Can I smell? Indeterminate. I can remember smells. Memory without passion, without pain, is perhaps a sort of omniscience. One becomes little more than a witness to one's life and everything, then, is changed.

I peer from side to side, trying to understand the situation. If I could breathe I would have retained control, but I do not appear to be breathing.

A white and yellow ambulance with a hairline crack in the rear window roars along the highway, no siren, gumdrop red light rotating. The highway has been closed. Traffic is being redirected. In and out of their cars people are yammering on cell-phones. But I'm right here, still here, a presence, a part of the ghostly landscape rising from the blood spot on the highway, about four inches from the median. I'm here and I'm there as they strap me on a gurney and take me to the ambulance. In the ambulance I'm just an anonymous corpse. But here I am—

—I am standing.

I'm standing and dressed as if my Anderson & Shepard double-breasted suit, Holl shirt, green silk tie and Ramon Tores ostrich-skin loafers have become part of me: loose flags of tattooed flesh. The DeSoto—an antique bought for too much a few years ago out of a misguided humor—is a crushed accordion; but then, even as I assess this, it becomes in a flicker exactly what it was before the accident: well-restored, cleaned, and serviced. I wedge my way in there. The door clangs on me. I always thought of this DeSoto as a refuge, which I could take anywhere and be free, a refuge against my life itself; but the difficulty is that I was wholly deluded, I could never have been free in this car, any more than I could have been free anywhere. More than physical reconstitution is being managed here.

I had exited through the side window, I remember, and been impaled on a sheer metal rail torn from the frame. Somehow being crucified had felt, still feels, right and just. As we were in life, so we are in death. Not that in being crucified I had any great heights from which to fall.

But here I start the engine and I drive away. There is no one to stop me or even notice.

Life—or rather death—is filled with possibility and in fact promise. Indeed, perhaps I am alive after all. Maybe this is merely a concussion. Perhaps I am being given another chance or simply misunderstood the situation. I feel a surge of gratitude to whatever source has accomplished this, although I do not believe in the existence of a higher, controlling intelligence. I do not in fact believe anything except the sound of the big engine throbbing, the soft clatter of radial tires, the soughing of wind flowing wretchedly, and the ubiquitous, infinitely gray LA freeway extending forever, sprawling, launching me.

Home, I think, go home. Take me home, you poor dumb, dead Dante. Go home to your own Beatrice. Go home to Janice and fuck your brains out.

I had not realized that dying would make me so horny. My erection presses against the tautness, this post-traumatic erection warm and pulsing. Take me home, I think.

It shouldn't be long because there isn't another car going either way on the six-lane highway. There is just grayness, the median strip and the DeSoto.

And, of course, me.

Horny as hell and dead as road-kill.

Trees blur, the highway blurs, all passage blurs, but in the car death makes all these spaces warm and safe. I am not so much driving as being driven, and outside the barren highway has become a vast tent pitched over desire. I think of Janice, of all I had wanted to say and would have if I had known where the DeSoto would bring me that morning ... but it is not so much the saying as the doing which overtakes. I want to screw her, enter her very heart, create an erection so enormous that it will touch and dangerously displace her heart. An erection so enormous—impelled by death, by that hangman's noose draped now upon me—that it will reach to her center. Small puffs of cartoon steam seem to purr from my groin, the little abscess of the car fills with steam, and I think of Janice lying against me, of the sounds which I helped her make.

Oh, it was all such a long time ago.

Suspended, then, hanging in that space, the soundless gel of the car dense and swaddling, I find at the center of my new purpose raw necessity and past that an agenda. I have plans. I have clearly defined plans, even for a dead man. Never in fact have I had so many plans as those which now assault me at this moment: a little schedule of accommodation that will be met, places to be revisited, contacts to be made, but all of that only after Janice, after the screwing. Death congeals into a helpful arrangement of priorities.

Lights prowl the highway; I seem to have been overtaken by light, and I think of myself again as a figure in a cartoon, steam from the pants, lights through the window, hurt in the head. At the end of this journey Janice and with her the commencement of true and meaningful plans, which will then vault me past all this and into a newer life (or colder death) more certain than any I have ever known.

In that suspensory place, fixed on anticipation, but placed now only in that deadly quiet, it is as if my father appears in the car, seated beside me, legs casually crossed, eyes staring madly through the windshield. His hands flutter with what surely must be the effort of travel.

He is pretty much, the old man, as I remember him on his deathbed twenty years ago, although certainly in a more advanced state of composition. Still, for a corpse, he looks terrific. He has retained most of his hair, and the mad light in his eyes shows an uncharacteristic enthusiasm. He was always distracted. He always had places to go. He was always half out of the room even when he was in the room. "How are you doing?" he would ask, and his lips would move, and he would stare at his watch, at the door. "Well, that's very good," he would say. "We must discuss this later."

But now he seems more sedentary, fixated in a way he never was before. "It isn't going to work," he says, "I know exactly what you're planning, but it can't happen. There's a catch to the whole business. I mean, you can come back, but you can't come, if you follow what I'm saying here." He coughs, shrugs his shoulders and stares out the side window. "There isn't enough speed to save. Believe me, I have been here for almost twenty years now, and I haven't been able to change a thing. Not in me, not in the situation."

"So what do you want?" I ask. Our first conversation in almost two decades. "Why are you here? If there isn't enough speed to save, why did you come back?"

"I didn't come back," he says. "You call this coming back? I'm just filling in the time. Dead is dead, a big hammer on the head. Then you just try to amuse yourself."

"A hammer? Whose hammer?"

"I told you not to marry that woman, didn't I? She's too cold for you, always complaining. I know the type. Saw it early."

"It didn't seem that way at the start," I say.

Die in a highway crash, get resurrected to live a partial after life and what do you find? You find your father beside you, questioning your judgment as if forty years had not passed.

"Dad," I say, "You live your life the best you can. It's not for anyone to judge."

"You've judged me every moment of your existence. You never let it go, never." He shakes his head, shakes his hands and peers out the window, squinting. "Sons of bitches. They promised fifteen minutes and now I have to go back after five? Well, what the hell is the difference? I couldn't ever tell you anything anyway."

"I listened to everything you had to say."

"And laughed at it," he says, distracted. "I told you about that woman. I could have saved you most of it. Also if you weren't driving antique junk, and if you had checked your brake fluid level, which I remind you should be part of your ordinary life, you would have had enough torque to spin out of it instead of driving right into that bus. But no matter," my father says, "No matter, you were ready to end it all anyway."

And he dematerializes.

Gone, the father! He has disappeared as quickly and mysteriously as he had arrived, and through the windshield I can see the familiar dead-white strip malls that form the gateway to my neighborhood. Surely at this moment Janice is also there, waiting, beginning to worry, some faint sliver of warning neutralizing her restlessness and contempt, bringing her alert to the inference that this is not an ordinary evening. I think of her anger, throbbing at the margins and wonder if my lustful dead thoughts are simply part of the common apparatus of death itself.

Into the drive, off the engine, trudge from the DeSoto, and I enter the blue glazed front door of our Greek revival home on Antioch Avenue … perfect Antioch Avenue with its huge lawns and blue-glaze swimming pools and just underneath the trembling reach of the unspeakable. The unspeakable here or there, it is one Earth, isn't it?

"I'm home," I say coming through the door, and Janice steps from the study that aligns the dining room and blinks at me.

"Oh," she says. "You're here after all. I was worrying, I didn't know—"

"Didn't know what?" I say. "What didn't you know?" She is flawless, staring back at me: white, white and gold, all of this streaming from her; and I notice that she's wearing the heart-link ankle bracelet I had given her when we were engaged, and that she is barefoot.

"Pregnant and barefoot," I mumble, grinning. Death has seemingly energized me at this moment: I feel free and light and young—yes, light as in weightless, but I can perceive the numinous light around me, the world itself glowing.

It occurs to me that this must after all be heaven and that Janice—the best version of her I have seen in years—must be a wingless big-breasted cherub. An Angel.

"I'm not pregnant, Nathan." But she stands stock-still, thinking. "Although I suppose I could get pregnant here. I don't know that it has ever happened, but there's always a first time." She giggles.

"What didn't you know?" I ask again, determined.

"That you were dead," she says matter-of-factly, as if I died every day. "You don't look dead, not really."

"Neither do you."

She smiles, that perfect, placid, oceanic smile that I first fell in love with when she appeared in a shaft of light at a Sunday afternoon cocktail party. "Oh, I'm very dead, my darling. You'll learn."

"What will I learn?"

"That being dead is alive." Another smile and she steps toward me, arms extended. I respond reflexively. I can smell her perfume;

surprisingly, I can feel her, and then suddenly I am standing alone as if not I but she had just dreamed that moment and torn the dream away. She is standing before me, looking sadly at me, as if … as if I'd died.

"You're not very substantial," she says.

"Well, you look pretty substantial to me," I say, and I move toward her then, put my arms around her, and I feel a slight vibration in the touch of her skin, at the touch of her dress—but it is a memory. I am not so much touching then as recollecting touch. I don't so much feel as stumble toward some recollection of that; and I inhale, trying to breathe in her scent, her perfume.

But there is only emptiness. Remembering how she smells, I cannot quite move past that thin perception. Stripped of erection and desire, I am flooded by memory alone.

She pulls away from me, pity in her eyes. "You're not quite dead," she says, "Are you?"

Well, yes, I am. So it would seem. Senselessly, numbingly, flaccidly dead. Nothing there but doomed assertion, dead in the exposed light.

There is nothing to say. I turn and leave the house. "Where are you going?" she asks, "Do you really think that this is the answer?" Her voice is bright, tinkles like that of a hostess. A tour guide for the underworld.

There is no answer, I think, but I do not say this.

Now there are some who might say that it is humiliating to be sexually rejected by one's own wife, particularly if one is dead and represents, then, no threat—but, on the other hand, being not quite dead can have a depressing effect upon congress. Janice's position, tilted that way, is certainly justifiable; conjunction would be a spooky position. Also the news that I am not quite dead has apparently become common knowledge. So Janice would, however unfairly, be viewed as some sort of variation of a necrophile. There is no possibility that she could in the aftermath pretend she thought I was completely dead. "How could I be expected to know the difference?" just isn't a valid excuse.

Little puffs of dust and steam encircle my shoes as I trudge to the DeSoto in which I died (or half-died), knowing that once again I am justifying Janice, granting her excuse for the inexcusable.

There is, after all, the matter of commitment. Death would not buy her out of marital obligation any more than it would buy her out of claiming the Estate. This thought, in its ugly practicality, impels me ever more rapidly; but I find as I near the DeSoto that it is not quite in the abandoned state of its desertion. It is, instead, encircled by a crowd, some of them strangers, others dimly remembered, college classmates or colleagues, a quick and scattered roster of my career. They stare at me bleakly, gesture, whisper to one another of my presence. More strangeness this as I raise a hand. "Are you living or dead?" I ask. "Where is this happening?"

No reply. They do hear me, it would seem. My father comes up from the rear, puts a confidential, paternal arm around my neck and shoulders and guides me to the car. "You might as well get out of here," he says. "There's nothing more for you in these places."

"Why? How do you know that?"

"Because I'm your father, obviously. Because before you were here I had checked out the situation. Believe me, I know this territory better than you. It's a stinker."

"So what does that make you?"

"It makes me exactly what you always took me to be ... that man you could never understand. You're not going to understand it here either. You know why? Because death doesn't make you any wiser. It may give you the last word, but you're still no smarter. Am I right?" He gestures to the crowd. "Tell him I'm right. He never listened to me."

They look at him without interest. Someone in the middle—it must be fat Jack my first mentor who taught me every expense-account trick I know—makes a derisive sound. "You tell him," Fat Jack says. "You keep him on the straight."

"I knew that man," I say. "That man taught me everything I know, and everything I know is wrong."

"Don't change the subject," my father says. "Face the bench, kid, they're going to pronounce the sentence."

"You changed the subject all my damned life," I say, pushing him aside and yanking open the car door. Cushions ooze toward me like blood as I move behind the wheel. I have absolutely no idea where I am going or what I might think this means. "You never settled on anything; you were never home."

"Well, then, you studied me well. The same applies, son. For one thing, you can't even decide if you're dead."

It is a strange thing to consider at this moment but never, I think, have we communicated quite so well. Death seems to bring a higher state of alertness, although it is no good for sex. "Fat Jack and advertising ruined your brains, son," my old man says. "They turned you into a louse."

Fat Jack had forced me to the 1958 DeSoto. Working the campaigns for an auto manufacturer, I had come to understand that the engineers had surrendered to the stylists, the cars—which Fat Jack taught me to insidiously undersell, no campaign makes explicit promises when the unsaid could be anything—had profound defects. Steering wasn't balanced properly for front wheel drive and overcompensating drivers would receive their final reward by being hurled through a guardrail or off a mountain. I'd better drive something old and heavy, I thought. If we're lying like this then all of them are lying, and then all of these new cars are killers.

The scandal had been building in my last weeks there; someone had turned over internal memos to the Government.

But it was I in the 1958 DeSoto who went hurtling first …

Well, this time I will be more cautious. Assume nothing, protect everything. Cautiously engaging the ignition, dropping the car into gear, I call from memory all of my considerable driving skills, all of the weight and simultaneity of memory.

The gathered crowd salutes me with curses as I move the car, my own gestures beseeching them to move, fade to inconsequence as I turn cautiously toward the highway entrance a hundred yards from my house. Auburn City-link Highway, one of the great conveniences, although the heat and dust of near traffic on summer weekends was occasionally unbearable. Behind me, like memory itself, the house; ahead of me the highway.

Driving, I think of the nature of death and the nature of being alive and wonder if there is any difference, or whether it is merely a matter of perception. On some of those intense summer nights, traffic streaming from upstate to the corridors of downtown, Janice and I would close the windows, swaddle ourselves while naked in the dangerous air conditioning, and exchange confidences as we exchanged with one another. I could at those times feel the world burning. Surely if that had happened, it could happen again. "We lift above the night, we are Shiva, consumer of worlds," I would whisper. Did we? Could we?

It seemed plausible at the time …

But what is plausible now is Highway #9W, that dangerous road: two lanes, blind turns, no-passing zones occurring and recurring like strobe. 9W which I fight with all the tenacity of the newly dead until, sprinting from a blind curve, I find a sports car oncoming in my lane, sliding quite helplessly toward impact. I yank the wheel and dive for the shoulder, that small, pale strip overhanging a suddenly disastrous cliff, and just like last time the car loses purchase and slides past the shoulder and into the air.

But unlike last time, I am able to find a thread of traction before the wheels definitively soar from the ground. But I know better now. I force myself to stop trying to intercede, to control the event. I allow the car to resume its slide off the road into emptiness. It is a terrifying yet exhilarating drop to that clang of rage and fused metal. The car bounces, tears, collapses around me, and then is still.

This time I seem able to emerge.

Although I breathe, it is really the steady, reassuring syncope of death.

I step from the vehicle and stand alone at the side of the road. There is no traffic, and my state is one of absolute and perfect emptiness. I neither think nor feel, but what I do is trudge. I trudge the thousand yards of road I had driven and the hundred yards to the house. Two cars pass, but they are of little concern, just two more whisks of death: more syncope. I walk toward my home. The vaporous crowd has succumbed to the night. Janice stands at the open door, her body an arc of inquiry. "Hello again," I say. "I could have lived. But this time I didn't. I was able to save it. To save us."

She says nothing, locked in that interrogatory posture. Living or dead? Caring or uncaring? Seeing me or not? Her face is implacable, unassailable. In her cool and stricken gaze I find myself refracted only as an impediment to her field of vision, and then as I move past her into the house, feeling her breath upon me, I come to understand that living or dead—

—That living or dead, it is all the same.

My fate has overtaken like a deadly animal. My future lies as did those crushed entrails earlier somewhere on that road I have trudged. I sit on the leather couch before the large-screen television, and Janice sits beside me. We greet one another. We make brief reference to the events of the day. We watch "I Love Lucy" reruns from the 1960's. It's just as it had been. We laugh, and I touch her hand tentatively. Yes, I can feel her, and, emboldened to embrace, I feel her up as we used to call it.

But she is stone. She is stone, and I am a mirage. An apparition.

I can't help myself. I laugh, and that's all I have: vibrating air.

I'm still just as I have always been.

Probably not dead.

Probably not alive.

Probably not here.

The Man Who Murdered Mozart

by Robert Walton and Barry N. Malzberg

What do you do if you are utterly out of sync with your age?

What do you do if your age is as wildly out of sync with you? We are not here to answer these questions or even to consider them at length. Life and circumstance sometimes conjoin, often do not: the dancer can despise the dance. What can we say of Howard Beasley? (2042 - ?) He is neither dancer nor dance, age nor circumstance, only a composite of the weird cacophony of time itself. His brow is slanting. His eyes are bitter. His heart is impure. He has small pretensions and less hope.

What can we accomplish if we do not consider Beasley? It is not as if other solutions are at hand, circumstances more amenable. If we do not consider Beasley, here before us, bitter of eye, impure of heart, then it is the age itself we are forced to contemplate and this will take us nowhere but to the heart of immemorial darkness. It is a hard age. It is a hard and lost time; its weight descending upon Beasley has turned his heart to stone, his hope to an overarching and implausible loss.

In earlier life, in times slightly less decadent, Beasley pursued women, drank lavishly, lay on one bed of pain after the next, seeking the divine but settling more often than not for soddenness and despair. William Shakespeare wrote with familiarity of this problem: The Seven Ages of Man (a sprawling text); Gertrude in bed with the Bloat King; Lady Macbeth of the dry breasts and stony complexion. Truly, there is no age which does not have its predecessor, no signs and portents which cannot be found littering the corridors of any generation. Beasley, however, thinks that he is exceptional. He believes that his woe is somehow singular, his determination unique, his love of Mozart the sole beacon in this time of overproduction and dross. He is certain. He is focused.

Of course he is quite mad.

"I believe it's time to end this lesson, Mr. Beasley."

Beasley lifted his bow and glared at the small, silver-haired man sitting across from him. The man sat alertly in a straight-backed chair, his slender hands folded in his lap. The silver hair was an affectation in this ageless age of endless cosmetic possibilities and extended life spans.

"Why?"

The man shrugged. "I don't feel that we'll make further progress today."

Beasley lowered his Stradivarius. "Look, Soccer, I'm paying you a lot of money for lessons. I'll say when they're over."

Soccer's brown eyes met Beasley's glare calmly. "I'm the teacher. I'll say when lessons end."

Beasley looked away. "I could have five holo-teachers for the money I'm paying you. I could have Paganini, Heifeitz, Oistrakh, Midori, and Chung for the money I'm paying you."

Soccer nodded. "Quite so. However, those program teachers, though interactive, are dead. I live and still learn nuances of our instrument. My capacity to learn enhances my ability to teach. That is what you're paying for."

Beasley raised his eyes. "What's the matter? Why can't we make more progress today?"

Soccer raised his hands, put them together palm to palm in an almost prayerful gesture. He said, "I'll be plain. This Mozart concerto's first movement is a collection of coy, teasing, playful, ephemeral musical thoughts. The bow should at least pursue them, at best fly with them. Your bow crushes each and every note. I can't listen to such butchery any longer."

Beasley snarled and flung the Stradivarius across the room. The violin cracked against a silver and onyx coffee table and fell in pieces onto the carpet.

Soccer rose and walked toward the door.

Beasley, his voice rough with unreleased malice, shouted, "Where are you going?"

Soccer stopped, turned, and looked mutely at the shattered violin.

Beasley glanced down. "All right. It will take twenty minutes or so for my fabricator to come up with another fiddle. Have some coffee."

Soccer shook his head. "I'll have no coffee and I'll not see you again."

"But I'm—"

"I know. You're paying me a great deal of money. I shall return it all to you. Good-bye." He turned to leave.

Beasley's voice rose even louder. "You can't do this! I've got to play this concerto for several thousand important people in two weeks!"

Soccer turned again. "Mr. Beasley, you play Mozart as if you wished to tie him up and torture him. Sadistic dominance is the only concept you convey in your playing. Performing Mozart should inform, upraise, and illuminate you and your listeners. You should approach joy, Mr. Beasley, joy."

"How do I do that?"

Soccer snorted. "That question is beyond me. Try asking Mozart." He turned and walked toward the door. It sensed his approach, altered its molecular structure to accommodate him, and became translucent. Soccer walked straight through it without pausing.

Beasley stared at the door as it again became opaque. He loosened his bow. Ask Mozart? Why not?

In his madness Beasley does not stand alone. He is surrounded by a large group who hold similar views, who believe that they remain the last believers in heightened circumstance, in beauty, in a way toward salvation for the lost occupiers of this time. They share the conviction, this misguided group (for they are terribly misguided) that the outcome of their odyssey will settle this issue beyond debate, that the only way into the future is a retreat to the past, and they have found the technology to manage this.

Pru slid sinuously into the cushioned chair next to the onyx coffee table. Beasley watched her appreciatively. Her pale blond hair contrasted well with her pale blue skin tone. He said, "You should put some clothes on before the others arrive."

She shrugged. "They've seen me before."

"That's not the point. You're distracting when you're naked."

"Thank you."

"We have no time for distractions. The Institute's conference is imminent. I've invited a few people to join us and they need to pay attention, as do you."

She shrugged again with intentionally provocative vigor. "Whatever."

"I mean it." He sipped from his chartreuse-colored drink. "I intend to carry off the most daring abduction in history."

Interested at last, Pru leveled her blue-black eyes on him. "Ah," she said. "Tell me more."

Beasley proceeded to tell her. He told her with great passion and force. Passion and force were Pru's own drowning point; "I am a serious person," she had said to him more than once, "with serious intentions, but each of the seven deadly sins makes me pant with desire. They make of me once more a totally unschooled person."

Knowing this, knowing of Pru's overwhelming and embracing avarice, he noted at the outset that abducting Mozart, first trawling through time for him, then dragging him stunned to the present, would cause a sensation at the grand conference and certainly draw large sums of money to the Institute. "Furthermore, we can accomplish this easily," he said. "The technology is available. There are legalities and prohibitions, but these can be circumvented." He went on to explain, in more detail than is necessary to record here, the nature of the technology that would enable them to reach into December of 1791, pluck the dying, consumptive, oracular genius from his deathbed, and, after pumping him full of palliatives, bring him to the florid present.

It is a marvelous age that Beasley occupied, an age in which technological ambition had conflated with accomplishment in a fashion not anticipated through all the centuries of the Industrial Revolution. Beasley, both beneficiary and victim of this abstruse and uncontrollable technology (his victimization is the most salient part of this tragic story) gestured forcefully, spoke wondrously, made clear to Pru how exciting and advantageous this could be. "A *Forty-third Symphony!*" he emoted. "A *Sixth Violin Concerto!* And of course a completed *Requiem*."

"Forget the completed *Requiem*," said Pru, who played an antiquarian viola in a consort she had assembled to perform in unassembled parts of Africa that had not yet learned to regard her feebly acoustic tours with pity. "The *Requiem* was never written to be completed. He had no plan, no intention. Furthermore, he was much too ill."

"But that's what we can address!" Beasley said with a poisonous enthusiasm. "We can restore him to health! Or at least stabilize him to the degree where he can compose." He felt himself seized by possibility, almost transfigured by an almost immeasurable possibility. "Of course there is the issue of culture shock but we can deal with that, at least for as long as we need him."

"Perhaps we can," Pru said. She was, for all of her embarrassing anachronism and failure of resistance, an adorable and passionate creature, much taken with Telemann and the importance of maintaining compassion in a metallic society. "I would like to hear your plan. I would like to discuss this somewhat less formally and without the intervention of clothing." She made a gesture that cannot be properly converted to print. "Like this," she said.

Chimes played a plangent passage from a Mahler lieder. Nothing moved in Beasley's apartment. The chimes sounded again and Beasley appeared wearing only a Roman-style robe. His dark hair was combed, but he looked somehow hastily groomed. He motioned toward the door. It became translucent and five young people, three men and two women, walked through it. The men were dressed in neo-punk black crusted with silver and crystal ornaments. Only one, however, wore his hair in the regulation six-inch purple spikes. The two women were more subtly attired in fitness leotards, neon pink and sunset gold. They stopped a few steps from Beasley.

Purple Spikes, the leader, spoke: "We're here."

Beasley pursed his lips. "Obviously."

Purple Spikes glanced around the room. "Where's Pru?"

"She's indisposed."

Purple Spikes smiled. "Sure." The others smirked and glanced at each other.

Beasley ignored the byplay. "Chad, this is not a social occasion. We have a chance to seize control of the Institute in two weeks and, therefore, of human destiny. I have devised an infallible means to do so, infallible if my lieutenants perform well. You," he indicated them all with a gesture, "are my most trusted companions. I requested you to come here to ask you one question. Are you able to perform as I need?"

Chad looked around at the others. They all shrugged and nodded. He turned back to Beasley and nodded. "Absolutely."

Beasley looked long at each of them in turn before he replied. "Good. In a few hours, we will travel in time to eighteenth century Vienna. We'll require specialized knowledge for this operation. Pru is presently spending implant time absorbing all there is to know about eighteenth-century music and composition."

One of the women, Pink Leotard, chuckled. "I'll bet that's not all she absorbed."

Beasley ignored her. "Each of you must undergo implant training. Chad, you and Hess will take two hours to ingest the programs I've forwarded to your implants."

Hess, the man to Chad's right, asked, "What's in it?"

Beasley looked at him. "Everything we know of culture, customs and conventions in eighteenth-century Vienna. You'll also acquire comprehensive geographic data. You two will be responsible for our interface with that society. Arzu? Pearl?" Gold Leotard and the other young man looked up. "You and Pearl have some mathematical adeptness. You must learn the basics of time travel, enough to manage regular operations and troubleshoot if any technological problems arise. We will have more than competent support on this end." Both Arzu and Pearl nodded.

Pink Leotard frowned. "What about me?"

Beasley smiled. "You, Tina, must learn more about weapons, theirs and ours. I don't intend to waste your aptitude for violence. You are security."

Tina smiled, revealing small white teeth filed to sharp points.

Beasley continued, "Instructions for initial actions prior to our liftoff have also been forwarded to your implants." Beasley turned and took several steps toward his private chambers. The others stared at his retreating back. Before any of them could speak, Beasley raised his right hand, made a gesture of dismissal, and said, "Begin."

A few more words about the age in which Beasley, however tentatively, dwelt—it was an age of Pru's metal and contempt, of distance and compartmentalization, and yet for a few like Beasley it seemed to smolder with a barely containable fire which that could leap barriers, soar through intervention, lead its confused and distracted masses toward an era in which for the first time humanity could truly observe and then model its destiny.

Beasley played the "Turkish Concerto" miserably, his rendition of the "Twenty-fourth Caprice" driving not only his instructor but any casual listeners to tears; he was not nearly as compassionate as Pru or as rigorous as his teacher, but then neither was the age itself, and the two of them were coterminous. In wanting to kidnap Mozart, Beasley—like so many of his time and through our rather awkward history—was trying as it were to kidnap himself, to extract, wriggling from circumstance, some purer element of reason or belief that would burn open Pru's metal enclosure and expose it to the purer winds of circumstance. Mozart revivified, Mozart displaced, would enable Beasley to displace himself and make the metal smile.

Ah, the folly! But remember before you detach yourself from this tormented protagonist and pronounce yourself ineffably resistant to his folly, remember that night when you stood against the sky, stood against the night, stood to the arrow of the Queen's high F. Was it any different for you? Would you have been any more resistant to that lust that made Pru helpless in Beasley's clutch, immune to her cries of falsified resistance?

Doctor Abigail Richards squeezed Joan Chin's fingers very gently. Joan, too weak to do more, responded with a slight upward curve of her lips. Doctor Richards said, "You'll be stronger soon."

Joan was the recipient of a lungs-liver-stomach-pancreas-gall bladder transplant. Part of her esophagus had been replaced, too. All the organs were clones, of course, perfectly matched to Joan's body. She had ignored warning signs, however, and waited too long to undertake a normal succession of outpatient procedures. A crisis had precipitated forced maturation and rapid surgical installation of her replacement organs. She'd almost died during the few hours it had taken to bring the cloned organs to a minimally functional state.

But she lived, and Doctor Richards squeezed her fingers again. Medicine, despite enormous advances in knowledge and technology, was still a human art. The enhanced, trained, and compassionate human mind was still the ultimate medical tool. Microprocessors in various places beneath her skin supplied her with the sum total of medical knowledge. A microcomputer within her abdominal cavity provided systems with which to utilize that data. Her judgment guided that use.

Doctor Richards exited Joan's room into a circular corridor. The corridor's walls were colored dusky violet, soothing to all eyes, tired or ill. She walked upon what appeared to be soft gray carpet, though this floor covering was capable of a great deal more than mere carpet. The elevator door became clear as she approached. Before she could enter, a hand gripped the back of her neck.

Chad whispered into her left ear. "Easy, Doc. I've got a stun package on my index finger. I'd hate to have to mess up your 'tronics by using it. Ready to come with me?"

Doctor Richards did not resist. She nodded very slowly. At the same time, her tongue pressed the roof of her mouth three times, activating a security alarm. Help was on the way.

Chad, now without his spikes, guided her into the elevator and touched the sensor panel for the transport level. The elevator launched into swift motion. It stopped a few seconds later. The door became transparent. Hess was visible on its far side. As they exited, Hess took Doctor Richards's right arm. A wheeled van waited a few meters beyond him. Tina, less colorfully clad, leaned against its paneled side.

Two heavily armed hospital guards approached from the other side of the van. They halted several meters away and the larger one, a woman, asked, "Is everything okay, Doctor Richards?" Hess let his hand drop away from the doctor's elbow. He stood more than two meters tall and was proportionally broad. Both guards kept their eyes on him—understandably so.

Tina stepped away from the van. She held out a wallet. "Here," she offered, "let me show you my ID."

The guards were well trained and experienced. They knew not to let a potential threat within striking distance. Tina, barely five feet tall and waif-thin, seemed harmless. The lead guard reached for Tina's wallet. Tina jabbed a concealed needle between the woman's fingers. She took one step back and uttered a surprised grunt before Tina's venom took effect. Paralyzed, she fell to the concrete floor. Tina's left foot rose in a wicked arc that ended in the other guard's groin. The shock package on the end of her shoe delivered its charge and the agonized guard fell to the floor. She reached down, touched his left mastoid, and rendered him unconscious.

Chad grinned. "Well, that's that. Let's go."

Tina straightened. Her plush red tongue passed briefly over the sharp, bright points of her teeth.

Falsified resistance for a falsified age. Mozart composed the first seven measures of the "Lachrymosa" and could go no further. He died with the papers strewn on his chest. Desperate, the destitute Constanze reportedly brought in Süssmayr to finish the piece but Beasley had heard from a Traveler that when Süssmayr had seen the "Tuba Mirum," he scowled with revulsion and crumpled the paper. "It cannot be completed," Süssmayr said. "Mozart himself could not proceed past the 'Dies Irae.'"

"I shall bring Mozart here. You will help me. I intend for him to proceed past the 'Dies Irae' and finish his Requiem*."*

Doctor Richards shook her head. "You're mad!"

Beasley smiled. "Not in the least. I intend to secure control of the Institute at the conference of worlds. Presenting the real Mozart conducting his personally completed Requiem *will be a sweeping tour de force. It will afford me a period of opportunity."*

"Opportunity to do what?"

Beasley shrugged and sipped champagne from the crystal flute he held. "Opportunity to become the leader humanity needs. Human culture has sprawled across the stars, but it is an amoeba. It needs a guiding intelligence." He placed the half-empty flute on the polished granite surface of his bar. He looked directly at Richards. "Mine."

Richards took a deep breath. "You can't do that!"

Beasley smiled coyly.

"You can't tamper with the Institute computers!" Richards continued. "Music flows, docu-streams, simulations, ancient videos—all those are locked, secure from outside content."

"Perhaps not as secure as you're led to believe." Beasley again picked up his glass.

Richards looked down. "I won't help you. You abducted me."

Beasley stepped behind her, allowed his fingers to trace a line down her shoulder. "Need I remind you that your nephew and niece live nearby in the lunar gardens?" He squeezed her shoulder. "Or that your valued friends and colleagues follow quite predictable patterns here in the city, quite vulnerable patterns?"

Richards stared at her lap. "What do you want me to do?"

Beasley removed his hand from her shoulder. "First, you are to stabilize Mozart so that we can transport him here."

Richards looked up. "We don't know anything about his condition."

"Doctor Richards!" Beasley looked at her disdainfully. "Surely your expertise and the tools of modern medicine with which we will provide you are equal to this small task."

Richards nodded. "What else?"

"You are also to supervise the complete cloning of Mozart once we reach Vienna and acquire him. We need a replica to take his place, you see. The conventions of time travel are murky, but we wish to cause as little disruption as possible."

Richards shook her head. "That would be murder. We can create such a clone with portable equipment, but we don't have the resources to support complete maturation. The new person would die within weeks."

Beasley smiled. "That is precisely what I'd hoped you'd say. It is, after all, what history dictates."

Richards gritted her teeth. "This is against our laws and against my oath as a physician."

Beasley shrugged. "True progress sometimes requires the breaking of laws, the violation of ethics." He looked at her. "Any laws. All ethics."

But no less than Beasley, we must disdain this, cast it aside. Problems of credibility, legality, morality: ptui! "What do they want? Dazzle!" he replied and spat, "Enchantment!"

There is no time for any of this, nor will it fit this context. Beasley's perverse and dramatic obsession: Extend the *Requiem*. Continue the *Requiem*. Bring it to a conclusion—and with it the eighteenth century itself. Here a quick connection, there a rapid scuffle in an anteroom with a surprised and resistant Constanze, soon enough neutralized. Frantic denials passed up the line. Who, us? Mozart? 1791? Most of life is falsification, manipulation. And so this synoptic way to conclusion—the abduction has been managed against all reasonable possibility.

"This warehouse leaks."

Pru shrugged. "It's the eighteenth century. What do you expect?"

Mozart lay on a sheet-draped table in front of Dr. Richards. She touched his left wrist with a blue ceramic instrument. Lights sparkled on the instrument and it uttered a chirp. A drop of water plopped onto the sheets next to Mozart. Richards sniffed. "Don't they have lead on the roofs, or something like that?"

"This isn't a church."

"Still." Richards adjusted a thin yellow tube attached to a needle in the back of Mozart's left hand. "Where's Beasley?" she asked.

"He's out playing."

Richards glanced up. "Playing?"

Pru smiled. "The eighteenth century is too much of a temptation for him. He's gone to court."

"Court?"

"You know: white wigs, satin, brocade, bowing, plotting, assignations if he can manage a few."

"Is that safe?"

"Safe enough. He took Tina with him." Pru motioned to Chad and the others who sat or reclined on various bales. "And left us with those vultures."

Mozart sighed and shifted beneath the sheets. Richards handed the blue device to Pru. "Hold this, please." She ran her fingers beneath his jaw and paused just below the left ear. Her eyes became unfocused as her implants processed data.

Pru looked down at Mozart's wan, still boyish face. "He's very sick, isn't he?"

Richards's eyes focused again. She nodded. "On the edge of catastrophic renal failure. I think I've got a handle on that. Something else is going on, though, some toxin or microorganism I haven't isolated. There are bugs back here that no computer has ever seen." Richards shook her head. "He's far too ill to be doing this to him."

Pru shrugged. "That won't matter to Beasley, as long as he lives long enough to sway the Institute at that conference next week."

"We may be able to get him that far, but afterward?"

"It doesn't matter."

Richards straightened. "It does matter. No human being is just a useful piece of meat, not the poorest beggar we saw out there on the streets."

Pru looked at her closely for several moments. "You really mean that, don't you?"

"I do."

Pru looked down. "It would be nice to believe in something. It might even be nice to care about someone." She glanced back at Richards. "You won't have to worry about Mr. Mozart anyway."

Richards's eyes jerked up. "What do you mean?"

Pru glanced idly at Chad and the others. They were chuckling about something Hess had said. Pru lowered her voice. "Beasley is rich and powerful enough to fake a legitimate use for the time travel machinery, but nobody can completely break the rules. If we take Mozart back, we've got to leave somebody here."

"Somebody?"

Pru smiled. "That would be you."

"Me?" she said. "Why me? What can I do? How can I replace him?"

"You're not here to replace him," Pru said. "You're here to occupy his room, his air, his circumstance. Temporal displacement. It is a matter of weight."

Mozart, apparently interested even on his deathbed, sighed, gestured, made a hoarse sound, spoke indistinctly. "Muss es sein?"

Was that what she heard? No, that was impossible. Those were Beethoven's words, not Mozart's. Recall pierced her in gleaming splinters. This is madness, she thought. *We can watch him die or we can make him die but we cannot do both. How did we come here?*

"You are both fools," Richards said and pointed a technician's hand to

the murmuring Mozart. "It can't be done. And certainly not by me."

The fleshpots of Europe, she thought absently. *That is where Beasley has gone. All of this, the whole insane scheme so that he could desert us and act out some savage fantasy.* She shuddered. She had a technician's soul. That was the problem; that was her undoing. "Give it up," she said. "This is madness."

Unless this was some insane collaboration between Beasley and Pru, unless she had somehow become entrapped in a *folie à deux* beyond comprehension.... "I'm leaving," she said. "It's a mad task, a mad outcome. I won't be part of this."

"But you are. You are more a part of it than you will ever understand." Richards felt sudden enormous weight upon her, a collaborative weight, the weight of air and crushing circumstance. "Poisoned!" she thought and plummeted.

"Poisoned?" she murmured.

"You said something?" Pru asked.

"Poisoned." She stared at dried dung in the wide cracks of the warehouse floor. "Poisoned."

Pru took her hand and helped her rise from the dusty boards. "You fainted. I didn't think doctors did that. What's this about poison?"

Richards looked bleakly at her hands. "No matter what I do, I'm poisoned. My life is over. I'll always know that I helped Beasley commit murder and hijack human knowledge."

Pru snorted. "Give me a break! We invent ourselves several times a day. There is no past, no history. If there is responsibility, it is to your own future."

Chad loomed above them. "Time to go, girls. Beasley said to get him loaded up as soon as you were done. You look done."

Beasley appeared behind Chad. "I'm back." He looked incongruously comfortable in blue satin and white wig. He nodded to Pru. "Pearl, Arzu?"

The two designated vultures detached themselves from their perches. "Yes?" answered Arzu.

"Warm up the transfer apparatus and go on through. Make sure it's working correctly before we attempt to transfer Mozart."

The locus of this story is Mozart and Beasley's doomed and illegal attempt to get the *Requiem* done through transport of the dying man. It is an accursed plan but it is the only plan with which he will contend.

Watch him contend. Let us witness his contention. Here he is, enormous in his desperation and hate, grasping Mozart, Richards at his side clutching the other foot. There they are, struggling; Richards, struggling and cursing with the heat in an attempt to push the dying

Mozart into the receptor they have smuggled into his room. Constanze has been distracted and sent on an errand with gold in her purse; Vienna is in distant tumult; they are focused upon necessity. Mozart, no longer a genius, never to be the composer of the "Sanctus," "Offertory," and "Cum Sanctu Spiritu," gasps heavily, unevenly for dying breath and slowly they move him toward the transporter.

Beasley curses the age to which he was born, his own vanity, his misdirected and poisonous set of conclusions. Richards, overcome with remorse, pulls; Beasley pushes; she tugs; he gasps; they groan, and slowly the dying composer passes into metal jaws which bite and snatch. In the distance is the sound of tumult.

Four cloaked shadows detached themselves from the sides of the alley and formed a loose globe around Tina. Her sharp teeth gleamed as she drew her rapier. Light from a torch one corner over revealed four masked men. Tina chuckled. "Eeek. Four muggers in black masks. What shall I do?"

The tallest man drew his sword and stepped forward. "I ask you to yield."

"On whose authority?"

"On that of a certain Count, my employer."

Tina's smile widened. "Count von Walsegg?"

The man stopped. "A certain Count. Now throw down your sword."

Tina nodded. "Sure. Any second now." She leapt, extended her sword arm in an impossible stretch. Her blade flashed in toward the captain's chest. He executed a counter-parry and bound her blade.

Tina grinned up at him and thrust her thorn into his groin. The thorn, loaded with lethal venom now, struck deep into a leather pad and stuck.

The captain gripped Tina's left wrist. "Nice try. I've seen that move before." A club descended on the back of Tina's head. The crack of oak meeting skull echoed from stone walls. Tina fell onto wet cobbles.

They stumble haplessly into a machine too small for two, unbearable for three, and, groaning, are encompassed by metal.

This is the point of the narrative for explication, invention, description—the part in which the flight itself should have been described, the scramble past the gates of known circumstance, a florid description of the escape.

And an inserted passage on the clumsily cloned Mozart brought to meet the superficial gaze of a superficial time. That cloned Mozart, fabricated and spiritless but superficially interchangeable. Such is the contempt of Beasley's age for what they take to be the mindless credulity of the eighteenth century. An imaging of the shrieking rattle of the clone as the clumsy substitution is made. If this is done properly, inclusively, we should not neglect the faint, high, lustful blush and tremble in Pru's face and hands as the substitution is made. It will be an opportunity.

Richards stepped out of the transporter and wiped a tear from her cheek. She looked at Beasley. "He'll need attention as soon as you arrive."

"Of course." Beasley looked around. "Tina will escort the clone back to Constanze's lodgings and then we'll be done." A tiny blue light flashed from a bracelet on Beasley's left wrist. His eyes went wide.

Pru asked, "What is it?"

Beasley's voice was hoarse. "Silent alarm. Tina is down. Something happened not far from here." Nixonian sweat gleamed suddenly upon his upper lip. "We'd better depart. Quickly! Chad?"

"Yes?"

"I'll leave now with Mozart. Pru and Richards can follow. You and Hess come last. Got it?"

"Got it. What about Tina?"

"What about her?" His eyes locked briefly with Chad's.

Chad nodded. "Got it."

Beasley continued, "Let the clone sit where he is. Somebody will figure out where he belongs."

Hess lifted Mozart like a baby and placed him, tubes and all, in the transporter. Beasley went in after Hess exited. He entered the activation code and punched the transfer button. Light built within the machine, flashed rainbow colors across the warehouse, and then went dark. It was empty.

Pru walked slowly over to Hess and Chad, a lazy smile curving her lips. "It was a real pleasure working with you boys." She put her arms around Chad and Hess. "Maybe we should get together at home, just the three of us."

Chad leered. "What a fine idea! I'd thought that myself, baby."

Pru suddenly slapped her palms against their shoulders. Chad and Hess dropped to the floor like bundles of rags. Pru glanced at Richards and grinned. "I have thorns too."

Richards stuttered, "I don't ... I don't understand."

"Help me get this meat in the machine. You'll go last with baby Mozart!'

Richards stood staring at her. "You tricked Beasley."

Pru's right eyebrow arched ironically. "He's a big boy. He knows I play my own game. Always."

"You want his plot to fail?"

Pru smiled.

"You betrayed him?"

"Come on!" Pru pointed at the fallen men. "Help me! We don't have a

lot of time here."

Richards bent to help Pru. Skinny Chad was not difficult to drag into the apparatus. Hess was another story, but at last they had him stuffed in on top of Chad. Pru entered the code, pressed the transfer button, and leapt out of the machine.

Richards confronted her as she turned. "You worked against him from the start, didn't you?"

The lazy smile again drifted across Pru's lips. "Do you really think that I want Beasley's personality impressed upon the Institute's supercomputers? His brutishness flowing unimpeded into the minds of trillions? It was diverting to screw him now and then, but to have him pawing in my mind constantly like an obsessed, huffing bull is far too much."

"But he's done it! He's got Mozart!"

"He's got trouble."

"You turned him in? The Time Condittiore?" asked Richards.

Pru shook her head. "I turned him in, but nothing so blatant as a public arrest will happen. He will be taken into custody at some point, but it will be hushed up. I suspect Beasley will suffer severely diminished capacity for a time and then all of his resources will be strictly monitored. His plotting days are over."

"What about you?"

"We're sending two Mozarts back. I'll stay here with Tina."

Richards looked at Mozart's clone. The innocent face shone like a flame above pure oil. Pru touched her arm. "Trust me, Richards, he'll be safe in the future."

Richards took Pru's hand. "Call me Abby."

In the swell and escaping light of that Parma to which they will return awaits nothing for Beasley and his crew but the blood of paradox. What they do not yet know, what they will learn, is that if the strain of passage does not kill Mozart, then the nature of paradox will. To come at the end of the journey to the place where one has begun, as Thomas Stearns Eliot is reputed to have observed.

But where did Beasley begin? Surely not hunched in the transporter like a beast, about to fall into the State. Surely not in Salzburg, that damned city which Mozart hated so. And surely not in that sacred place with Pru when, staring into her widening, frightening eyes, he came to understand that there was no place within her which he could ever occupy, no tenderness which he could ever know. That knowledge had driven him to the *Requiem Aeternum* and the "Dies Irae"; he had sought in K. 626 what nothing in this place of metal and desire could ever give him, and now, with Pru stolen from him and the dying Mozart lolling in his place, he had nothing but failed resource, loss, and of course paradox.

Mozart would emerge from the transporter alive, if only barely, they would get him into a protected place, they would administer balm and detoxification and prayer, but it would be the shock of passage which would kill the composer.

"You'll take care of him?" Pru nodded toward Mozart's clone, now sitting within the time transporter.

"Baby Mozart?" Abby looked at his puzzled, smiling face. "I'll take care of him."

"Good. Who knows what he'll do in our time."

Abby nodded. "Who knows? You won't, for sure. Do you really intend to stay?"

Pru smiled. "I do. I must. Eight came. Only eight may leave."

"What about Tina?"

Pru chuckled. "Don't worry about Tina. She's in a dungeon now, but her skills are too useful to be wasted in Vienna. I might hire her myself."

"Isn't this risky?"

Pru shook her head. "I doubt it. All that rant about paradoxes and changing the future is crap."

"You're sure?"

Pru shrugged. "Pretty sure. Current theory predicts infinite futures, so whatever I do to change a few million of them won't matter. I hope."

Abby thought about this and then looked up. "Why do you want to stay? What's here for you?"

Pru was silent for a moment and then she tapped her right temple with her index finger. "The Requiem needs finishing. I'll do it quietly, secretly. I'll make sure the mystery is preserved. Mozart will die a secret, shrouded death here and the Requiem will appear when needed. After all, Constanze always needs ducats. She'll cooperate and keep her mouth shut."

Abby shook her head. "That won't take a lifetime."

Pru grinned. "Hey, my immunities are good and there are a couple of people here I'd like to meet."

"Who?"

"Beethoven, for one." She licked her lips. "And I've always been curious about Napoleon. What was he like in the sack?"

Abby laughed. "You're incorrigible!"

Pru nodded. "Always."

And surely now there is a scene to be written about incorrigible Pru, intrepid Pru, time traveler and reprobate, explorer and party girl. More than a scene, a series. In one she clutches Beethoven tightly, leans him into her breasts, explores with her free hands the wizened genitals of the Master. "Ah," she says to him, "I am your Immortal Beloved," and later he is conducting the premiere of the *Ninth Symphony*, deaf as a post, totally lost, and all that he can recall is her thundering against him. That would be one scene and here is another: Napoleon on Elba, Pru sneaking into his quarters in a surfeit of cunning and technological mastery, and his half-salute to her in cover of darkness. There are other scenes that could be written: a charmer, Pru, mad as a hatter as you have noted and equally obsessed, but they are not for this narrative. She will find her way through the compass of history free of our attention; her role in this narrative, like her role in Beasley's strange and unaccomplished life, is done. Those no longer part of our odyssey are subsequently detached from its history no matter how we may clamor for them, and of Pru I can tell you little more. Just as the technology of time travel has not been made available in this recollection, so Pru's further adventures must be purely speculative.

Remember: it is an explanatory age, an expository time. The need for detail in narrative was a product of its formal origin earlier in Mozart's century.

Good-bye, good-bye, Richards had said.

Perhaps the concept of certainty is an illusion. Meanwhile, in this reconstituted, brassy century, the real Mozart lies abed, shocked into deepest slumber, heedless of the composition paper that lies scattered beside him. The slumber touches on coma, is perhaps indistinguishable from it; the savaging of time conversion and the toxic gasses of this distant century have conflated to create great risk, irreversible damage.

Swaddled in paradox, Beasley thinks, looking upon this pathetic, aseptic, hardly domestic scene. Mozart and he alike have been trapped here by self-canceled circumstance. So this is how Mozart died, Beasley thinks. If not a victim of temporal displacement, then ravaged by the toxicity of our time. He wonders if that cobbled version Richards had conveyed to 1791 looked like this, was reacting similarly. Were these two versions linked?

The problem is too complicated for Beasley, far beyond his feeble power of rationalization. It is not an age contrived for paradox or resolution, this post-technological time. If it were an age open to the possibilities of paradox, none of this would have ever happened.

All he knows for sure is that he misses Pru, mired two centuries away, trapped in a historical context she cannot fully understand. Pru and her sense of doom had so powerfully attracted and centered him. Where has it gone? And in that going what has Beasley himself become? *Requiem aeternam cum sancto* spiritu—Beasley sees his circumstance, his entire history, as a mirror; it casts back at him only his own strangled features. Who could have known?

Quivering, the comatose Mozart feebly raises a hand, makes the motions of handwriting. The gestures become swift, desperate. Beasley has no way of knowing that K. 627 has been inscribed upon the empty air.

And so then, seeking to break history apart, we become that history; our own efforts become part of the temporal flow. Going back we endlessly move forward; staggering forward we penetrate nothing other than our past. For this is the sum of the chronicle: each of us is Mozart, each of us his assassin.

And our own.

THE RAPTURE

by Jack Dann and Barry N. Malzberg

Schwartz was an atheist. Had been now for about fifteen years. It was a position he had reached (or so he rationalized) only after a credible journey; it was not for him the lazy way out. And he would not hedge his position, none of this, "I'm a cultural Jew and a literal agnostic" nonsense for him. No, he had made all of the Stations of the Atheist's Cross, the cold mornings in Synagogue sometimes without a minyan, diarrhea in an Ashram in the backblocks of Lahore, Nepalese guides with magic mushrooms, vision-quests in the Dakota badlands, all those energetic exercises of disillusionment-in-the-making. "I have come to terms with my life," Schwartz thought. "Rather than embrace one of many onetrue-gods, I will choose the cold solace of science." Cold solace of science, that was a good one. Better this than the warm embrace of belief. "Warm embrace of belief." Now from whom had he first heard that? It must have been that Nepalese beggar: "I seize you in the warm embrace of belief." Schwartz had wrenched himself from the trembling grasp, fled at a brisk limp. Disproof of any higher power poured out from the Nepalese landscape, and from everywhere else. The rationality of flight, the solace of science, the wise counsel of emptiness ... ah, that was the way to go.

It was all delusion and politics; at least he knew and understood politics.

Schwartz was now seventy-one. Broke, like most seventy-one year old good Americans, stumbling along on the penury of Social Security, no family to speak of except his estranged son, Freedom (born during Schwartz's Ashram period) who lived circumspectly in a white collar prison in Scottsdale. Schwartz might be weakened by penury, but at least he was intellectually consistent. Thus he did not swoon, did not mumble the *Sh'ma Yisrael*, did not shout *"Gewalt in Himmel!"* when he saw his long dead friend Louis Kandinsky (a name like the painter's but no artist old Louis) alive and breathing and waving sunnily to him. Alive and breathing right there at what had thirty years ago been their usual table in front of the big greasy window at Milton's Famous on Surf Avenue in Coney Island.

Surf Avenue in Coney Island in Brooklyn, New York.

Who could have figured this to be the place where the Book of Revelations would be marvelously transmogrified into living truth?

Certainly not that atheist, William Saroyan Schwartz. Nor his long dead, supra-rationalist friend Louis not-the-painter Kandinsky.

William had no intimation whatsoever of this miracle. He lived in Sea Gate, once a ritzy upscale community, but now just another remnant of the lost city; and every Wednesday he would walk a mile to Milton's for an artery-clogging potato salad and some illusion of youth. It was on just such a Wednesday, a hot day in June 1963, with the humidity, you should be aware, right off the scale, that the One True God—or the one true series of gods or some synchronistic quantum not yet discovered in this parlous, pre-plasma-physics time—brought the dead back to life.

High and dry all of them, just two blocks away from the ocean on Surf Avenue.

It would be later on this Wednesday, after their initial quiet occupancy, that the dead—all of them apparently male and what an insufficiency this was—were to come ride the F train, drink cans of Piels beer and catcall certain pretty young girls who were showing off their miniskirted legs on their lunch break. The dead would come back to play on that very day that William so admirably kept his composure and belief system intact, even as he rode the Cyclone rollercoaster again with his dead best friend Louis.

But this would be some mortal hours in the future.

Right now, however, this was the present and Louis gestured to the white plastic chair beside him, motioned the speechless and shaken Schwarz to a seat. There they sat for just a moment, taking in the salty air, the exhaust fumes, and the amusement park noise, just like old times.

"You're not even going to ask how I got back here and what's doing with all the rest of us?" Louis asked as he gestured toward a trio of Chassidim guiding three empty bicycles carefully toward the corner. He smiled at Schwartz and pointed at his half-eaten sandwich. "Not too bad," he said, "although they've gone downhill a little in the eight years I am dead. But so has everything I begin to see."

"I disagree," Schwartz said with some determination. "And I think that restaurant critic is no job for a dead man."

"Dead," Kandinsky said, as if savoring the word. He smiled. "Dead is a state of mind. So now tell me something important, such as how are the Dodgers doing? Did they win the World Series again? It was no coincidence that I died that November. There was"—he twirled his finger in the air for emphasis—"a completeness."

"There are no Dodgers in Brooklyn anymore," Schwartz said. "They moved to Los Angeles and took O'Malley with them."

Kandinsky scowled, shook his head, then waved desultorily at a very tall, stooped, and ugly angel passing by. The angel had huge and magnificent wings, the white wings of an enormous butterfly, and their narrow, marked tips extended high in the air, creating a breeze and snapping noises as he passed. The angel wore a brown corduroy suit; his wrinkled shirt and jacket cut out in the back to accommodate his wings.

"What the hell is *that?*" Schwartz asked.

"Someone who believes that the Dodgers should have stayed in Brooklyn."

Thus was the afternoon spent: hot buttered corn on the cob from Nathans, later two hot dogs, a wild ride on the Cyclone because Kandinsky insisted that being dead shouldn't affect one's *jeux de vivre* (his words), and Schwartz protested that he didn't need to get sick on a roller-coaster to be French; but he paid the fare nevertheless and got into the cart with his old dead friend and yelled and screamed and shouted "Sonovabitch" in joyous rapture and uncharacteristic abandon, suddenly understanding that being French—or dead—might not be so bad, after all; and later, his legs aching, his bladder full, his shirt sticking to his armpits, he and Kandinsky whistled at young girls and Schwartz gave a crisp twenty dollar bill to the over-the-hill prostitute who patrolled the block east of the Cyclone. Her white-blond hair was stiff and ruined from eternities of peroxide applications. She was big breasted, dressed in a faded black evening gown with frayed red shoulder straps, and her name was Daisy. She had always treated Schwartz kindly; and, if truth be told, he had just a little bit of a crush on her.

"*Boychik,*" Daisy said, "for twenty dollars, I don't even pat what you got in the front."

"I wasn't expecting anything," Schwartz said, embarrassed. "It was meant to be a nice gesture. A ... tip."

"You tip a girl once you've paid for a girl. I'm not a beggar on the street. I'm a professional woman."

"I apologize," Schwartz said, taken aback by his impulsive action and her response. "I meant no harm."

"You want to go have a little fun?" Daisy asked. "Would perk you up, and I thought you'd never ask." She giggled. "How many years is it now that you pass by, say 'Good Day' and then cross the street to get another look?"

If she lost about twenty pounds, she'd be a good looking woman. Maybe a little wrinkly in the face, and the neck had those folds, but—

"Well," Daisy asked, "you going to stand there grinning at me or are you going to be a man and take me away from all this?"

"I'm sorry, but I'm with my friend Louis, I should be ashamed of myself for not making proper introductions, Louis, this is Daisy, Daisy, this is ..."

But Louis Kandinsky, who was dead in the first place, had disappeared. Just like that. One second he was standing beside Schwartz and saying "A woman is a woman," and then, poof, off he went, salubrious hallucination that he was. Schwartz had no illusions. You don't see dead friends who eat hot dogs, you don't ride the Cyclone and the Ferris wheel and look at girls together, no, no, not when you're dead; and Schwartz wasn't dead yet. Louis was dead. Schwartz ... Schwartz knew what was the matter.

He was hallucinating.

He was losing his marbles, going senile, and who knows what else.

That would explain everything.

That would make sense.

For all he knew, Daisy wasn't Daisy. He probably wasn't even here. He could just as easily be asleep, sitting in his worn leather chair in front of the television (he allowed himself at least that), and snoozing, dreaming about old whores and dead friends.

And angels?

Sure, angels. Why not? A dream could contain anything.

"Hey, you, are you okay?" Daisy asked.

"What?" Schwartz said. "I'm fine."

"You just started talking like a crazy person, that's all."

He grinned. "Maybe I am."

"Then maybe I am too. Come on, we can be crazy together, providing you have a hundred dollars."

"Well, *I don't*. I'm very sorry."

Schwartz really had to pee. It was the damn prostatitis; whenever he got worked up, he had to pee. But he never had to pee in his dreams. He started coughing, asthma, and fumbled for his inhaler. He gave himself a spritch, felt the medicine fill his lungs, and held his breath.

"You okay, Mr. Schwartz?"

He nodded, shook the inhaler—he'd need to buy another soon—and exhaled. Better. He took a deep breath.

Sonovabitch.

He wasn't dreaming.

He guessed he was just plain crazy.

"I'm sorry, Daisy. I'm old and not dead yet."

"Well, that's a relief."

"And I've got to pee."

"So come up to my place."

"I don't have a hundred dollars."

Daisy patted him on the bottom as if he was a baby and said, "This one's on the house. Think of it as a gift from your invisible friend."

Schwartz hadn't been laid in twenty-two years, and here he was humping and bumping around on Daisy's creaky satin-sheeted bed with the smell of the ocean coming in from the open window and the sounds from the boardwalk blending with his wheezy, nasal huffing and puffing and Daisy's oohing and ahhing; and she was clinging to him and dancing on top of his erection (he was proud of that erection; so maybe it wasn't as hard as it could be, it was hard enough) as if he was twenty years old and had a full head of hair—no pot belly then, no scrawny arms, no hernias on both side of his groin—and ... and it was *wonderful*. As his father used to say, "A miracle."

Schwartz didn't believe in miracles, but this was simply a response to the pragmatic pleasure prescribed by biology. Well, perhaps not pragmatic. This tumbley mating could not lead to offspring, so this once let it be a miracle.

"Was it good for you?" Daisy asked.

Schwartz looked out the window and said, "The very best."

"Then we'll do this again."

"I don't have money, I—"

"Don't worry, Mr. Look-I'm-getting-an-erection-again. You can be my boyfriend."

"Boyfriend?"

"Everything for you is free, except meals. You have to take me out and treat me like an important person."

Schwartz turned his gaze away from the window, smiled, and said, "Well, you are an important person."

"Then give me another one, big boy."

But before he descended once more into seemingly miraculous but scientifically rationalizable bliss, he glanced out the window. Why he didn't know. But something seemed to be pulling him away, like when sometimes he'd feel a pressure on his neck and he would turn around and see someone staring at him, as if eyes could radiate some special kind of heat.

Down below—standing on Neptune Avenue right in front of Daisy's apartment block, as if he was waiting for the bus—was Louis Kandinsky.

Waiting as patiently as only the dead could.

Waiting for Schwartz.

"So what are you, some kind of peeping Tom?" Schwartz asked Kandinsky.

"I couldn't see what you were doing from the street," Kandinsky said.

"I could *feel* you seeing."

"How could you? I don't exist according to you."

"You exist in my mind," Schwartz said. "For all intents and purposes that will have to do."

"Because you're crazy and hallucinating, right?"

"Right."

They walked back toward Famous. They could at least have a coffee together.

"And you think you're asleep in your apartment in front of the television, right?"

"Probably," Schwartz said. "That's almost as good as proof that I'm not here, or you couldn't have been reading what I was thinking about earlier."

"Why not? I'm dead, and I'm here. Why shouldn't I be able to read your mind? It's not that difficult, you know. You're what your Mother, may she rest in peace, would call an open book."

"How would you know about my mother?"

"You think the dead don't enjoy a cup of tea, and maybe a little of what you were doing up in that apartment?"

Schwartz just snorted. He couldn't imagine his mother fooling around with Kandinsky, of all people, dead or alive.

"Well, if you were dreaming, you wouldn't have to pee again so soon, would you?" Kandinsky asked. "You never pee in your dreams."

"Well, I guess this is something new."

"You should take Finastride for your problem. It'll shrink the prostate, and if you're going to keep schtupping your new girlfriend, you'd better get it fixed."

They took their regular seats at Famous, ordered coffee and Danish.

"I waited for you because I wanted to explain something to you before I go."

"Where are you going?"

"Back to being dead, which according to you would be nothing, nothingness dissolution of self, everything that scares the crap out of you," Kandinsky said.

"Damn right."

"So that'll be your state of death, William. But I'm going to do you a favor after I'm gone."

"Yeah …"

"Do you like Charles Dickens?"

"He's okay, too long-winded and moralistic for me," Schwartz said. "What has Dickens go to do with—"

"Remember *A Christmas Carol*, your favorite *goyisha* book?"

Schwartz nodded, in spite of himself.

"Remember how Scrooge got sent all those spirits?"

"Yeah …" Schwartz said warily.

"Well, I'm only sending you one," Kandinsky said. "You saw him earlier, the angel, the tall guy who needs to eat more and get himself a new suit."

"So instead of hallucinating you, I'll be hallucinating him?"

"Pretty much. But before you get up to pee again, old friend, remember you're not the only one ever to see an angel ... or a demon. Did you know that Rilke composed his *Duino Elegies* by taking dictation from an angel and Kepler was inspired by a demon of scientific bent?"

Schwartz just shook his head and went to pee.

When he returned, Kandinsky was gone.

Schwartz knew it from the start. No, it could never be enough; bantering with an angel, even a sardonic angel, even a self-deprecating angel made no more sense than trying to engage in a coherent discussion with Kandinsky. If you accepted the premise, then you would have to accept the conclusion; and that wasn't Schwartz's way. None of this Pascal's wager stuff for him; as far as Schwartz was concerned, Azazilel—angel, demon, or awkward and skinny figment of the imagination—was as entrapped by the scam as any of them.

Schwartz, who was being trailed by Azazilel at a discreet distance, walked back to his one bedroom apartment on Neptune Avenue. The old neighborhood looked exhausted, a brick and mortar bum in need of a bath and a make-over; Brooklyn in these years of the fading Wagner administration and the wake of the Dodgers' exit was an unhappy place, populated by sullen, tight-faced inhabitants outraged by inverted circumstance and condemned to isolated, empty, and useless lives on this side of the bridges.

Schwartz was often given to thoughts of this nature; "isolated and useless" was the fatal position of Man in the modern world, or so Heidegger thought ... and Schwartz was a big fan of Heidegger.

In the days following his inadvertent and unappreciated reunion with the dead and supercilious Kandinsky, Schwartz continued to ascribe their meeting to hallucination and exhaustion. This was exactly the kind of thing that happened when you were old and living in a spiritually abandoned time and Borough. Everyone his age had a right to a little senility. It was as normal as losing pubic hair.

Thus Azazilel continued to lurk, sometimes following at a discreet distance, sometimes presenting himself in thinly shielded disguise on the sidewalk. Once he appeared as a beggar with a chipped teacup and haunted expression, once as a police officer with big feet and martial intent in his eyes. He was a fat man passing out political leaflets, a Parks Department Supervisor distractedly buttoning and unbuttoning his uniform, a chestnut vendor with a bandaged finger.

All disguised manifestations of Azazilel.

Indeed, Schwartz could respect the wit, attention to detail, and persistence of this spirit who, rather like Duchamp, might carry a urinal into a synagogue on Shabbat to gain the congregation's attention and advertise the unexpected duality of material existence. Schwartz yearned for the old days when an expression of atheism stimulated rather than threatened and brought needed distance and objectivity to embedded notions such as common prayer, patriotic duty, political will, and whether enough angels existed to fit comfortably on the head of a pin.

Now and then Kandinsky made short appearances at the rim of Schwartz's attention, but he no longer attempted to communicate: The shuffling Azazilel was the communicator for both of them and most of the time had little enough to say.

So matters might have persisted in uneasy accommodation ... for a while.

Schwartz was in no hurry. Any forward motion would be motion off a cliff. Azazilel was obviously in no hurry; he was an agent of temporal paralysis. And the Borough of Brooklyn, New York at this time was in no hurry either; it had in Schwartz's view stabilized into a kind of balanced misery, a New Frontier of accommodation which might well last until the millennium. Schwartz himself had no such expectation; he was as hopelessly trapped in the 20th century as the tailfin or the Hot Five; the only way out was no way out at all.

Uneventful weeks passed—well, the weeks had become uneventful after Daisy had given him the ultimate brush-off (she didn't answer her phone, was never home, and couldn't be found streetwalking in Coney Island)—weeks populated only occasionally by an angel who seemed too distracted to have any kind of agenda. Thus, after this pair of spectacular interventions and the aforesaid ultimate brush-off, resigned once again to a monotony of days edging toward uninspired obliteration (maybe God, like O'Malley, would deposit him on the Other Coast, all in a quickening), Schwartz found a certain valor in his casual temporality.

Ignore signs and wonders, miracles and angels, boredom and loneliness, and concentrate on self-sustention. In this monochromatic mood, near the end of a gray New York autumn, Schwartz cashed his Social Security check and returned to his apartment, only to find both Azazilel and Kandinsky ensconced on a couch. As he entered the dusty, newspaper-stacked living room, they regarded him with disapproval.

"You look terrible," Kandinsky said, "Matters have been weighing on you."

"Keep your analysis to yourself," Schwartz said. "What, you had to bring him? The two of you are intimate colleagues now?"

"Just forget about him," Kandinsky said, tapping Azazilel lightly on a wing, which fluttered reflexively. "Things are not so good for him either, but he felt he should tag along. He has nothing to say. These are difficult times for him. He is in a state of transition. Going from here to there with nothing to say about it isn't such a nice thing, let me tell you. But let us not discuss this. It is time for *you* to make a choice. Large events portend, and you are called to their necessity."

"What large events?" Schwartz asked; he felt suddenly confused, put out, and exhausted. "What necessity?"

"We are now approaching some true polarity," Kandinsky said, insistent and suddenly agitated. A new thought seemed to have struck him; dead all these years. His old friend displayed an energy, not to say a level of distress, that Schwartz had never seen before.

"Polarities," Kandinsky continued. He said it again, as if to confirm in his own mind that it was indeed polarities. "It's the illusion of time as aggregation rather than as a linear journey. Instead of going from here to there, we are *really* going here ... and here ... and here ... while imagining that we are *there*. Everything is in the oneness; all of it is together." His hands shook, and he appeared to be on the verge of suffering some profound and terrible personal insight. "If it has happened, it is always happening. If it is happening now, than it will never, never stop happening. It is all synchronicity, compilation, an infinite massiveness of event."

Unimpressed by his old friend's temper, Schwartz shrugged. "Here," he said, "Here, there, everywhere. You're still dead and I am still alive. Not that it is doing either of us any good."

"That's not for us to say." A sudden sourness twisted Kandinsky's features. He gestured at the angel, who for reasons known only to himself—or itself—had levitated out of the couch and sat suspended just below the ceiling. "Haven't you had enough of him?" Kandinsky asked Schwartz. "I dispatched him for purpose, not so that you would have a grubby old angel on the premises at all times."

Azazilel stirred uncomfortably, rotated slowly as if he were suspended by a rope, and mumbled or grumbled in an angelic undertone.

"And something else," Kandinsky said, as if suddenly realizing his purpose, as if suddenly struck by an entirely new, a shocking idea. "A bullet in the brain."

"I have absolutely no idea what you are talking about," Schwartz said. "And will you please ask your colleague to stop hovering?"

The angel dutifully returned to the couch beside Kandinsky, although some ghostly afterimage remained near the ceiling.

A bullet in the brain ...

Schwartz glanced toward the ceiling, suddenly paranoid that he was being watched from on high; and he imagined the ghostly wisp of ectoplasm that remained near the ceiling was a baleful unblinking eye, the clear and perfect eye of God ... the eye of circumstance, of mortal and heavenly fate.

Schwartz shook himself like a dog shaking off rain and said, "Louis, you never made any sense when you were alive. So you're right, some things never change, but I am quickly approaching the end of my patience. Could you please take your companion and leave me be. Go be someone else's hallucination."

Kandinsky and his angel levitated to that particular place below the ceiling where Azazilel had left his ectoplasmic signature; and in a blink of the ectoplasmic eye of God, they both disappeared.

Bullet in the brain, Schwartz thought.

From whence comes such talk of a bullet in the brain ...?

Two weeks later and Schwartz was strolling through Dealey Plaza in Dallas, Texas. How he got there, what Dallas has to do with this, do not ask just yet. If all goes as planned, you will soon comprehend it all with rented omniscience.

Two weeks before, as described above, Azazilel and Kandinsky had levitated, floated ceilingward in Schwartz's dismal room, and then disappeared through a skylight. Or the ceiling. Or something. The two of them—deaf friend and mumbling angel—had left clouds of speculation and discontent, quandary and bewilderment. As might be recalled, Schwartz had suddenly found himself bereft of the company and delights of Daisy (no doubt the fault of Kandinsky and Azazilel). Suffice it to say that he was unwilling to remain in Brooklyn any longer than he had to. Brooklyn was not an answer. Brooklyn was simply a familiar path to the certainty of a dusty, imminent, procrastinated death. Schwartz had an inch or two of life left in him. He contained multitudes. His memory contained childhood, adolescence, maturity, death, and the spectral visions (and teachings) of dead friends risen and angels in-waiting in corduroy suits.

If Brooklyn wasn't the answer, what was?

What coruscated through his unconscious thoughts, as yet unrevealed?

What words could move him to ... move?

What deeds could be done or undone by an old man with but an inch or two of life left?

Bullet in the brain—

Perhaps he should look outward. Beyond himself. Beyond habit, beyond petty needs, beyond ...

Bullet in the brain—

Bullet in the brain—

Perhaps a Presidential political tour was the answer.

Take the train Bulletinthebrain.

Yes, a vacation into polity. Perhaps he could follow John Fitzgerald Kennedy—the best president since Roosevelt—on his travels. A grand tour. A

Bulletinthebrain

Fly drive take the bus Bullet in the brain

Perhaps, at some point, he could get the chance to talk to him. He was a citizen, wasn't he? A senior citizen, in fact. Indeed, he had a few questions for the President. If the dead were capable of reappearance and levitation, why could America not in the aggregate be in the province of miracles and reconstitution? Those were questions any serious citizen had the right and obligation to ask. And Schwartz was a serious citizen determined to ask them.

That he might be running away from himself and the pain of losing a woman before he even had enough of her was irrelevant. That his sudden re-infatuation with politics, great personages, and the doings of the rich and successful was irrelevant. Schwartz, a 71-year-old American with the ruins of a life behind him and the whiff of a recent strangeness which went beyond explanation, familiarized himself through the press with Kennedy's travel schedule.

He would have an adventure in polarity, just as Kandinsky foretold. He would have an adventure in necessity and political reconciliation, an atheist's adventure in God's chronometry.

Ah, to dream, to meet Yarborough in Dallas with Connally, to sit with both of them and tell Goldwater jokes. Tell them a few anecdotes.

Lyndon would be there, too; and he would get these two old rivals and enemies to shake hands in anticipation of the 1964 election. Schwartz could see them doing it, possibly in public, maybe in a hotel room, maybe in the back of a limousine; the affability of politicians in public and private, never more desperate than when they felt themselves challenged, had never been a mystery to Schwartz. Schwartz had always considered himself politically savvy. But for the unfortunate turns of his life, he would have made a good politician. Perhaps not as good as JFK, but then again, who on earth was?

Now.

Dealey Plaza.

Surrounded by Texans, surrounded by thoughts of resurrection even if not his own, Schwartz could see the limousine approaching. Agents ran beside it, flags streamed in the wind.

Schwartz felt himself transported, yet captured in diorama and belief and powerful conviction.

As the limousine approached, he felt light as pollen. He felt expansive, as if he were the light *and* the pollen. He felt himself on the verge of levitation, understood the luminous joy that his old friend Kandinsky must have felt on the occasion of his first return, and then he caught a glimpse, a quick afterimage of a levitated Kandinsky hovering over Kennedy's oncoming, expanding limousine.

And then Azazilel was suddenly beside Schwartz.

"*You!*" accused the angry, distraught angel. "What are *you* doing here? You weren't supposed to be here."

Schwartz could sense an unangelic confusion, a desanctified mystification; and reflexively he reached for the distraught Azazilel.

"It is too late for that," Azazilel said. "Too late, too late," and Schwartz found himself enormous, distended by helium, floating free of the ground.

He was the pollen and the light. He contained time and multitudes.

Bulletinthebrain

"You can't say the city of Dallas doesn't love you Mr. President." Underneath now the scramble of rifle fire; strewn roses.

Schwartz held on to his life ... held on to Kennedy. He was mist. He was smoke. He was fire. He was as fulgent and substantial as the sun. I want to be here again, he thought, past this happening.

I want to be here.

I want to be in Dallas again.

Azazilel showered him with ancient Hebrew and Aramaic curses.

Kandinsky made a sudden appearance on the trunk of the

Continental. He scowled at Schwartz and tried to levitate. But he was heavy as lead, heavy as flesh and blood, unlike the new polarized Schwartz, who through Kandinsky's misguided guidance had become as light as any mortal could ever hope to be, and who could be here ... and here ... and here.

Unlike Kandinsky, who could only talk the talk.

Signs and wonders, Schwartz thought. Nothing needs to be as it was/is. Time is illusion. Time is event, an infinite massiveness of event.

Bullet in the brain. Age of miracles.

Now that Schwartz had more than an inch of life left, perhaps he would return to the golden enveloping folds of religion, ah, yes, go back (here) to *shul*. Try it as he once had. After all, he wanted/wants the political life. He understood/understands politics. And he now knew/knows that *everything* is simply time and politics.

And so with all his newfound *nous* and revelatory knowledge, which, of course, he *always* had, Schwartz ran into Daisy in front of her apartment block on Neptune Avenue.

"So, nu, Mister No-goodnick William Saroyan Schwartz?" Daisy asked. "What brought *you* back to the neighborhood?" She looked radiant in a brand-new strapless evening gown—black satin hemmed with yellow lace—and she had lost at least twenty pounds. Her Marilyn Monroe hairdo was smooth and permed.

"Me …? I was away for maybe a week. I deserved *something* after you left me."

Daisy shook her shoulders slightly, a gesture which always excited Schwartz.

"I didn't leave you, buster. You left me. I was right here in my house sitting like a *meshugge* by the phone and waiting for *someone* to call. Waiting for *someone* to ring the buzzer and tell me he wanted to take me out on the town and show me off. Waiting for *someone* who said he was going to make an honest woman of me and take me away from all this."

"I called ... I knocked."

"And …?"

"And you weren't there," Schwartz said. "I looked everywhere."

"Well, obviously, you didn't look hard enough." After a beat, she said, "Of course, I might have had a few ... appointments."

"Come, we'll go up to your apartment and talk."

"We are talking."

"You know what I mean."

"You got money, Mister No-goodnick who can afford a vacation and now thinks he's also entitled to free nooky?"

Schwartz shook his head and sighed.

"So you think you've got proprietary rights like I was your girlfriend?"

"You *are* my girlfriend," Schwartz said, surprising himself with newfound assertiveness.

"And that's it? I'm supposed to just sit around and wait for you while you—where were you, anyway?"

"In Dallas. Texas."

"Ohmygod," she said. "You were in *Dallas?* Were you there when—?"

"Yes, of course I was," Schwartz said and, remembering his conversation with the angel Azazilel and his dead friend Kandinsky, added, "I was taking a vacation into polity. Having an adventure in polarity."

"Well, the next time you go to take a vacation to polarity or anywhere else, you sure as hell better take me with you ... if you want to keep your privileges." Then she led him up the creaking stairs into her apartment.

"I watched it all on television," she said. "You must tell me everything."

"Nothing to tell. Like you said, it was all on the television."

"I'm glad they shot the bastard who tried to assassinate the president. He should be shot a thousand times for what he did."

Schwartz sat down on the sprung sofa, and Daisy brought him his favorite scotch in a heavy, cut crystal glass.

"Well, it was lucky for the president," Schwartz said, "but not so lucky for Jackie."

"Yes, it's a tragedy, a national tragedy."

Daisy sat down beside him.

"You always said you thought Jackie was a stuck-up bitch."

"She is ... I mean she was. But she was also the First Lady, may she rest in peace." Daisy shook her shoulders fetchingly.

Schwartz reached for her and grinned with satisfaction as he felt her spongy flesh in his hands. He didn't care if she was alive or dead. He didn't care if he was alive or dead. And later, he would take her to *shul* to pray for the eternal soul of the poorly done First Lady. After all, this was the age of miracles. Life and death were simply time and politics.

Schwartz understood this.

Perhaps now the good spirit Azazilel did too.

TOURIST TRAP

A Companion Piece to Gene Wolfe's "The Marvelous Brass Chessplaying Automaton"

by Mike Resnick and Barry Malzberg

***On Gene Wolfe**: Gene has a worldview and a way of expressing it that is uniquely his own. He has never genuflected to the so-called needs of the field, but has, over the course of his admirable career, made the field genuflect to him and his unique voice. There are worse legacies.*

—Mike

***On Gene Wolfe**: I've been reading Gene Wolfe since "Trip, Trap" appeared in an early* Orbit. *We began to publish at about the same time; he's been far more successful ... but then again I am eight years younger. His magnificent short story "Cues" was the subject of one of my earliest essays, which was published in Andrew Porter's* Algol *pulp four decades ago.*

—Barry

I was just bringing Lame Hans his lunch when he looked up at me excitedly.

"What do you see?" he demanded.

"I see a lame man waiting for his meal," I answered.

He shook his head vigorously. "The *game*," he said. "What about the game?"

"Same as always," I said. "You're sitting in your cell, the computer is right outside it, you're playing white, and since the computer is an empty shell, you're playing black, too."

"*No!*" he yelled. "It moved on its own!"

"Hans, even if it still had a brain, it's not plugged in."

"I don't care! It moved its Knight to King's Bishop three!"

"Hans, it hasn't moved a damned thing since you hid poor Gretchen inside it when you and Professor Baumeister attempted to defraud the others. And we all know that she suffocated. That's why you're here."

"Just *look!*" yelled Lame Hans. He pushed his Queen's Bishop forward, leaving her Rook unprotected—and while he held his hands up in the air to prove he wasn't touching anything or leaning on the board, the Black Queen slowly slid on the diagonal and took the Rook.

"There's someone inside," I said with certainty.

"Look!" he urged me.

I pulled out the side panel, and could see nothing, but remembering how cleverly they had concealed Gretchen, I walked around the other side, removed that panel, found that I could see clear through to the far well, and then felt around inside it. There was no one there and, of course, no mechanical brain.

"Well?" demanded Lame Hans.

"I don't know how you did it," I admitted.

"*I* didn't do anything!" he shouted at me. "The machine's alive."

He pushed a Pawn forward, and the machine responded by taking it with its Knight.

"I am the best chess player in all Bavaria," said Lame Hans. "The machine is not only alive—it's brilliant!"

Brilliant, I thought, but did not say. If the machine was indeed brilliant, then why was Lame Hans in his ongoing competition ahead by one hundred and sixty games to twenty-two? Why, time and again, did the machine succumb to Knight forks and fianchettoed Bishops, stumble into doubled Pawns two games out of three? The machine had its instances, to be sure—twenty-two of them in fact—but it was impossible to conceive of it as anything other than a dull refraction of Lame Hans's madness.

Or so I thought. The thoughts of a jailer are not, however, profound by nature, and it is possible that I misunderstood the situation. Perhaps the brilliant Lame Hans had created a machine *persona* cunning enough to deliberately lose eight-ninths of the time, thereby inflating the already enormous ego of its perpetrator. Summers were hot in Bavaria, at the time of which I am writing, even hotter than they are now, a peak of solstice that fried brains and damaged reputations. The thoughts of a jailer are not to be dismissed; we see aspects of prisoners that they do not see themselves.

"It is time for another game," Lame Hans said deliberately. "Please redistribute the board. I will not ask you this again. If your mind is to drift, let it be when you are not in my presence."

Clumsily—I have never quite understood the initial posting of the thirty-two chess pieces even after all this time—I bent to the task. Lame Hans regarded me indolently, perched in the shadows of the cell. He called it his "Plato's Cave." Under no circumstance have I pursued this subject. It has something to do with idealization as opposed to the grim actuality furnished within the Bavarian compass, but I am not a reflective person (no jailer possibly could be and keep his position), and I leave Lame Hans to his own speculations. With some difficulty

("Queen takes her own color; Knights adjoin the Rooks on the first line," I mumble subvocally) I completed the formation and pushed the board into proximity to the prisoner. Rubbing his hands, he contemplated the fresh formulation with delight. "Are you ready?" he asked.

"Of course I am ready. Go ahead."

"Not this time," Lame Hans said. "It is time now for you to play, You have the white pieces. Move."

The invitation was unprecedented. Hans had never before asked my participation. I admit that I looked at him with some confusion. "I don't understand," I said. "It is your move. Both times."

"This is the second series," Lame Hans said. He moved in spindly, erratic fashion from the deep shadows to the front of his cage. "In the second series there are two participants. The previous series has reached its conclusion. It was mediated that the winner would be the first to achieve one hundred and sixty victories, and I have now done so. The machine is therefore eliminated, and it is time for you to take its place."

This announcement was dismaying. I barely knew the rules of chess, as I have made clear—and in the role of human, entrapped opponent, Gretchen suffocated. While I am sturdier than Gretchen and considerably less naive, I have my own disability as well as only the shakiest command of chess. "I would rather not," I said. "This was never provided."

Perhaps I should explain the conditions. Bavarian tenets and folkways can be mystifying to tourists or the uninitiated. Through the years we have had occasional wavelets of visitors, some of them interested in mountain passages, others in hearty adventures in the local pubs and resorts. A few of them have been drawn by news of the legendary Lame Hans and his bizarre penitentiary in the aftermath of Gretchen's horrible but rather necessary death. We are obliged to enact this strange tournament for their edification and ours. It is a laborious and stultifying circumstance, but I assumed my role without complaint. It had been my plan to abscond to the North and somehow change my life, but I had been embarrassingly caught at the border and returned in chains and humiliation to the authorities and, after a perfunctory trial, to my rather peculiar fate. I had not objected. There were worse penalties. The delectable Gretchen, for instance, had been sentenced to the machine and subsequent suffocation. I had in contract been given privileges of the cell block and occasional periods in default during which Lame Hans had been subject to interrogation, and I had been permitted to sleep or otherwise amuse myself. Of course, there were limits to my own freedom, and my life contained no more possibility than that of

Lame Hans.

The good aspect of totalitarianism is that it grinds all of its subjects into a monotony of feeling and circumstance. Everything feels pretty much like everything else after a while. There is a glittering similarity and a fascinating restriction of emotional range that, once accepted, tends to pass rather quickly.

"There was never any intention to enlist me in place of the machine," I pointed out. "I was never meant to be a participant."

"*Au contraire*," Lame Hans said. Sometimes he lurches into terrible French, a language he comprehends as poorly as I do chess. "Provisions were clear. You would enter at the conclusion of the one hundred and sixtieth victory for either side. You are white and therefore on move. I suggest an aggressive game. King's Gambit? Of course it will be King's Gambit declined."

All of this rather tense and barely comprehensible exchange is taking place between a man in a musty corridor, barely pervaded by light, and another locked in a cell. The question of who is the prisoner, who the guardian, seems quite abstract at this moment.

"Gretchen suffocated," I observed pointlessly.

"So she did. Life itself is a dismal affliction, an imposition upon us. We breathe, we do not breathe; it is all the same. Like totalitarianism. Life itself is a species of suffocation. We are now on the clock. An imaginary clock of course, but no less determinant for all of this. I await your move."

I understood, finally, that the situation was somewhat more complex than I had previously thought. Bavaria is more than Bavarian: It is the world itself. This is a species of contemplation with which I had never been previously engaged.

In consequence and somewhat reluctantly, I moved the King's Pawn two spaces. I know this much at least, and of the necessity to bring out the Queen's Pawn on the subsequent move and the King's Knight shortly thereafter. In the wake of this rather daring accommodation, I survey the board glumly, awaiting Lame Hans's subsequent move. His eyes appear to glitter with purpose.

He moved his own King's Pawn, folded his arms, stared at me. "Mate in ten moves," he said. "By the way," he added, "all of this is in your imagination."

As if from a great distance, gasps and throttles come from somewhere behind him, deep in his cell.

Gretchen is suffocating again.

LET THE GAMES BEGIN

by Robert Friedman and Barry N. Malzberg

Barry,

Sorry for the delayed response to your last email. Week from hell. Super weird job interview on Monday, a root canal on Tuesday, big Zoom presentation on Wednesday where I basically had to tell half the staff they're about to lose their low-paying jobs because no venture capitalist wants to venture any capital on us. Who wants or needs another streaming service, right? So our startup has stopped. Everyone who got promised a big share of success just got a bigger share of failure and it won't be long before upper management comes for me.

Hence the interview. Sounded from the ad on the job site like it was a typical consulting assignment, i.e., we need you to do internal and external communications, change management, public relations, advertising, social media, etc. but would rather avoid paying you a dime if at all possible. We got like three admin assistants and two interns with English degrees so maybe we'll just let them do the work instead. But then I get there to this place way downtown in the financial district and here's where the super weird part comes in.

The building a block below Wall Street looks abandoned—just one guard in the lobby—and the guy who ushers me through a side door into a cubicle for my interview literally looks uncomfortable in his own skin. While he's asking me these questions he found somewhere online—"what are your key strengths and weaknesses?", "how good are you at handling job pressure?", etc.—in this odd staccato murmur you can see him kind of adjusting his body inside the outer shell. Thought I was hallucinating. Then I really thought I was hallucinating when the dude offers me $500 "earth dollars" per hour plus travel expenses and asks when I can start. I ask, "when do you need me?" he says, "this Friday," I say, "I'm your man," and I'm abducted by aliens first thing this Friday morning.

I'm not joking here, Barry. You of all people should get it. And I don't mean aliens-as-symbols-of-alienation or any of that other metaphorical bullshit you play around with in your fiction. We're talking dudes from outer space. Right now I'm on a ship heading for my new, high-pressure consulting gig in a galaxy far, far away. And I don't mean New Jersey. The only good news is that those travel expenses are going to add up pretty fast.

Let me put this more bluntly: help!

Bob

***

Bob,

But why the cry for "help?" Did you not put yourself into this (alleged) situation deliberately, even eagerly? Assuming of course that this is a "situation;" 1950's GALAXY science fiction (and lower-class rejects from that excellent magazine) is choked with stories of first contact, second contact, continuing contact between rather confused but sincere Terrans and alien invaders in the guise of ordinary folk looking for an angle.

In sum I take this to be a put-on, a short opening draft for a story of immersion, execution, first and second contact and ultimately FUBAR. I don't want to say that the field (not the television or comic book offshoots but the field which James Blish called "true quill") has outgrown this kind of ploy but okay, it has outgrown this kind of ploy; your situation reads like the discarded opening of a failed Robert Sheckley story.

You remember Sheckley, don't you, 1928-2005, NYU graduate, fell into the field the way of most of us and found, maybe to his dismay, and to his editor Horace Gold's satisfaction that he had a real gift for absurdity? Better yet, science fiction seen from one angle was absurdity grown to a shaky maturity, populated by distracted aliens and wacky, displaced humans who magnified the similarities, exploited the differences.

Am I being too "technical" here, too much inside stuff? I do not mean to be; I assume that your letter is not a Sheckley (or "William Tenn" who was really Phillip Klass) pastiche as it should be but a genuine put-on, complete to the last detail of funny hats and office restrictions at this presently unnamed terminal point. I am ready for more. Perhaps we could collaborate. Perhaps this could be my Big Comeback. Keep the faith as I must say most of the film and comics industry have not.

I like the offhand corporate evocation, by the way. THE MAN IN THE GREY FLANNEL SPACESUIT. Bravo.

Barry

***

Barry,

I utter a desperate plea for help and get trenchant literary criticism and obscure history instead? What the hell, dude? You know me, Al. And you know my 20-century-literary frame of reference (B.A. in literature, Swarthmore, 1995; MA in literature, Columbia, 1997) well enough to recognize that I'm parroting Ring Lardner by using that phrase, which means you know it's really me. You also know I'm not big on practical jokes or, for that matter, science fiction, the lost orphan of literature.

This isn't a put-on. This is exactly what I get anytime I try to improve my circumstances. You want absurdity? You want irony? I aim for a better gig and end up on a hyperspace hop to Palookaville. Your boy Robert Sheckley never had to put up with this kind of shit. As for your comeback, and thanks for the self-involvement instead of help, if you're not willing to suspend your disbelief, why would anybody else be?

I wonder why I'm so calm. I think maybe there was something in that drink the stewardess gave me.

That's right—stewardess. And, apart from that third leg, she looks just like stewardesses looked in pictures of what it was like to fly in the 1970's. For that matter, I'm sitting here in the window seat of what looks like a Boeing 727 from that same period. Either the aliens have a fondness for retro pop culture or they're a little behind the times when it comes to earth normalcy if that's not a contradiction in terms.

Some words of advice in case this ever happens to you—don't look out the window even if they give you a window seat. Remember that Twilight Zone episode where poor crazy William Shatner looks out the window of the plane and sees a monster on the wing trying to destroy the engine? I wish that's what I had just seen. It would make me feel better than the starless, lightless, infinite void out there right now. Chilling.

Needless to say, although I'm saying it anyway, I closed the curtain fast and downed some more of my drink even faster. It's oddly soothing and I should find out whether they sell this stuff wherever I'm going.

What makes you think this is a so-called first contact story, anyway? Has it occurred to you that this could be a last contact story? Well, it's occurred to me, and it sure doesn't make me feel any better about the situation.

Here's the thing, Barry. I don't have any experience with this stuff. You're the one who's read and written so much about aliens. I need some guidance here, old buddy, old pal. What the hell do you think is about to happen next?

Bob

***

Bob,

If I knew what was going to happen next it would have happened. I remember wandering the streets of Greenwich Village on New Year's Eve in 1962, a fathomless year. "Hey," someone passing shouted, passing at a run, "I hear there's an orgy going on around here. Anyone know where?" "Hey, fool" a stentorian voice (maybe a derelict, abandoned Father Christmas) replied, "Anyone who knows is already there."

And so it applies: If I knew, if I could give advice, it would have been given. I will accept that this is not a put-on or at least a put-on of some industry and emotional force. Maybe you have caught hold of something: Maybe this is universal clean-up and emergency repair and you have been enlisted in its service, made conterminous with the alien objective. How would I know? You know me, Al ... Lardner died in his forties, ruined by the Black Sox scandal and his son Ring Lardner II got himself blacklisted from scriptwriting during the McCarthy era. Ill fortune stalks the fortunate; maybe this is one of the numerous lessons classic science fiction was able to pass to the disbelieving.

But I do not wish to wander; our reasonably close acquaintance justifies your request for help, however peripheral to my own reliability and of course the situation overall. Perhaps you *have* been recruited to assist in some kind of Terran makeover, perhaps you are not trying my patience but patiently cajoling my trying. Silence, exile, cunning is obviously not going to work with the stewardi, not in this unusual situation. Perhaps ancient, embryonic Bradbury is to be evoked. Regard the cosmos through the panel of the window, that soaring justification for our own existence, try to fixate upon a plan. Maybe you can persuade them to offer a return journey. Maybe you can convince them that they have the wrong customer. If they don't take to that remind them that GALAXY Magazine and all of its intrepid, maddening editors are no longer on this earthly plane and the common fate may indeed be the common fate.

Barry

***

Barry,

I'm not asking for a prediction. I'm asking for extrapolation. Isn't that what you SF writers are supposed to do? And if SF is the literature of ideas, as you've often told me, then I could sure use a few of them right about now.

But never mind. All that matters is that you seem to believe me, which makes me feel a whole lot better but also frankly makes me worry about your own mental status. Been getting enough Vitamin B-12 lately? I may be having a psychotic break of some kind, so that explains me, but it doesn't explain you going along with me.

What's that old saying about neurotics building castles in the air and psychotics living in them? Who knew I would have a housemate?

The good news, so to speak, is that this is all real. How do I know? Because I'm sitting here in a conference room waiting for our kickoff meeting to start after a bumpy landing and then a rapid trip through countless underground corridors to an office building that looks exactly like every other office building ever built.

I know these places. I've worked in hundreds of them. That's the life of a communications consultant and, apparently, it doesn't matter what planet you're on or galaxy you're in. The only thing different about this one is that it looks like the discarded set from a 70's television series. Very mid-century modern. My laptop is a blatant anachronism on the big wooden conference table.

You know how you can tell if you're working for a good client? It's easy—the chairs. The cheaper and less comfortable the chair, the more budget-conscious and difficult the client is going to be. These chairs were like bad IKEA knockoffs and I could already feel my lower back announcing its displeasure. I was about to stand up and stretch when the guy who interviewed me, who claimed his name was Darrell, arrived with a big grin. And when I say with a big grin, I mean it—he was carrying a big grin in his left hand that he then merged onto his face.

"Sorry," he said. "Protoplasm issues. We haven't quite ironed out all the kinks of being human yet."

"Welcome to the club," I said. "Where the hell are we? And how the hell do I get an intergalactic Uber to take me back home?"

He frowned, or at least partially frowned while still grinning. "I'm afraid that's not possible."

"Why not?"

His left eyebrow went up while the right one went down. He held his hands up but they pointed in the wrong direction. More kinks to iron out. "You accepted the assignment, did you not?"

"Yes," I said with reluctance.

"Then please understand that, in our culture, you've essentially signed a blood oath. You can quit at any time you like but, as our contract states, the penalty for quitting is death."

"Sounds reasonable. Uh, could you repeat that in my good ear?"

"Are you having hearing difficulties? I'm certain that our doctors—"

"No, no, I'm fine! No doctors! Did you say death?"

"Yes, I did. Really, it's miraculous that you're still alive after your undocumented journey through hostile space. Deadly enemy species, unscrupulous pirates, sentient black holes with anger management issues, fatal hyperspace glitches—have you ever seen an organic implosion? It's not pretty and a mess to clean up—etc. Quite glad and surprised you made it. Ah, Joanne is here. And Ted. Ted, Joanne, this is Bob. Bob, this is Ted and Joanne. Please commence with enacting your human social norms. It will be good practice for Joanne and Ted."

We shook hands. Theirs were ice cold but with strong grips that I matched. Never try to overwhelm a client—just meet them halfway.

"Now that we're all here," Darrell announced, "let's get started."

Started? The only thing I wanted to get started on was stopping. But it doesn't seem like there's anywhere to go, Barry, except forward. Thoughts?

Bob

***

Bob,

Well, let us stretch a point and treat this as if it were "real" whatever that might be, life being real and earnest and these events "reality" in one sense or the other. Let us stipulate or at least speculate that and act as if you were on the verge of a potential negotiation.

These aliens, imagined or real, this situation, put-on or to be taken seriously at least by you, seems to have you on the verge, the precipice, the posturing arietta of a definite negotiation; they appear equally interested (although it all may qualify as deception). Regardless, I suggest that you go to the table, so to speak.

Barry

***

Barry,

I'm already at the damned table as you well know. My new friends have excused themselves to feed, as they put it, and I'm trying very hard not to think about how or what they might be feeding on after Darrell's protoplasmic mask slipped and exposed his serrated black pincers. I'm just glad it's not me.

This is not a negotiation, as you suggest, because the time for negotiating is over. This is a planning session.

What are we planning, you ask? Just take a look at the whiteboard because—as always—there's a friggin' whiteboard. Where would corporate America be without one, or corporate wherever this is?

Whiteboards are the core of both the problem and the solution. Walk up and down the corridors of any office building from sea to shining sea, or apparently from galaxy to shining galaxy, and you'll witness a procession of obscure diagrams and indecipherable handwriting on hundreds upon hundreds of whiteboards. The epitaph for the 21st century will be written on a whiteboard and the eulogy will consist of bullet points in a presentation.

Darrell returned first. He was wiping his lips before carefully reinstalling them on his face. I tried hard not to watch.

"Ah, Robert, so good to see you again. I trust you've been working on a plan during our brief but necessary absence?"

"Yes, I finished and implemented it ten minutes ago. Um, can you remind me of what you need planned?"

He chuckled. "I so appreciate your sense of humor and easygoing nature. It's a good part of why I hired you. Everything is right there on the whiteboard."

"I know but could you summarize it for me again? Give me the elevator pitch, so to speak? Just some background and then your goals."

"Certainly. Ted? Joanne? Please commence."

So they did and it was weirder than anything in one of your stories or the stories by any of your fellow SF scribblers from the 1940s until now. Ready to hear about it?

Bob

***

Bob,

Of course I am ready. I have been ready since the dawn of curiosity in the cradle, ready since the mysterious power of sex was more to me than a punchline and a giggle. They want to enslave us. They want to take us over through our apparent administration; it is the old fascism-as-anti-fascism trick which has worked so well from time to time in our Republic and has destroyed nations not so remote that we could not emulate them.

They want to make us free before cosmic forces and politics embrace and destroy us. Am I right? Could I have centered on anything else? But even as you withhold the actual information, so I must withhold my reply; it cannot be wheedled away or extracted through false promises or manufactured crises. So I await patiently and semi-muted, knowing that this atmosphere of crisis is contrived, is merely a reply for solution modeled upon response and in the meantime I have nothing to convey. I will not assist in our destruction however fashionable it has become in our politics. I will await your presentation as the blind prop and will hence leave nothing rather than mottled figures atop a mysterious mountain. There was never any choice.

Heigh-ho. I await. What do they want? What will they give in proxy? Questions for the ages.

Barry

***

Barry,

Okay—you asked.

Ted cleared his throat. "The background is this. We've encountered a new species of intelligent life on a planet in this sector. Let's call them the Tandorans, which is not what they call themselves but, really, who cares? Such discoveries are always cause for celebration because our goal, as usual, is to open up new markets for exploitation and ruin. This is something you will be familiar with since we've modeled our entire culture during this quarter on that of 20th century corporate America."

"May I ask why?"

"Because it's fun. Why else? We don't have much culture of our own so we just borrow them from other species as we see fit. Last quarter we modeled ourselves on the war-mongering Zelavians in what you call Bode's Galaxy. That was a brutal quarter and we posted many losses."

"I'm sorry to hear it."

"Oh, no matter. You place your bets and you takes your chances. But it was a nuisance whenever the Zelavians tried to maim, torture, and kill us and we felt compelled to respond. Left a bad feeling all the way around. So we picked something more entertaining this time."

Joanne stepped in. "It's proven to be more of a challenge than we anticipated, though. We thought it would be easy to establish contact with our new customer base and peddle them products they would otherwise never want or need while conquering them. But we've encountered solid resistance. It's almost as if the customers have minds of their own."

"Perish the thought," I said.

Added Ted, "Not just that—I think they're kind of sarcastic about us and our efforts. We've done everything to present a likeable, honest image but that hasn't worked at all."

"Probably because they see right through it."

"And that," Darrell said, "is where you come in. We need to reach out to these people with a solid communications plan that addresses their typical customer profile and talks their snarky language. And we need products that will appeal to their cynical, anarchistic nature. I have no idea what any of this involves or even means but assume you do. This is all within your wheelhouse, so to speak—I do love your slang!—correct?"

"Absolutely."

I didn't bother to mention, Barry, that much of my resume is more fictional than your novels and short stories or those of the SF writers you admire. And, okay, yes, I admit it, I've read and loved them all despite my Columbia lit MA or my PhD dissertation long in progress (if I live long enough to finish it), "From Babbit to Rabbit: The Businessman in American Literature." That's right—Asimov and Heinlein and Bester and Pohl and Kornbluth and Kuttner and Moore and Sheckley and Dick and Brackett and Silverberg and Russ and Ballard and LeGuin and Zelazny and Butler and Gibson and all the rest of the poor doomed dreamers from yesterday until today—including you, Barry, you magnificent bastard. Time to return some of that love and help me out of this fiasco.

"So let's throw some of it on the porch and see what the cat licks up. Would you care to place a wager?"

"On what?"

"Your success. I can tell you're a bettin' man. Besides, you have no choice. We're quirky but deadly."

"Fine. What do you want to bet?"

"Your planet and your life. Isn't that how it always works?"

"And if I win the bet?"

"Your planet survives, at least until we get bored and invade it for the sheer entertainment value, and you go home with your fee and some astronomical travel expenses. Should cover the cost of your ongoing therapy and maybe you can even toss a few bucks to Barry."

I felt a chill. Don't show your fear, I thought, don't let them sense your concern.

"Barry?"

"Yes, your writer friend. The one you've been emailing. Quite a fascinating exchange that we've been monitoring and forwarding from the start. How else did you think your emails could reach Earth? We're very fond of your so-called science fiction, by the way, since it acknowledges our existence. Even we aliens need to feel validated sometimes. "

"I'm so glad you're enjoying our collaboration. That was our goal."

Darrell stared at me for a long moment and then burst into sudden applause with the back of his rubbery hands. He was either very credulous or very stupid but either way he seemed to believe me and was delighted.

"Excellent. You backward species sometimes do and say the darnedest things! I look forward to reading your future exchanges. How about if we leave you in peace for a while—it's feeding time again and we like our meals fresh—and see what you come up with?"

I shuddered. "Sounds like a plan."

And a plan is exactly what we need to come up with, Barry, or we're both shit out of luck.

Bob

***

Bob,

You want a plan? here is a plan: your friends or confreres, your jokers of the apocalypse, your ever so-self-motivated crew should partake of their plan for invasion: they should return, they should manifest, they should blend into the masses of this planet and do so for the cause of protecting the planet against invasion, saving their freedoms by seizing or at least infiltrating their devices.

In his wisdom, Podhoretz the Elder noted well over a half-century ago, "If fascism comes to our world it will do so in the guise of anti-fascism" and if the aliens invade, infiltrate, seize they will do so in the cause of *defending against other aliens*.

I can work up a protocol for this; perhaps you will assist, you better assist you galaxy-jaunting metaphysician because you and I together are going to need the closest accord and outside help to bring this off. We will turn over the joint—it is damned time that we do so—in the cause of protecting the joint, of walling us against the nefarious project your aliens have dreamed and I will be with you at every step. Sheckley has left the room, poor old Phil Dick rules a culture but he is dead, H.G. Wells launched the Martian invasion but settled for two World Wars, abandoning as it were, the project. We survivors must do this the right way.

And the right way is to give permanence, solidity, rationale to the wrong way. To merge the possible into the impossible. Schrodinger's Cat stirs in the vacuum and yowls. We enter the end of times as, well, the origin of times. Forward the Foundation!

Barry

***

Barry,

Easy there, big guy. Take a few deep breaths—and maybe a Xanax or two. Not sure what you're saying but you say it eloquently as always.

So sorry you got caught up in this stuff. None of it was real but it sure seemed real to me. I can't believe they let me email you throughout my session—the Wi-Fi on my laptop was supposed to be disabled—but mistakes happen.

What session, you wonder? You should know—you invented the whole idea in a short story many years ago. I'm talking about virtual reality therapy, where they jack your brain right into the hardware and then use your own imagination to help you work out your most daunting conflicts, phobias, barriers, and desires. The latest twist on this is the augmented reality feature, which blends fantasy and fact to an until-now unprecedented degree. Hence my ability to interact with the laptop while also inhabiting the recesses of my own psyche.

Look, I didn't want to mention it to you or anybody else, but it's been a rough few years. I'd lost my confidence after a few bad breaks. Potential clients could tell I was off my game and stayed away in droves. It was a self-perpetuating cycle and bad news all the way around. So when I read about this new approach to therapy, which came right out of the pages of a science fiction magazine, I figured it might help and couldn't hurt. Not many people know about this yet but I think it's going to revolutionize psychotherapy just as you predicted.

Did I believe everything while it was happening? I sure as hell did. That's why I reached out for help. But it turned out that I didn't need any.

Here I was, confronted with my toughest clients ever and with more on the line than I could ever have imagined—and I won. I'd forgotten what winning felt like. But I gave them exactly what they asked for and deserved.

Those dudes ate up every last piece of marketing communications I wrote, or at least fantasized about writing, and good 'ol Darrell was thrilled. He and his creepy crew went ahead and built the products I imagined—each one of which was designed to maximize anarchy and discord on the planet they were trying to conquer. It didn't go so well for them with the hostile natives and that couldn't have happened to a more appropriate group. And, as for me, the whole adventure was a reminder of how damned good I can be at playing all the angles in just the right way.

Anyway, again, I'm sorry I dragged you into all this but I'm doing much better than before. It's you I'm worried about now. You sound pretty caught up in your imagination, which I guess is an occupational hazard for someone in your line of work. You might want to check out virtual reality therapy yourself one of these days. The only problem with it is that I'm honestly not sure anymore what was real and what I imagined.

Bob

***

Bob,

So now the truth, the truth at last. Great performance. And I fell for it.

But you say you're uncertain about what's real. You know, of course, that the VR technology you describe is still in its earliest infancy. If it exists, as you claim, it is not, could not, be of earthly origin. So perhaps the true and terrifying question is whether the aliens—both literally and metaphorically—are already among us.

Or, perhaps, you better give this some consideration, superannuated New Wave relic that you are, we might be literally as well as metaphorically the aliens. With false recall, false history, and a determined, controlled, terrible mission of galactic conquest to enact. Forward the empire! Let the games begin.

Barry

THE END

Barry N. Malzberg Bibliography

FICTION (as either Barry or Barry N. Malzberg)

Oracle of the Thousand Hands (1968)
Screen (1968)
Confessions of Westchester County (1970)
The Spread (1971)
In My Parents' Bedroom (1971)
The Falling Astronauts (1971)
The Masochist (1972, reprinted as Everything Happened to Susan, 1975; as Cinema, 2020)
Horizontal Woman (1972; reprinted as The Social Worker, 1973)
Beyond Apollo (1972)
Overlay (1972)
Revelations (1972)
Herovit's World (1973)
In the Enclosure (1973)
The Men Inside (1973)
Phase IV (1973; novelization based on a story & screenplay by Mayo Simon)
The Day of the Burning (1974)
The Tactics of Conquest (1974)
Underlay (1974)
The Destruction of the Temple (1974)
Guernica Night (1974)
On a Planet Alien (1974)
Out from Ganymede (1974; stories)
The Sodom and Gomorrah Business (1974)
The Best of Barry N. Malzberg (1975; stories)
The Many Worlds of Barry Malzberg (1975; stories)
Galaxies (1975)
The Gamesman (1975)
Down Here in the Dream Quarter (1976; stories)
Scop (1976)
The Last Transaction (1977)
Chorale (1978)
Malzberg at Large (1979; stories)
The Man Who Loved the Midnight Lady (1980; stories)
The Cross of Fire (1982)
The Remaking of Sigmund Freud (1985)
In the Stone House (2000; stories)
Shiva and Other Stories (2001; stories)
The Passage of the Light: The Recursive Science Fiction of Barry N. Malzberg (2004; ed. by Tony Lewis & Mike Resnick; stories)
The Very Best of Barry N. Malzberg (2013; stories)
Ready When You Are and Other Stories (2023; stories)

With Bill Pronzini

The Running of the Beasts (1976)
Acts of Mercy (1977)
Night Screams (1979)
Prose Bowl (1980)
Problems Solved (2003; stories)
On Account of Darkness and Other SF Stories (2004; stories)

As Mike Barry

Lone Wolf series:
Night Raider (1973)
Bay Prowler (1973)
Boston Avenger (1973)
Desert Stalker (1974)
Havana Hit (1974)
Chicago Slaughter (1974)
Peruvian Nightmare (1974)
Los Angeles Holocaust (1974)
Miami Marauder (1974)
Harlem Showdown (1975)
Detroit Massacre (1975)
Phoenix Inferno (1975)
The Killing Run (1975)
Philadelphia Blow-Up (1975)

As Francine di Natale

The Circle (1969)

As Claudine Dumas

The Confessions of a Parisian Chambermaid (1969)

As Mel Johnson/M. L. Johnson

Love Doll (1967; with The Sex Pros by Orrie Hitt)
I, Lesbian (1968; as M. L. Johnson)
Just Ask (1968; with Playgirl by Lou Craig)
Instant Sex (1968)
Chained (1968; with Master of Women by March Hastings & Love Captive by Dallas Mayo)
Kiss and Run (1968; with Sex on the Sand by Sheldon Lord & Odd Girl by March Hastings)
Nympho Nurse (1969; with Young and Eager by Jim Conroy & Quickie by Gene Evans)
The Sadist (1969)
The Box (1969)
Do It To Me (1969; with Hot Blonde by Jim Conroy)
Born to Give (1969; with Swap Club by Greg Hamilton & Wild in Bed by Dirk Malloy)
Campus Doll (1969; with High School Stud by Robert Hadley)
A Way With All Maidens (1969)

As Howard Lee

Kung Fu #1: The Way of the Tiger, the Sign of the Dragon (1973)

As Lee W. Mason

Lady of a Thousand Sorrows (1977)

As K. M. O'Donnell

Empty People (1969)
The Final War and Other Fantasies (1969; stories)
Dwellers of the Deep (1970)
Gather at the Hall of the Planets (1971)
In the Pocket and Other S-F Stories (1971; stories)
Universe Day (1971; stories)

As Eliot B. Reston

The Womanizer (1972)

As Gerrold Watkins

Southern Comfort (1969)
A Bed of Money (1970)
A Satyr's Romance (1970)
Giving It Away (1970)
Art of the Fugue (1970)

NON-FICTION/ESSAYS

The Engines of the Night: Science Fiction in the Eighties (1982; essays)
Breakfast in the Ruins (2007; essays: expansion of Engines of the Night)
The Business of Science Fiction: Two Insiders Discuss Writing and Publishing (2010; with Mike Resnick)
The Bend at the End of the Road (2018; essays)

EDITED ANTHOLOGIES

Final Stage (1974; with Edward L. Ferman)
Arena (1976; with Edward L. Ferman)
Graven Images (1977; with Edward L. Ferman)
Dark Sins, Dark Dreams (1978; with Bill Pronzini)
The End of Summer: SF in the Fifties (1979; with Bill Pronzini)
Shared Tomorrows: Science Fiction in Collaboration (1979; with Bill Pronzini)
Neglected Visions (1979; with Martin H. Greenberg & Joseph D. Olander)
Bug-Eyed Monsters (1980; with Bill Pronzini)
The Science Fiction of Mark Clifton (1980; with Martin H. Greenberg)
The Arbor House Treasury of Horror & the Supernatural (1981; with Bill Pronzini & Martin H. Greenberg)
The Science Fiction of Kris Neville (1984; with Martin H. Greenberg)
Mystery in the Mainstream (1986; with Bill Pronzini & Martin H. Greenberg)

www.ingramcontent.com/pod-product-compliance
Lightning Source LLC
LaVergne TN
LVHW010210070526
838199LV00062B/4522
9798886010466